"Obviously, there's something illegal going on."

Bobby paused. "And it has something to do with you, doesn't it?"

Reluctantly Jolene nodded. She lowered her head. Glad she couldn't see the disappointment in his eyes. But she could feel it. Bobby lived by the law; in his mind, she had probably crossed to the other side.

More quietly he asked, "Does it have to do with you and this Monteverde woman? Are you trying to protect her memory? Did she confess what she'd done while she was visiting you and then commit suicide by taking the boat out? Is that it?"

She hesitated. Then she remembered Nina, whom she had never been able to find. And then the cabdriver, dead by a gunshot to the head. Bobby was right. The important thing now was to stop the violence before more innocent people got hurt.

Oh, Terry, forgive me.

"It's not her memory I'm protecting, Bobby," she confessed. "It's her."

"Who?"

"Terry."

"But she's dead."

"No, she isn't, Bobby. I believe—I hope—my friend Terry Monteverde is still very much alive."

Dear Reader,

It's been very exciting for me to be part of the TRUEBLOOD, TEXAS series. What writer wouldn't love to step into a world of missing persons, strong family ties and passionate romance, with an element of danger thrown into the mix?

Especially when she gets to create a dark-eyed hottie like Bobby Garcia, the hero of *Her Protector*. Bobby's a Texas Ranger who is shouldering a load of guilt, and carrying a torch for the one woman he should try to forget. But when that woman, Jolene Daniels, is stalked by a man who's been known to resort to murder to get what he wants, there's no keeping Bobby away from the sultry country-western singer.

Jo's got trouble in her past, too—including a tragedy that Bobby's mere presence reminds her of. Problem is, she can't get Bobby out of her blood. And now that he's made it his business to ensure her safety, she's not entirely certain she wants him out of her life….

I hope you enjoy reading *Her Protector* as much as I enjoyed writing it!

Best Wishes,

Liz Ireland

TRUEBLOOD, TEXAS

LIZ IRELAND

Her Protector

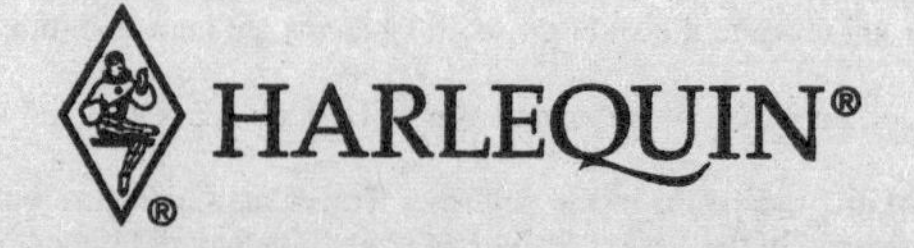

TORONTO • NEW YORK • LONDON
AMSTERDAM • PARIS • SYDNEY • HAMBURG
STOCKHOLM • ATHENS • TOKYO • MILAN • MADRID
PRAGUE • WARSAW • BUDAPEST • AUCKLAND

HARLEQUIN BOOKS
225 Duncan Mill Road, Don Mills,
Ontario, Canada M3B 3K9

ISBN 0-373-21745-5

HER PROTECTOR

Elizabeth Bass is acknowledged as the author of this work.

This edition published by arrangement with Harlequin Books S.A.

Visit us at www.eHarlequin.com

Printed in U.S.A.

Liz Ireland is the author of numerous contemporary and historical romances for Harlequin and Silhouette Books. She began her writing career in 1993 with the publication of *Man Trap,* a Silhouette Romance that won the *Romantic Times* Reviewers' Choice Award for Best Silhouette Romance. Liz grew up in a small town in east Texas, then lived in Brooklyn, New York, and Austin, Texas, before getting married and moving to Oregon. She enjoys exploring her new northwest U.S. home, as well as watching classic movies, reading, antiquing and hunting for old jazz recordings. But her favorite activity, by far, is writing, and she feels incredibly lucky to get paid for doing something she absolutely loves.

CHAPTER ONE

HE COULDN'T BELIEVE he'd found her. And *here,* of all places.

Leo Hayes squinted through the boisterous, smoky atmosphere of Tumbleweeds and shuddered in disgust. The defunct downtown Houston warehouse had been transformed and tricked up to resemble an old-time western honky-tonk, with unfinished pine floorboards underfoot, red-checked curtains, dead animal hides tacked up everywhere, and even a longhorn skull mounted behind the long, Old West-style bar. The garish result looked like some interior designer had been overexposed to *Gunsmoke* and *Hee Haw* at a tender age.

And did teeming masses love it? Naturally! Leo seemed to be the one person in the crowd without a brainless Fridaynight grin on his face. Everywhere around him patrons were laughing, chugging down beers, and half listening to the live entertainment. The dance floor was crowded with Texas two-steppers. Leo, ironed and pressed in Armani, was the only man in the room who didn't resemble a Garth Brooks wanna-be. Most of the men wore Western-cut shirts tucked into tight jeans with belt buckles as big as their heads, and the place was lousy with Stetsons.

Nice-looking women, though. He didn't mind admitting that.

And for his money, the finest specimen was standing up on the bare pine board stage in front of a microphone, belting out an old sappy song Leo remembered from a movie or something. He normally didn't care for country-and-western garbage—if he thought about music at all, his taste ran more to classical—but this particular chanteuse could have made a country fan out of a diehard rap junkie. Jolene Daniels's low, throaty voice wouldn't even need words to sound suggestive. And the woman herself was a seductive package as well. Juicier than a yellowed newspaper photo had led Leo to expect.

He couldn't believe he was staring up at her now. If he wasn't so irritated he would have laughed at the rich irony of it. For months his bumbling drones had been down in Rio trying to get information. Leo had even been forced to fly there himself last week. And all the while what Leo was looking for was right here in Houston—mere hours from where he lived!

Stupid, stupid Gilberto and his two sidekicks. He should have the idiot killed for wasting so much time. And maybe he would. But that could come later.

Leo was exhausted from tracking Jolene Daniels, and he had vital work yet to do tonight. Still, he found himself lingering over a third whiskey sour and basking in that sexy voice. While he was at it, he admired the way those tight jeans of hers hugged her generous curves. The way her bosom pushed flirtatiously against the buttons of the fringe-trimmed Western shirt she wore, giving her performance an added edge of suspense.

Jolene Daniels was five foot eight inches of pure woman. Leo was a smallish man, but he favored shapely females. Not fatties, of course, but tall ones with long legs and figures with a little muscle that gave a man something to grab on to.

He felt himself growing agitated. It had been a long time since he'd had a woman, and the last sexual encounters he'd had were with prostitutes. He preferred them; he didn't like to get tangled up with people and their problems. And women always seemed to have problems. Most of the time Leo was too concerned with business, legitimate and otherwise, to give a damn. Now was no exception. Jolene Daniels was just his type…but he couldn't afford the distraction. Especially not with her.

He dug his free hand down into his right pocket, fingering a couple of marbles, quietly, so he wouldn't draw attention to himself. The effect on his nerves was like plunging a burn into ice water. Relief came immediately, and as he finished off his drink and prepared to leave, he gave the singer a last, more businesslike once-over.

She had a pretty face. Curly auburn hair. Good skin. Startling hazel eyes.

Startling, because this was another thing about Jolene Daniels that Leo hadn't expected. The woman couldn't see a thing. Her eyes didn't alight on one spot, then another, as a regular entertainer's would, but looked out at her audience as though she were actually focused on something beyond them. She was as blind as a bad.

In other words, she would be helpless. That small bit of luck brought a rare smile to Leo's lips. For once, things were going his way. After weeks of working under pressure, searching for his precious diamonds, he could take care of this next bit of business quickly and easily.

Maybe he wouldn't even have to kill her.

JOLENE BELTED OUT the words of that old Patsy Cline chestnut about a woman falling to pieces, and felt herself…falling to pieces.

She could swear someone was watching her.

Of course, she scolded herself, *there were nearly a hundred people watching her.* The usual Tumbleweeds crowd for a Friday night, Tammy had told her. Jo pictured Houston working men who, under the influence of her old country-and-western songs and a pitcher or two of Shiner Bock, transformed into weekend cowboys. And urban cowgirls, too—women with tight jeans and big Texas hair poofed, piled and sprayed until it stood as tall as Marie Antoinette's wig. They were Jo's bread and butter; fun-loving folks here to dance and flirt and listen to Jo, who on a good night could raise the roof off this old shed.

Nothing ominous about that. And yet her skin pricked with apprehension.

Was she losing her mind? Gripping the mike, she tried to scan the crowd, but as had been the case for the past two months, all she could make out were shifting shadows and light. In bright light, she could usually manage not to walk into trees or trip over large pieces of furniture. But here at Tumbleweeds they kept the lights down except for three hot klieg lights over the stage, which used to blind her even before the accident. And yet even now her sightless eyes kept darting to the left corner of the bar as if she could feel a presence there. She could have sworn a dark-haired man was standing there, even though she couldn't possibly have seen him.

Could she?

A dark-haired man.

Bobby.

Just the name practically stopped her heart. She tried to hold herself together, finish the song. Thinking about Bobby Garcia could be dangerous—she had ample proof of that fact. She'd been having a particularly erotic daydream about the man nine weeks ago while driving down the street near her home when she'd run a red light and slammed smack into the side of a UPS truck.

She closed her eyes, crooned into the mike, and tried to

conjure up another dark-haired man. But the next name that popped into her head was Greg. Greg, her big brother, best buddy, and number one fan. How often had he been front row center on Friday nights at Tumbleweeds? Even after all this time, six long months, she could still see him there....

As the last strains of "I Fall to Pieces" tumbled from her lips, a teardrop spilled down her cheek and she bowed her head, embarrassed to be putting on such an emotional display in public. But if the audience noticed, they must have thought it was all part of her rendering of the song, because the crowd burst into furious applause and appreciative whoops and whistles. Flustered, Jo spun on her heel, then grabbed the mike stand to steady herself. She felt dizzy.

Willie, her bass player, was at her side in a second, his strong hands bolstering her shoulders. "You okay, Jo?"

She nodded mutely for a moment, gathering herself. Since her car accident, she often had dizzy spells, which was apparently just part and parcel of having suffered a concussion that was the medical equivalent of eight point five on the Richter scale. The doctors said the vertigo was also the result of being able to see only flashes of light and blurred impressions, like pictures snapped mistakenly at the end of a roll of film. Her whole being had been thrown off-kilter, rattled, and she would need time to adjust. They promised her that one day she would recover her sight, maybe fully, but Jo wasn't banking on it. She just hoped. Most of all, she hoped that the dizziness and headaches would end.

"I'm okay, Willie, just rattled."

He rubbed her shoulder in an avuncular way. Willie was one of the old-timers of the Houston music scene; he'd seen a lot and been through more. "Just give yourself time."

She blinked back another tear. Was there time enough in the world to get over all the losses this last year had dealt her? First her friend Terry Monteverde was gone, then Greg had been murdered. And she'd lost Bobby, too. And in their wake, what had they left her? Guilt... sorrow...heartbreak. A deadly secret she alone would have to take to her grave.

Willie squeezed her shoulder. "You ready to go home?" Clint Black was already blaring from the jukebox, signaling that their jobs were officially over.

She nodded. "Give me a few minutes, will you?"

"Sure thing, Jo."

With the help of her trusty cane, and knowing Tumbleweeds like the back of her hand, Jo started making her way through the milling crowd toward the ladies' room. She brushed against several people and tried not to let herself imagine that any one of them was her mystery man. Her *imagined* mystery man. She knew Bobby wouldn't show up here. She hadn't heard from him since her accident, and that had just been a duty visit on his part. The meeting had been tense and obligatory; Bobby was stiff but courteous, while she was all defensiveness. She'd wanted him so much, but she didn't want the reminder of the past, of their shared guilt over Greg's death.

Most of all, she didn't want his pity. The idea of him coming back to her because she was blind was repugnant to her. So she'd been curt enough to chase him away, probably for good.

So if it hadn't been Bobby out there, then who? Dreaming about Greg being in the front row was just a morbid form of self-torture. Medical folk probably had an explanation for that, too. Craziness, they called it. First her retinas had detached; now her sanity.

''Hey girl, you were fantastic. Can I get you a beer?''

The voice was unmistakably that of Tammy French, longtime Tumbleweeds waitress and Jo's personal nominee for supportive friend of the year.

Jo shook her head. ''Could I trouble you for an iced tea and an aspirin instead? My head is killing me.''

''Sure thing,'' Tammy replied. ''Meet you back at headquarters.''

In the ladies' room, Jo ran cold water over a paper towel then pressed it to her forehead, trying to chase the headache and gather her wits. Terry...Bobby...Greg...they had been the triumvirate that had kept her going over the years. Her emotional safety net. It was still so hard to believe that they were all, either literally or figuratively, dead to her now.

''Here you are,'' Tammy singsonged as she pushed through the door to the ladies' lounge. She placed a cool glass in one of Jo's hands and pressed two tablets in the other. ''Bottoms up.''

Jo gulped down the tablets and the tea and prayed for quick action. Maybe the aspirin would obliterate the headache before it got too bad. She only wished there were a pill that could obliterate memories. ''Thanks, Tammy, you're a gem.''

Tammy's boot heels clicked. ''At your service. Anything else you need?''

She hesitated. No sooner had she scolded herself for even thinking of asking the question than it was out of her mouth. ''Is there anyone...strange...out in the bar tonight?''

Tammy laughed. ''Strange? Everybody in this place

seems strange to me. Only odd thing tonight was that we actually had a guy in a spiffy suit come through."

That wouldn't be Bobby. The man would rather eat worms than dress formal. She smiled, remembering that she'd once asked him if he'd even wear a tux at his own wedding. And what had he answered?

If you were my bride, Jo, I'd wear a monkey suit. Or even a gorilla suit. Or any damn thing you wanted.

Her smile faded. That conversation seemed like a lifetime ago. "Tammy, do you remember Bobby Garcia?"

"Texas Ranger?" Tammy asked. "Bedroom eyes? Temptation in boots?"

"That's the one."

"Nah, I've forgotten him completely." Tammy cracked up at her own joke. "I thought y'all were all washed up."

"We are, but... You didn't see him tonight, did you?"

Tammy tsked under her breath. "No, Jo, he hasn't been around here. Did that rascal stand you up?"

"It's not that." Somehow she couldn't bring herself to tell Tammy about the imaginary dark-haired stranger by the bar. "I guess it was just wishful thinking on my part."

"You shouldn't pine over Bobby, Jo. There are plenty other fish in the sea, in case you haven't heard."

"I wish I could want some other fish," she said wistfully. "I wish I could want anything besides what I know I can't have anymore."

Tammy swore under her breath. "Aw, Jo. Put the past behind you—get on with your future."

"That's what I want to do," she answered honestly. But the truth was, the only man she'd thought about at all in a coon's age was Bobby, and she couldn't have him for so many reasons.

She felt Tammy's concern during the long pause in which she sipped awkwardly at her tea, and could just imagine the thin blonde's furrowed brow. ''I gotta get back to the salt mines,'' Tammy said finally. ''Don't forget your ride's waiting. Leave Willie to his druthers and he'll start up a poker game and you'll never make it home tonight.'' The words were half joke, half warning. Despite being a member of every twelve-step group imaginable, Willie was still apt to stray in all directions.

Luckily, it wasn't difficult to pull Willie away from Tumbleweeds this night. In no time they were scooting through Friday night traffic in his '68 Chevy pickup. This was one of the few fringe benefits from her accident. Jo loved riding in this old tank with its springy bench seat that felt about a mile from the dashboard. It reminded her of the truck her father had owned in Galveston when she was a girl—another part of her life long gone. She even enjoyed the smell of old vinyl that seemed to have soaked up three decades of tobacco before Willie finally kicked that particular habit.

Since it was a hot July night and the air-conditioning, according to Willie, had given up the ghost sometime during the Carter administration, they rode al fresco with the windows down. The wind tunnel effect made it a constant challenge to keep her unruly shoulder-length hair out of her face. She finally gathered it in a ponytail at her nape and held it there.

''Okay, Jo, what's on your mind?''

She turned, surprised by the question. ''What do you mean?''

''You flipped out tonight, Jo. Onstage. I could tell. And you might not be able to see it, but the strain's been on your face since we finished up. So out with it. What's tormenting your innocent young soul?''

''Innocent?'' That was a joke. ''And the last I heard,

thirty-two wasn't exactly considered being a spring chicken.''

Willie's deep laughter filled the pickup's cab. ''Don't throw bunk at an old-timer. To me you're still as green as grass.''

She smiled. Maybe Willie would understand. Or at least wouldn't think she was crazy. Heck, he'd told her enough about his comings and goings through rehab clinics and divorce courts and *she* hadn't raised an eyebrow. ''Well, it's nothing...just a feeling, really.''

''What kind of feeling? Feeling your career's stalled? Feeling lovesick?''

''Not exactly.'' She hesitated just one more moment and then blurted out, ''Did you notice anyone strange out in the audience tonight?''

''Good lord, no! Didn't I tell you that I never look out into the audience?''

Jo frowned. ''Never?''

''Never.''

''Why not?''

''Because I've been in this business a long time, and over the years I've looked out into that crowd of faces, and whenever I did, it seemed disaster always was nippin' at my boot heels. I'd look out into the bar, and maybe a young lady would catch my eye. Especially if she was a blonde—they stand out in the dark better. So then maybe after a set I'd go ask that lady if she'd like to have a drink...and maybe I'd forget that I was wearing some other lady's wedding band.''

Jo clucked her tongue in disapproval. ''You old skunk!''

He howled in protest. ''You think I came by four divorces honestly?''

''I didn't think you picked up groupies in bars.''

''That was years ago, hon, when this old leathery mug

of mine could still attract a groupie. Now all the folks out there in the dark are coming to see you.''

The assertion, which normally would have been gratifying as all get-out, tonight gave her pause. People coming to see her, when she couldn't see them. It had been bothering her a little in the weeks she'd been performing since her accident. She had no way of knowing *who* was out there. It didn't have to be Bobby or anyone she knew. Or even anyone wishing her well. Maybe some nut case was fixated on the husky way she could belt out old country standards, sad songs about love gone wrong, about cowboys who wandered, about women left lonesome and sorry.

Or maybe—more likely—she was borrowing trouble, dreaming up crazed fans where there were none. After all, Tumbleweeds wasn't exactly Radio City Music Hall. In her memory, no local singer in Houston had ever required a bodyguard. She wasn't Whitney Houston by a long shot.

''It wasn't fans I was wondering about. I don't think. Actually, for a moment tonight, I thought maybe I saw Bobby.''

''For real?'' Willie asked. ''I mean, could you really see?''

She let out a huff of frustration. ''I guess not. It was just a blur of dark hair—for a moment I even thought I'd seen Greg.''

Willie swore under his breath. Nobody knew more than he how torn apart she'd been since her brother had been murdered. She'd cried on Willie's shoulder more times than she could count. ''You probably just thought you saw somebody who looked like him.''

''Probably,'' she agreed quickly.

''But that's good, isn't it?''

''That I'm seeing ghosts?''

''That you're seeing anything.''

''Blurs. Shadows.'' She shrugged. ''Willie, Tom Cruise could have been in the front row tonight and I wouldn't have known it.''

''Sure you would have. Tammy would have shrieked then fainted.''

She laughed.

Willie lowered his voice. ''And if it'd been Bobby, believe me, you'd have known it. That boy wouldn't come by without sayin' howdy to you.''

Only Willie could get away with calling Bobby Garcia a ''boy.'' Bobby was a Texas Ranger, and he didn't need a badge to show authority. His five feet ten inches were carried with a pride few could match, and he had cunning, intelligent, and incredibly sexy dark eyes. The short time she'd been with him, she'd more than once noticed women's gazes—consciously and unconsciously—following him as he walked across a room. His magnetism was powerful.

Hell, it was so powerful she could feel it even now when she hadn't been anywhere near the man for a couple of months.

She steeled her hand against the armrest as Willie turned the pickup into her neighborhood. She smelled cut grass and sage; sprinklers swished mechanically, adding a trace more moisture to the already humid Houston night air. Was the oleander blooming? Were there lightning bugs? It was so frustrating not being able to see; she missed all the simple summer touchstones she'd taken for granted all her life.

Last summer she'd been at a policemen's picnic with Greg and they'd palmed lightning bugs like they had when they were kids. Thinking back on that July evening, they seemed as innocent as babes then, not knowing the turmoil of the year ahead. Within months, their friend Terry Monteverde would be gone and Jo and Greg would have to share the responsibility of silence about her death. Then Greg would bring Bobby, a Ranger he was working a case with, home for Thanksgiving, never guessing she and Bobby would fall in love. And because of them, Greg wouldn't live to see another policemen's picnic.

Tears threatened, but she blinked them back. "I'm just all mixed up, I guess."

The pickup slowed, then stopped. The seat springs squeaked as Willie turned to her. "Have you called Bobby lately, Jo?"

"God, no."

"Betcha twenty bucks he'd be glad to hear from you."

She folded her arms defensively. "Listen to you—Gamblers Anonymous has worked wonders!"

"Don't change the subject."

She pivoted toward his voice. "Bobby Garcia and I can't be together anymore, Willie. You know that."

"No, I don't."

"Not after what happened...not after Greg was killed."

Willie sighed in exasperation. "Listen to me, Jolene Daniels. I'm no expert on love. But I have reached one conclusion the hard way, and I'm gonna pass it on to you for free. Life doesn't come up all rose petals and sweetheart serenades for two people. Most of the time, it just provides problems, which is handy because if you're looking to end a relationship, you can always find a reason. But if you've got love there gluing the thing together, a relationship can withstand a lot of what the smart guy in tights called slings and arrows."

"Maybe Bobby and I just didn't have the right glue."

"Did you try to find out? Really try?"

Maybe she should have been grateful to Willie for sharing his wisdom, but this part of her private history was just too painful. ''Everyone's always telling me to forget about the past, Willie, and yet at the same time they want to yank me back in that direction.''

Before he could launch into another sermon on the subject of love—a subject she'd just as soon avoid like the plague—she opened the pickup's door and darted out. And tripped over the curb.

''Whoa there!''

Her ankle stung, but she winced quickly then forced a smile. ''Don't mind me, I'm just a klutz!''

''You want me to escort you in?''

Oh, lord, wasn't the love sermon over? ''No thanks—I'm sure you've got a poker game waiting for you somewhere,'' she kidded. Actually, he probably had his girlfriend waiting. And Lena had been understanding enough about his nightly detours to Jo's house without her prolonging them. ''Besides, I've finally mastered the feat of making it up my walkway by myself.''

''You left your porch light off,'' Willie pointed out disapprovingly.

Her lips tugged into a rueful smile. ''It doesn't make a lot of difference to me whether it's on or off.''

''It makes a difference to burglars.''

She chuckled. ''Greg checked the crime stats before buying into this neighborhood. I'm in the little old ladiest part of Houston. Lights out at ten, and plenty of peeking through the venetian blinds.''

''Okay, then. But you really oughta turn your porch light on.''

''Thanks, Willie. I don't know what I'd do without you.''

''No problem, Jo.''

She stood and listened to the truck grind into first gear

and sputter down the street before turning back to her house. Then she tapped her cane ahead of her on the rough concrete, shuffling along as fast as she could. She had only had rudimentary training with her cane after her accident—she kept hoping that by the time she could get around, her sight would have made that miraculous recovery the doctors had predicted. Unfortunately, all this stubborn optimism had garnered her was stubbed toes and multiple bruises.

A little eyesight, it turned out, could be a dangerous thing. The only special equipment she'd installed in her house since the accident was a talking alarm clock. With Tammy helping her with grocery shopping and annoying things like memorizing the buttons on her TV remote, she got by well enough. Still, sometimes in her house she felt like a human pinball, getting from one destination to another by a slipshod series of bumps and crashes. Outside, she felt even more vulnerable. There was a whole wide world out there for her to trip over, bash and collide into.

She made it up the two front steps without any mishaps and was still congratulating herself on a job well done as she leaned against her front door and began to fish through her purse for her keys. The front door gave way, and she staggered across her threshold.

She gasped in surprise. "What the—"

Before she could get the question out, a hand from inside the house grabbed her neck, yanking her backward. She stumbled, then instinctively tried to lurch around the other way, toward the outside again. Her heart was pounding like a hammer, and the only thought going through her mind was to get back out the door, where she could scream for help.

But the intruder stopped her with a quick wrench to her arm and she buckled, falling to the floor. She made a move to crawl over the threshold but a man's body fell on top of her, pinning her down, his hot breath stinking of whiskey. She wiggled violently, then felt a cylinder of cold metal against her temple.

Jo froze. She hadn't been a cop's sister for nothing. She knew guns. Unfortunately, she also knew too well the damage they could inflict when they were in the wrong hands.

Nausea rose in her throat and she realized she couldn't cry for help, couldn't make any sound at all.

But he could. In a chillingly flat voice, the man pinning her down growled, ''Where are they, lady? Where'd she hide them?''

CHAPTER TWO

IF HER ATTACKER had given her the choice between her money or her life, Jo would have handed over her purse, no problem. She had no desire to be a hero. If he'd advised her to say her prayers, she might have crumpled.

But *Where are they? Where did she hide them?* Those questions sent one-hundred-proof panic racing through her veins; they also made her fight back.

Jo bucked against the man's weight and attempted to inch her way out the door. He continued to hold the gun against her and to hiss in her ear, the same words, the same alcohol breath, the same creepy voice. Fueled by adrenaline and fear, she twisted and reached out, groping around for anything she could use for a weapon. She could hear her heart thumping beneath her tight, fringed shirt. Her body was drenched in sweat, and being halfway over the threshold, between the hot humid outdoors and the air-conditioning, only made matters worse. Her slippery fingers stretched out and touched the rough clay of a flowerpot. No good.

Then, finally, her knuckles bumped against something cold and hard. Her palm clamped down on her brother's old brass armadillo boot scraper.

Ridiculous, she'd declared the object when Greg had dragged it home from one of his Saturday morning yard sale expeditions. It was also hideous—a frightful statue of a crouching varmint with a long edge curving around the top of its shell. Right now Jo sent up a silent thanks for Greg's bad taste and seized on it as if it were her most treasured possession.

Wielding the boot scraper wasn't easy. It was heavy, cumbersome. She wrenched against the man's weight to face him and flailed the object blindly until it made sound contact with human flesh. She didn't know whether she'd bashed the guy on the shoulder or the head, but whichever it was, the blow got him off her and she heard the gun clatter against the cement porch.

The split second he let go of her was all she required. For once in her life, she was grateful for those steamy afternoons she'd spent training for track and field. Right now she did the fifty-yard dash to her neighbor's house.

Only she couldn't see to clear the hurdle of the azalea hedge between their yards. Not that it mattered. She plowed right through the bushes, tripped from the grass to the sidewalk, and felt her way to the front door in record time. She didn't bother to hunt for the doorbell but instead pounded against the door.

Her voice, lost only seconds before, found itself. "Bertie! Dean!"

She didn't care if she woke up the entire neighborhood. In fact, she hoped she did.

In seconds the door flew open and her fist swiped at air. Bertie Winston, who was about a half foot shorter than Jo and at least thirty pounds lighter, grabbed her wrist and yanked her across the threshold with ease. For the first time in her life, Jo felt fragile. As if her whole body might shatter like glass dropped on marble.

"Land's sake, Jo, what is it?"

Jo was panting. It was hard to get any intelligible words out. Harder still to know how much she could actually say. "My house—there was a—a burglar!"

Bertie sucked in a breath. "A burglar!"

Beyond the entrance hall she heard Dean Winston, Bertie's husband, spring to action. "A burglar, you say?"

"Yes. He was in my house when I got back from work."

"He won't get out of this neighborhood. Bertie, dial 911. I'm going over."

Jo whirled on the man, alarmed. "Don't, Dean. He's armed!"

"So am I." A closet door slammed. "I got my hunting rifle!"

Yes, but could a retired appliance salesman with a bird gun hold his own against a man Jo felt certain was a vicious career criminal?

Apparently Bertie didn't think so. She stopped speaking to the 911 dispatcher long enough to yell at her spouse. "Dean, don't be an idiot."

"He might get away!"

"Or he might kill you," Bertie warned. "Get your carcass back in here!"

But Dean's heavy footsteps shuffled past Jo and he was off. Jo's heart flipped in dread, and she reluctantly followed him out the open door, retracing more slowly her hectic run of moments before. Suddenly, she felt exposed, unguarded. She half expected her intruder to run up and clap his hand over her mouth, but then she heard doors being thrown open and familiar voices shouting across the street.

Her poky, lights-out-at-ten neighborhood was coming to her defense.

"What's going on, Dean?"

"A burglar at Jolene's!"

"Is he there?"

"Don't see him."

"The police are on their way," Bertie shouted from her doorway.

"They won't find anything here now," Dean said. "Looks like he's gone."

Jo stopped and felt her shoulders sag. He was gone.

That should have made her feel better. She was safe. For the time being.

But there was no doubt in her mind that he would be back. No doubt at all.

THE SECOND Bobby Garcia heard the address over the police dispatch radio he did a highly illegal U-turn on Montrose and scorched a trail straight in his Dodge Intrepid to Jo's house.

Adrenaline pumped through his body. What had happened? If anything had happened to Jo, by God he'd find the person responsible and wring his sorry neck. He prayed she hadn't been home when it happened, that she was safe.

And if she wasn't, whose fault would that be?

He swore at himself under his breath. He just couldn't do anything right these days. He'd always been a man to take his responsibilities seriously, but events of the past year had mocked his efforts. First there was Greg, the friend he'd failed completely. Not only did he feel responsible for Greg's death, he had promised Greg to look after Jo, a task that seemed as impossible as it had been to save Greg.

How could you look after a woman who didn't want your help? Who didn't want you around, period.

When he'd visited Jo at the hospital after her accident, he could barely get her to say hello to him. And he'd failed to give her any kind of comfort. In fact, his presence there only seemed to make things worse. The trouble was, he'd arrived too late to help her. Just like with Greg.

And now this...

He winced at the guilt that coursed through him. *God, please let her be safe.* If she was, things would be different. *He* would be different. He wouldn't let her out of his sight.

The normally quiet street was lit up like a Christmas tree. Neighbors in pajamas and bathrobes lured away from Jay Leno or the late movie by the excitement gathered in clusters in a few front yards. Parked outside the two-bedroom ranch house Jo had shared with her brother were two police cars, their lights flashing, so Bobby figured he could leave his Colt .45 in its resting place in the glove compartment. Nor would he need his evidence or fingerprint kits, which he kept in the trunk.

Inside one of the cars talking on the radio was a man Bobby recognized as Ed Taggart, a good cop. He'd worked with him several times in connection with various cases the Rangers had teamed up on with the Houston police.

Bobby got out of his car and was rushing up the sidewalk to see Jo, when Ed stopped him. "Hey, Bobby!"

Bobby pivoted quickly, waving. "I gotta check on Jo."

"She's okay. Mark Hartell is talking to her, and evidence is fingerprinting the back door."

She's okay. Right now those sounded like the dearest words in the English language. His feet stopped moving, and he allowed himself to take a breath.

Ed caught up with him. "Some kind of amateur robbery job," he explained. "Might have been a nitwit kid. That's what Jo said. She was able to chase him off without much trouble, sounds like. We got police cars scouring the neighborhood to see if he's still around."

Bobby frowned. "A robbery? What did he get?" Jo's house wasn't filled with valuables. She didn't even have many electronics, if he remembered correctly.

"Not a thing, so far as we could tell. Did a tidy job breaking in the patio door, though."

Bobby took note of that odd detail. Nitwit kids didn't usually pull tidy jobs. In fact, they usually made a mess, grabbed stuff willy-nilly, left a gazillion clues, and got caught. The jails were full to bursting with incompetent juvenile criminals.

"What did Jo say?" Bobby couldn't be sure that she'd be willing to talk to him herself.

Ed shrugged. "Said she'd just gotten home and was opening the door when she discovered it already open. Perp jumped her in the entrance hall. She scuffled with him, dashed next door, and when the neighbors came back over to catch the guy, he'd already vanished. Pretty fast runner, I guess."

Even Ed's tepid description made Bobby's blood boil. *He'd jumped her.* "Was he armed?"

"Said she thought he had a gun."

Maybe it was a good thing the perp had vanished, because right now if Bobby had seen him, he would have wanted to strangle the sorry SOB, police brutality be damned. When he swallowed, his Adam's apple had to leap over the dry lump in his throat. "And Jo…how's she holding up?"

"Oh, you know Jolene. She's a tough egg. Terrible to have this happen to her, what with all the problems she's had this year. Seems like she's hit a real patch of bad luck."

Bobby nodded. "Yeah." Regret and guilt pricked at him.

"I'll bet she'll be glad to see you," Ed prattled on. "She knows all of us, of course, but not close like you know her."

They continued up the sidewalk. Precinct scuttlebutt apparently wasn't what it used to be. If Ed had been aware of exactly how things stood between Bobby and Jo, he'd know that Bobby was the last person Jo would want to come knocking on her door during a crisis. Bobby couldn't be sure what kind of reception he was going to get in that house.

They stopped at the front porch and Ed picked up a brass boot scraper shaped like an armadillo that had been Greg's. ''She clunked him on the head with this.''

Bobby pushed his hat back and studied it for a moment before his gaze snagged on another object—a white cane, red-tipped. The sight of it sticking out of the petunia bed caused his heart to stall.

''I hope she pounded him good.''

''She did,'' Ed replied. ''Hard enough for us to get a couple of hairs and a skin sample.''

That would be useful if they ever had a suspect and could match up hair samples. For now, the hair color would help them start forming a description of the person they were looking for.

When Bobby stepped into the living room, memories assaulted him. The couch where for a few happy months he'd watched the Super Bowl, basketball games and the latest video blockbusters with Greg and Jo; the dining table where he'd partaken of lousy home-cooked meals and had laughed so hard he thought he would pass out; the exact spot next to the sickly ficus plant where he'd first kissed the only woman he could remember loving so fiercely it hurt.

And though she was encircled by three police officers, when he walked in Jo looked up, her hazel eyes focused straight at him. Her gaze threw him—it was so direct. It seemed almost as if she could see him, and yet the way she stared it was more like she was seeing through him, beyond him.

The effect she had on him was amazingly familiar. She stirred his emotions and his blood. Right now she was a mess. Her green Western shirt looked like someone had put it through a shredder. It was torn in several places, and some of the decorative fringe was missing; other strands had been snagged and now hung longer than the rest. Her jeans were grass stained at the knees, and there was an azalea twig trapped in her auburn curls.

Despite it all, his every muscle seemed to tighten and desire hummed through him. It had been a while since he'd seen her, and all he could think of was how beautiful she looked. She knocked him for a loop every time.

"Hello, Jo."

Her wide lips parted in an expression that was neither smile nor frown. For a moment, he didn't know what to expect.

"Bobby!"

He didn't know how it happened, he didn't care. In the very next moment she was in his arms. He hugged her tightly, completely, burying his face in her mane of coily auburn hair. His chest heaved in a sigh; he was so relieved to know she was okay, so glad to hold her again. She smelled the same, like an exotic flower, yet he could sense that she wasn't the same. That she was afraid. She leaned her weight against him as if she might topple over if he stepped aside.

It wasn't like her.

A knot formed in his stomach, as if somebody had kicked him, and he loosened their embrace just enough to take a second look at her. Still beautiful, still Jo. Still the woman he wanted and feared he could never have. But he'd never seen her like this. Afraid. She was practically trembling in his arms.

"Hello, Sergeant," one of the policemen said awkwardly.

Bobby sent a curt nod to the young cop. He didn't know him; the man was obviously responding to the silver badge on his white shirt. Maybe the novice thought Bobby, a Texas Ranger, was here on official duty.

The Rangers, an elite division of the Texas Department of Public Safety, often did help out on cases with local police and sheriff's departments—cases involving murder or kidnapping. Or long-running problems like the drug smuggling investigation that had resulted in Greg's death. They also occasionally worked in conjunction with the FBI, U.S. Customs, the ATF and even international agencies such as Interpol. But in Houston, Rangers weren't usually on the scene at burglaries.

Mark Hartell, an old friend of Greg's, sent a look that told the younger guy to beat it. "We're about finished here, Bobby," Mark informed him. "You can check with me or Ed tomorrow if you want to see what evidence makes of all this."

Bobby nodded again, but didn't let Jo go, even though he could feel her body stiffen when the others spoke. It was as if, for a moment, she had forgotten anyone else was there. As if she had forgotten that their breakup had happened and they weren't supposed to want to touch each other, to love each other.

It was as if Bobby's wildest, most deeply desired dreams had come true.

He waited until Mark and the younger guy were out of earshot before speaking to her again.

"Shaken?" he asked quietly.

"I'm okay."

She tilted her head and pushed against him with a subtle pressure he didn't want to acknowledge. He could feel the barriers going up again, could feel the past lapping against them like the tide coming in. She looked a little embarrassed.

Her brow furrowed. "How did you know to come here? Did one of the men call you?"

"I caught your address over dispatch. I had to come check on you."

"I see." Her voice was suddenly stiff, her tone brittle. "A duty visit."

He shook his head violently before realizing the gesture wasn't registering. "My being here has nothing to do with my job, Jo."

"I meant your duty to Greg."

Greg. The name was like a land mine exploding between them, ripping through the moment of closeness they'd just shared.

She freed her arms from him, then took another step backward and leaned against the bar dividing the living room from the open kitchen. She was trying to appear casual, though he knew she felt anything but. Her face was tense with worry, and hurt.

The same brew that had him all stirred up. "Jo, I wish..."

His words trailed off; he didn't know where to begin. Looking into her face, her beautiful face that had haunted his dreams for months now, he found it impossible to speak the laundry list of regrets that plagued him. *I wish we could erase what happened six months ago. I wish I had been a better lawman, that Greg hadn't been killed. I wish we could be together....*

For a moment he saw anticipation in her hazel eyes, but

at his inability to put feelings into words, she blinked twice and let out a ragged breath. ''Yeah. So do I.''

There was no point in dredging up the past right now, when they were distracted by more pressing concerns. ''Look, can you clue me in on what happened tonight?''

''Didn't one of the guys here tell you?''

''I want to hear it from you.''

Reluctantly, in a tight, nervous voice, she recited the same information Bobby had received from Ed, with the added detail that she'd smelled alcohol on the attacker's breath. Ed hadn't mentioned that. Perhaps Jo had left the detail out when she'd been talking to the cops.

On second hearing, the story struck Bobby as being just as peculiar as it had the first time round, though he couldn't put his finger on exactly why it was odd.

''They think it was probably just a kid,'' Jo finished up, parroting Ed.

''They told me they thought that because that's how you described him.''

She cocked her head. ''Well, yeah, I did. He seemed about the size of a teenager.''

''Last I looked, teenagers came in all sizes.''

She cleared her throat and gestured in a flustered manner. ''I mean...he wasn't big. Not a heavyweight, that's for sure, if I could take care of him.''

''Hmm.'' He wasn't so certain about her modest assessment of her abilities. Jo had never been a wraith-thin model type. She was five foot eight, in good condition. At least she had been before her car accident. ''You still lifting weights?''

''Just three times a week.''

Her tone was a little embarrassed, as if two or three times a week at the gym could be considered slacking off.

"And you've been out of the hospital for three weeks now?"

She nodded. "Right. But I had to go back a few times for physical therapy. I call them blind lessons. People who help me figure out how to get around. And I've started a water aerobics class at the Y. I can't sail or swim in the ocean anymore, but at least I can jump in the water and move around every once in a while."

The thought of her not being able to sail anymore pained him. When she was a girl, her parents had owned a boat rental in Galveston, and she was a natural. A master sailor. He'd never seen her happier than when she was at the helm of a sailboat. They'd gone out on a lake a couple of times last winter. "Are your eyes better?"

She released a mirthless laugh. "Sure, now with all the lights on, I can tell that there's somebody standing right in front of me. That's why I always flick on all the lights when I'm in a room—I think the contrast helps. Unfortunately, my intruder wasn't considerate enough to turn on the lights so I could see him."

"What do the doctors say?"

"They're as optimistic as ever. Easy for them, right?"

"Right."

He looked around the room in amazement. How did she get along around here? How had she possibly managed to fight off an intruder? The fact that she had impressed the hell out of him, even though he knew if he told her as much, she'd shrug it off as nothing. She was infuriatingly modest about her singing and everything else.

"This man...did he say anything to you?"

Her brows knit together, and her eyes focused on the carpet. "It happened so quickly...."

"But you must remember if he said something."

Her brows beetled in concentration. ''He—he told me to hand over my money.''

''You didn't recognize the voice?''

She shook her head. ''No.''

''And did you hand over your money?''

''No. I hit him. Then I ran.'' She shrugged. ''And that was it.''

''And this happened when you came home from work?''

She nodded.

''Willie still driving you?''

Her face turned up to him, her eyes wide, almost startled. ''How did you know?''

''How do you think? Willie told me.''

''That old coot! He never mentioned that he'd spoken to you.''

Bobby had told him not to. He turned, looking back toward the doorway, and spied a crocheted knit handbag in a heap by the couch. ''That your purse on the floor?''

''I think that's where I dropped it,'' Jo told him.

Bobby went over and picked it up. The first thing he noticed was that her thick wallet was still there. ''How much money did you have?'' he asked, handing it over to her.

She opened the wallet and pulled out thirteen dollars. The ten had been folded at the corner. The ones were all folded in half. ''Probably about this much,'' she said, fingering the bills with a frown. ''I guess I scared him away before he could go through my purse.''

And yet the man had told her to hand over her money. Her purse was right there. Why hadn't he just grabbed it?

Bobby looked around the living room. ''Anything taken from the house?''

She put the wallet and purse away and shrugged. ''I'm not sure. The police say they see no signs of anything being ransacked. No open drawers, at least. Nothing tossed. The television's still here, and the stereo, and my jewelry box wasn't touched. I checked those things.''

Now that was interesting. A burglar, professional enough to make a ''tidy'' entrance from a patio door, failed to snatch anything on his way out? That would indicate someone looking for a specific item. ''Seems odd. That bash with the boot scraper you gave him must have really knocked him silly if he didn't even stop long enough to grab your pocketbook.''

''I did my best,'' she declared.

He took another good look at her. She was leaning back, those long legs of hers crossed at the ankles. Her arms were folded, tightly hugging her body. She looked defensive, tense; for a woman living alone whose house had just been broken into, that wasn't a shocker. But for some reason, she didn't sound at all interested in rehashing the events of the evening, which was remarkable. Usually crime victims *wanted* to tell their stories in great detail. To anyone who would listen. Unless…

As a terrible thought occurred to him, a wave of anger washed over him. When he spoke, he had to strain to be calm. ''Jo, this guy. He didn't try to…''

He didn't even have to finish. She shook her head adamantly. ''No, Bobby. It was not a sexual assault.''

His breath released, he unclenched his fists, and he mentally sifted through the facts again. ''It doesn't seem a little suspicious to you that he didn't bother to snatch your purse?''

This time Jo merely shrugged. ''I told you, it all happened really quickly. I hit him and then ran. The next thing I knew, he was gone.''

''Did you tell the police that he asked you for your money?''

"I forgot." She shook her head. "I mean, they didn't ask me."

Bobby sighed. Why was he not surprised? Those guys probably stepped inside their old buddy Greg's house and started shooting the breeze with Jo like it was old home week. Granted, there wasn't a lot here to be examined. A neatly broken door, an aborted attack, nothing even taken. To men who were used to seeing the grislier side of Houston's nightlife, this incident probably seemed like a happy ending.

Bobby thought it was damned peculiar.

Jo shifted slightly and cleared her throat. His hands itched to reach out and pull that silly twig from her hair.

Aw, who was he kidding? He longed to pull her into his arms and bury his face in that mop of curls again. Their brief contact earlier had only served to remind him how their bodies fit together perfectly, how good she felt against him, how soft her skin was, how lightly springy and sweet smelling those curls were. He'd asked her once what kind of shampoo she used to get her hair to smell like that. Freesia, she'd answered.

Freesia. He didn't even know what a freesia was, whether it was a root or an herb or a flower, but he would probably remember that smell until his dying day. He couldn't count the number of times that he'd lain awake at night, remembering it. Remembering her.

"We're finished here, Bobby," Ed announced from the doorway. He spoke as if he thought he needed to report to him—as if Bobby were somehow now in charge of the investigation. Then he turned to Jo. "We're going to be sending a patrol car around every so often, so you don't need to worry, Jolene."

She smiled. "Thanks. And thanks for coming out so quickly. I really appreciate it."

Ed's cheeks reddened. ''Sure thing. Don't be surprised if I don't come around to hear you sing one of these nights, either.''

''I'd like that,'' Jo said. ''The first round of beers will be on me.''

The pleasantries went on and on until Bobby wanted to scream and boot Ed and his fellow officers out the door. When the police were finally gone, he turned to Jo, ready to get back to questions about this intruder. Instead, his gaze snagged on her torn shirt and a lump formed in his throat once more. ''I don't know if you realize this, but you look sort of the worse for wear.''

She sent him another rueful smile. ''A few new scrapes and bruises to add to my collection.''

''Do you need help cleaning them up?''

From the way she stiffened, you'd have thought he'd propositioned her. ''I can take care of myself,'' she said stonily.

He caught the eye of that silly brass armadillo. ''Apparently so.''

They stood uncomfortably; it was unnerving, seeing her, yet having her unable to look back at him. He felt like a voyeur. Especially when he could sense how tense she was, as if she wished he had left with the others. ''Maybe I'd better take a look at that broken door.''

''The boys already fingerprinted it,'' she said, following him through the kitchen. A breakfast nook looked out through a long sliding glass door to the patio and backyard. The door was closed now, but still bore the oval hole the burglar had cut through the glass.

''Ed said it was a neat hole,'' Jo said.

''It is.''

''The man must've used a glass cutter.''

''I thought you said it was a kid.''

Two red stains appeared in her cheeks. ''Whoever it was.''

He nodded. The hole was tidy, all right—just big enough for a hand to reach through and flip the lock. ''This locking mechanism is too flimsy for security anyway. At the very least you need a shim as a backup.''

''Right now I need a whole new piece of glass.''

''That, too.'' He looked around, wondering what he could use to cover the hole. ''You have any duct tape?''

She smiled. ''To keep burglars out?''

''Mosquitoes,'' he said.

''Somewhere...'' She started opening drawers, investigating them by feel.

He spotted a roll of silver tape, snatched it from the drawer, and started taping over the window. ''I'll call a glass company tomorrow to come fix this.''

''I'll call, Bobby.''

''You don't want to put this off.''

''Believe me, I know.'' Of course she did. ''And I've got a piece of wood to wedge in the door for tonight. Greg cut it a long time ago, but I got lazy and stopped using it.''

Bobby bit his tongue to keep from lecturing. She needed real security. On the other hand, his experience in law enforcement had taught him that all the locks in the world couldn't keep a determined criminal out of a house.

She tilted her head up at him. ''Were you on duty when you came over here?''

Was the question a not-so-subtle hint that perhaps he should get back to work...and leave her alone? ''Just getting off. I was on my way home.''

''You must be tired then.''

Yup—definitely trying to get rid of him. ''I don't want to leave you, Jo,'' he confessed.

Her lips parted, and she stepped back again, her hands tensing into fists at her sides. ''I'll be fine. You heard what Ed promised—he's going to send a patrol around.''

He let out a ragged breath. ''I don't care about that. You've been through a lot tonight. I don't think you should stay here alone.''

''I'll be fine,'' she repeated.

In Bobby's experience, most break-in victims were unnerved at the thought of being alone in a home that had been invaded. And Jo had seemed truly rattled when he'd come in. Now she appeared to be shrugging it all off. ''I know you think you'll be fine. But wouldn't you sleep better if I were here with you?''

A ragged laugh exploded out of her, and he realized how ridiculous his question had been. If he stayed, neither of them would get a wink of sleep. They probably wouldn't sleep anyway, just remembering their all-too-brief hug. That hug would tease his memories and his senses for weeks to come.

''I don't need a nursemaid, Bobby. That burglar's not going to come back here tonight.''

''If he was a burglar.''

''Of course he was.''

Frustrated, he stepped forward and took her hands in his. He'd expected warmth; instead, her skin was ice-cold. She jumped back, bumping the edge of the dishwasher.

''You're nervous, Jo.''

When she looked up, those gorgeous hazel eyes were full of moisture—and their expression! The sheer anguish nearly tore his heart in two. ''Can you blame me, Bobby? This hasn't exactly been your typical night in the life of Jolene Daniels. A gun-wielding stranger was in my house. It's creepy.''

''Then why—''

"And just when I was getting my nerves back in line, *you* stepped into the picture."

"I had to come when I heard about the break-in."

"I realize that, but..." She drew in an uneven breath. "Remember the last time you were here, Bobby?"

The last time he'd been inside this house was the night Greg had been murdered. They'd gone to dinner together that night, then whiled away far too much time on the couch saying goodbye before he had to go to work. They had never made love before, but they had come close that night. Only lack of time had stopped them. Bobby hadn't wanted to leave her at all, had wanted to stay and make love with her with every fiber of his being. But he knew he was already late to join Greg at the stakeout of what they suspected was a methamphetamine lab. Ten minutes late.

And if he had arrived ten minutes earlier—on time—he might have been there when an armed thug approached Greg's car with a loaded Glock. He might have found Greg waiting for him, smiling that goofy smile of his, rather than sprawling across the front seat in a pool of shattered window glass and blood.

He might have been able to save his best friend, his girlfriend's brother. Instead, he'd had to deliver the worst possible news to Jolene. It had torn him apart. And worse, it had torn them apart.

As ever, the memory of last February shook him to his very core. Nothing would ever erase the responsibility he felt for that night. It was a long moment before he could gather himself enough to speak again.

"Of course." He felt like a jerk now. "It was thoughtless of me to blunder in here like this...I heard the news and I couldn't help myself. Would it have been right for me *not* to come?"

She shook her head. "No...I don't know. I appreciate your concern, Bobby, I really do. But I assure you, I'll be okay. I'm a big girl. I can take care of myself."

Bobby gave in. For now. "Sure, Jo."

She promptly escorted him to the front door. "Don't worry about me," she admonished him again.

He didn't reply to that. She might as well ask him not to breathe.

When the door shut firmly behind him, he realized that Ed and his gang had received a friendlier send-off. Bobby retreated to his car and started the engine, fully intending to go home.

Go home. Sure. And do what—sleep?

Not likely. He'd slept fitfully at best for months now, anyway. Every time he closed his eyes he was tormented by memories of Greg. Or incredible memories of Jo, and how happy they'd been during those short months they were together. Sometimes he dreamed that last February had never happened, that he and Jo and Greg were all still pals, that Jo had become his lover. After dreams like that, waking up to the sobering memory of what had happened was excruciating.

He circled the block. When he was back on Jo's street, he cut his lights and eased to the curb two houses down from her place.

The police might pat themselves on the back for sending a patrol around every few hours, but he wasn't about to take his eyes off her house for one instant. He hunkered down in the seat, keeping a sharp eye on Jo's front door. It was going to be a long night. But then again, seeing Jo had given him plenty to think about.

Like wondering at how close they'd been once—and how far apart they were now.

Like marveling at how beautiful she was.

Like figuring out why she'd felt compelled to lie to the police. And to him.

CHAPTER THREE

JO CLOSED the door behind Bobby, bolted it, then sagged bonelessly against the cool wood. It was hard to put an exact name to the rush of feeling racing through her. Was it lust, relief or pure fear? Probably, she realized, a mixture of all three. She felt dizzy and more than a little wobbly but she was too damned freaked out to sit down.

She pushed herself away from the door and did something she hadn't done since losing her sight. She paced. Back and forth across her living room in a monotonous path she walked, her mind snapping from one problem to the other.

What was she going to do?

Bobby. Thank heavens he was gone! The whole time he'd been here she could feel his eyes on her, studying her. Watching her. It was unnerving. She'd wanted to hug him, to cling to him, to be absorbed by that surefooted strength of his. Heaven help her. All those months they'd been involved in their tentative mating dance, she'd been so careful. A kiss here, a necking session there. She'd spent three months soaring in the clouds, she'd been so happy. They had known, always, that they would become lovers, but they were friends first, and so they had taken the romantic part of their relationship seriously. They hadn't wanted to rush it.

That was then.

But tonight, oh, God, tonight. She could kick herself at

the way she'd thrown herself at him, hurling herself into his arms as if he were her savior. Her incredibly sexy savior. In truth, she'd felt safer in his arms than anywhere...until his questioning had begun.

Only after Bobby had started interrogating her did she remember that he was, first and foremost, a Texas Ranger. A detective. Having a detective around was dangerous. One question too many from the law could be her undoing.

She should have known better than to let her guard down around him. She'd managed to handle the police okay. But when Bobby stepped into the room, everything changed. You would think that all these months apart would have given her a little bit of distance, of composure, but no. Why couldn't she talk to him without feeling the heat of a blush in her cheeks? Why did his voice still make her feel flushed and warm? Why did being in his arms, smelling his familiar scent of leather and starch and Obsession cologne, make her fall in love with him all over again?

If he'd stayed another fifteen minutes she was sure she would have gone to bed with him. She was that unsettled, and confused. That desperate for the kind of physical solace she'd known instinctively she could find in his arms.

But of course making love with Bobby now, of all times, would only cause problems. She had enough of those. More than enough.

She heard a noise—a breeze rattling a windowpane, probably—and nearly leapt out of her boots. Her fingers worried her lower lip as she squinted around the living room as if she could actually detect if someone had broken in again or not.

But of course no one had. The police were just here.

But he would be back.

Where did she hide them?

Chills swept through her as she recalled that flat voice. It had sounded like a combination of Christopher Walken and Hal the Computer. The creepy guy had been looking for something. But what? There was no way to know for sure because the one person who could tell her was long gone.

The only thing Jo knew for certain was who the *she* referred to. Terry. Someone had traced Terry to her. But what did her assailant know? How much did he know?

She needed to call Nina Monteverde, Terry's sister, in Rio. The number was written in her address book by the phone. But of course she couldn't read it. She could call information, but she didn't know the slightest bit of Portuguese. Even her English felt shaky tonight.

She could ask Bertie to read the number for her. That was it. She crossed the room toward the spot where she'd last had the address book, then stopped. It was late. And wouldn't Bertie think it peculiar that she suddenly felt a burning need to call Brazil?

Tomorrow. She'd wait until tomorrow. She didn't want to go back outside anyway. If she went outside she'd have to come back in…and she would be terrified.

But she was terrified anyway.

Someone was looking for something that Terry had been carrying before her accident. Someone was willing to resort to violence to get it. That someone would not be put off because she'd whomped him on the head. He would be back.

Oh, lord. Maybe she should call Bobby and tell him that she'd changed her mind about having him stay with her….

No. All that would lead to was more emotional turmoil—the last thing she needed. The attacker would not come back tonight. He would know that the police were watching her house.

Instead, the man would wait. And watch.

He might be watching, even now.

Jo stood stock still in the middle of her living room and realized there was not a single person she could turn to for help. Not Bobby, certainly not the police, not anyone.

She'd never felt so alone, so exposed, so damned afraid.

LEO GINGERLY touched the egg-size lump on his temple and winced in pain. His head felt as if it were about to explode. Who knew a blind woman could pack such a wallop?

Now he was even worse off than when he started. No doubt the police would be prowling around the singer's neighborhood today, making it more difficult for him to make his next move. Just what he needed. More problems.

He just prayed they wouldn't search her house again and discover the bug he'd planted in the potted ficus tree by her door. At least he'd had the presence of mind to get that tended to—the one thing that had gone right last night. He should get a few chuckles eavesdropping on Jolene Daniels and her retinue. And he should also glean some valuable information as well.

He looked down into his empty coffee cup and muttered a curse. It didn't help matters that he seemed to have walked into the most inefficient greasy spoon in Houston. Half an hour ago his waitress, a beluga whale of a woman who reeked of cheap drugstore perfume, had dumped him at this half-cleared table, slapped a cup of inky coffee in front of him, and hadn't been back to take his order.

"Excuse me?" he snapped across the restaurant to her. Actually, calling this place a restaurant, with its smell of last year's grease and filthy floors and sticky menus, was dignifying it all out of proportion. He'd only chosen the interstate café because it was near his hotel; so much for convenience.

Beluga looked up from the beefy truckers she was flirting with at the counter and sauntered over, annoyed. ''You decided yet?''

He let out a huff. ''I'll have a side of toast.''

The waitress's penciled-on brows shot up. ''Just toast?''

It was probably the only safe thing for breakfast here anyway. ''Toast,'' he repeated tightly.

She twisted her garish fuchsia lips at him, no doubt calculating how paltry her fifteen percent cut of an order of toast was going to be.

Yeah, right. Like he was going to tip this cow. *Dream on, sister.*

''And could I get it sometime this century?''

As the waitress waddled away, visibly ticked off, and the truckers began glaring at him, Leo realized that he was losing his composure. He needed to get hold of himself.

He reached into his pocket and his fingers brushed against the four marbles he always carried with him. They even made a tantalizing clicking, beckoning him, but he resisted the urge to pull them out. He was trying to kick the habit. Instead, he fished for the little container of Tylenol he'd bought in a drugstore last night. He should have purchased an economy-size vat.

But he'd had no idea how taxing this errand was going to be. It had seemed like such a breeze compared with what he'd already been through. Waiting while his goons tailed Terry Monteverde's sister and her American flat-foot boyfriend all over Rio had been a real exercise in frustration. In Leo's opinion, whoever first remarked on how hard it was to find good help had hit the nail on the head. His man Gilberto and his two sidekicks had spent months coming up with exactly zip on their own, but Leo had known as soon as a bounty hunter like Rick Singleton started hovering around the Monteverde business that something had to be up.

Which all just proved that if you wanted something done right, you had to do it yourself. Within hours, they had found the picture of Jolene Daniels in Nina Monteverde's apartment. Leo had recognized her as the woman who had been present in the newspaper photos taken at the time Terry Monteverde had drowned. Terry's old college friend, Jolene, he put together, was the last person to have been with Terry before her death.

Added to that, Gilberto had discovered Nina and her boyfriend were on their way to Texas, no doubt to see dear old Jolene and twist her arm to get the diamonds themselves. But they hadn't reckoned on Leo Hayes.

People like that slew him, they really did. Did they actually think that he was going to let them waltz off with his loot? *He* had been the mastermind behind getting Terry suspected of smuggling. He had personally seen to the theft and transportation of those jewels. They were *his,* not the Monteverdes'. He wasn't going to let that simpering snot Nina Monteverde act as if the diamonds he'd gone to all the trouble to steal were now her family's heirlooms. The very idea enraged him.

Well, he'd taken care of her and her American lover. Leo had found the pilot of their plane and put slow-acting poison in the man's soft drink. Nina and Singleton were at this very moment splattered to bits and pieces on a mountainside somewhere in Brazil.

That's what really had his head pounding. Shaking a few diamonds out of a blind woman should have been a cakewalk after what he'd been through already. And he'd had his mitts on the woman last night. He knew she knew what he wanted from her. If he hadn't been a sap, hadn't stayed too long at that hick bar watching her sing and soaking up way too much liquor, he would have handled everything better. But no, he'd assumed that he had the upper hand, that he could scare the information out of her. Unfortunately, he hadn't reckoned on Jolene Daniels being the Mike Tyson of the country crooning set.

He'd sure like to kill her now. Like to, but he couldn't. Not until he recovered those diamonds.

He struggled to stay calm. With Nina out of the way, he could take his sweet time. Really plan this out nicely. No one had ever linked him to the contraband gems that Terry Monteverde had been caught with. No one ever would. For years Leo had been smuggling gems, using his business, Old Tyme Toys, as a shield. On paper at least he'd been the most upright of businessmen for over a decade now. And all the while he'd smuggled jewels in dolls from an assortment of countries and in wood figures from Africa and Mexico. Lately he'd been using cheap kaleidoscopes—the diamonds blended in seamlessly with the colorful plastic chips. All these years since he'd got out of jail he'd risked his own name, his reputation as an honest businessman, and he'd never been caught.

Of course this time he hadn't worked alone—he'd partnered with that strange woman and she'd gummed up the works!

Never collaborate. That was the lesson. Especially with someone with an ax to grind. And then Terry had unexpectedly fled the country and died, creating yet another complication.

Sweat broke out on his brow. He could do this, he could get his diamonds back. Last night's failure was just a setback, just a—

Oh, to hell with it!

He dug inside his pocket again, pulled out the marbles,

and rolled them in his hand. A relieved sigh issued from his lips. Screw it. If it made him feel better, why not? It wasn't like nicotine, it wasn't going to kill him. The cool shiny orbs in his hands gave him a lulling feeling.

More important, they gave him reassurance. He could overcome this last obstacle. *He* was the victim here. Experience assured him that he was smart. Smarter than customs officials. Smarter than the police. And he was certainly more cunning than a simple country-and-western singer.

THE KNOCK at the door nearly scared Jo to death.

Of course that wasn't hard to do. She'd been on pins and needles now for the past forty-eight hours. Locksmiths had doubled the security on her windows and doors; Greg's old Remington shotgun was always within reach. Yet despite these additional security measures, she felt more vulnerable than ever. There was no one she could turn to—no friends, none of the guys in the band, not the police...and certainly not Bobby.

Her thoughts now were so filled with Bobby that by the time she reached the door she had half convinced herself he would be standing on the other side. But of course that was ridiculous. She hadn't heard a peep from him since the attack.

"It's not Bobby," she scolded herself.

Still, just in case, she smoothed her hand over her hair to make sure it wasn't frizzing any more than usual. Never mind that it was ten in the morning and she was still in her ratty old terry cloth bathrobe, still exhausted after a third sleepless night. How could she sleep when every time her head hit the pillow, Bobby's deep sexy voice rang in her ears?

Doesn't it strike you as suspicious...?

Another knock sounded, more insistently this time.

"Who is it?" she called through the closed door.

"Jolene, it's Bertie. Can I come in?"

Jo let out a sigh. It wasn't Bobby. Relief and disappointment warred inside her as she flipped the dead bolt and pulled the door open.

The minute the door was cracked enough to allow entrance, Bertie slipped through and quickly closed it behind her. Jo heard the tumblers of the dead bolt flip again, then her neighbor grabbed her by the elbows and said breathlessly, "Now don't panic, Jolene, but I have reason to believe you're in *serious* danger."

Duh, Jo was tempted to retort, but she made do with a nervous laugh instead. "What makes you think that?"

There was a disturbing pause. "Oh, dear."

Jo frowned. "What's the matter?"

"You don't look so good. Is that mascara under your eyes?"

She suppressed a groan. Say what you will, not being able to see oneself in the morning sometimes had its advantages. "Try dark circles from not sleeping for three nights running."

"Oh! After what you went through, I'm not a bit surprised."

Jo nodded. "Yeah, I guess I'm a little shaken up." The century was still young, but she was willing to bet she'd just uttered the understatement of it.

"Well, naturally. You poor thing!" Bertie sighed. "And now here I come with even more bad news!"

Bad news. The words struck a dire tone in her heart.

Yet what could Bertie have to tell her that was worse than what had already happened to her? "What bad news?"

In the silence that followed, she could feel Bertie peering up at her. "Have you tried Dozy-Dose?"

The question, so unexpected, took a moment to register. Once she realized that they had taken a conversational step backward, she shook her head. "I don't take sleeping pills."

"Well, don't mind my saying so, hon, but it looks like you should start. And Dozy-Dose isn't addictive—oh my, no," Bertie chirped helpfully. "Dr. Hopper recommends them to me when I can't sleep."

"Bertie, about that bad news you were—"

"You can buy them right over at the Food Save."

Jo thought she was going to scream if her neighbor didn't spit out pertinent information, pronto. "Bertie, what makes you think that I'm in danger?"

"Oh!" Bertie sounded surprised to be reminded of what she'd come rushing in here to tell her. "Dear, I don't mean to startle you. In fact, I think this might be the beginning of the end."

"The *end?*" Jo felt a full-fledged panic attack coming on. She reached out and grabbed Bertie by the shoulders. *"Why?"*

"Because there's been a car parked outside your house ever since Friday."

"Just a car?"

"No, someone's in it. Watching this house, I'll wager."

It shouldn't have surprised her. The eerie sense of being watched wasn't just paranoia. She'd known she was in danger. But suddenly a fine layer of sweat broke out all over her skin. *She was being watched.* What could be more disconcerting, more creepy? Who was doing this?

Her heart palpitated irregularly, and she stepped back, crossing her arms over her chest. She wanted to run to her bedroom, stuff everything she could into a suitcase and flee. But where could she run? The man had found her house, and that had probably been the tricky part. Tailing her when she tried to escape would be child's play. Was her old assailant just toying with her now, trying to unnerve her utterly? Or was he just waiting for the perfect opportunity to attack her again, so he would be better prepared to get information out of her?

What did he want?

She felt sick again.

"Oh, honey, I know," Bertie said, fluttering closer. She patted Jo comfortingly on the shoulder. "It's terrible. But Dean's taken steps for your safety. He's already talked to the police about all this."

The words, meant to soothe her, had just the opposite effect. The police were the last people on earth Jo wanted poking more deeply into this matter. She'd had a hard enough time getting rid of them Friday night; now she'd have to answer more questions—lie again. Pretty soon, she might forget the lies she'd already told. If they tripped her up, more trouble than she could handle could come raining down on her.

But she couldn't tell them the truth.

She took a step backward, then another, slowly, until the backs of her shins nudged upholstery fabric and she could sink into the generous arms of Greg's old recliner. She had to think. She couldn't run; trying to lie low somewhere would be pointless. Besides, she had her work. Two gigs this week. Tumbleweeds and her band depended on her being there, and she'd never missed a show before.

That left her few options. She couldn't confide in the police, which would put herself and someone else in grave danger. What could she do?

"I didn't want to tell you about it," Bertie said worriedly, "but of course you had to know."

"Of course," Jo agreed.

"And now maybe the police can catch this crook, or pervert, or whatever he is. Dean gave them a description and a license plate number. The police can sometimes solve these things," Bertie assured her. "Remember how quickly they figured out who stole Myrna's silver flatware?"

Jo took cold comfort in this example of police efficiency. She couldn't think of a punishment that she didn't want for the man who attacked her; on the other hand, if he was caught, he could tell the police things she didn't want revealed. She had no choice but to keep wobbling along this tightrope woven of half-truths, utter fabrications, and stone-cold fear.

But of course well-intentioned Bertie didn't know this. Jo tried to pull herself together. "Thanks, Bertie. And thank Dean for me, too. Maybe the police will come through for me."

Bertie sighed. "It's a shame your brother's not still with us, Jolene. I bet none of this would have happened if Greg was still living here."

Even the mere mention of Greg could make tears well in Jo's eyes. Before she could react, however, there was a loud pounding on her door. She shot out of her chair as Bertie let out a startled gasp.

"Don't open it! It could be him!"

Jo laughed anxiously. "At ten in the morning?" With a bravery she didn't exactly feel, she made her way to the door. "Who is it?"

"Jo, it's me."

Bobby!

After the terror Bertie had injected into her, it was all she could do not to throw open the door and leap into his arms again. Never mind that she had just been scolding herself for tackling him the moment he walked through her door Friday night; never mind that Bobby's questions could undo a secret she'd sworn not to reveal. Right now he felt like her last, oldest friend on earth.

More important, just having him here for a few minutes would give her respite from this numbing fear. She was safe from her attacker when she was with Bobby. Even if she wasn't safe from herself.

But what was he doing here?

She opened the door, trying to keep up the appearance of being in control. "Bobby?"

His footsteps burned a path inside. "I guess you heard," he said, a trace of annoyance in his voice.

She frowned in confusion. "No..."

Before Jo could get another word out, someone else was at the door.

"That's him!" Dean Winston hollered, blasting into the room. "*That's* the man who attacked you!"

Jo heard the sound of a rifle being cocked and gasped in alarm. "Dean, no!"

Bobby was a fraction calmer. "Sir, put your weapon down," he told Dean.

"I seen you parked here, mister," Dean barked at him. "You can't intimidate me. Bertie, call the police and tell 'em we've caught the guy."

"Bertie, don't," Jo interrupted. "Dean, you're wrong. This is my friend, Bobby Garcia."

Dean grunted. "They say it's always the people you know that you've got to watch out for."

"Bobby's a Texas Ranger."

"Huh?"

She imagined the barrel of Dean's rifle going south. Bewildered silence followed her revelation. It didn't take long for Dean to register Bobby's uniform-that-wasn't-exactly-a-uniform. The boots, the perfectly pressed snowy white shirt, the white Stetson that was the standard garb for Texas Rangers. And finally, the badge. The silver star inside a circle that denoted a sergeant in the Texas Rangers. Bobby, proud of his position in this elite branch of law enforcement, was rarely without it.

"Well, I'll be switched!" Dean grumbled. "I been watching you, Sergeant, and I sure thought your behavior seemed suspicious."

"I've been looking after Jo."

He had? His low voice reached out to her like a reassuring caress. Maybe there was no stalker. Maybe the other man, the attacker, really had been frightened off and wasn't coming back at all.

"Well, why didn't you just say so?" Dean asked.

Jo could have asked the same question. He might have saved her some panic...although she would have been equally alarmed at the idea of him watching her too closely, poking into her affairs. She reminded herself to be very careful.

"I didn't think Jo would want me here," Bobby explained. "See, we used to be...well, involved."

"Oh."

"Oh!"

Bobby couldn't have chosen better words for clearing the room. Within two minutes, she was alone with him again. Which, she realized, wasn't necessarily a good thing.

"I got a call from the police this morning saying they'd had a complaint and that my car was reported as suspicious," Bobby explained when her neighbors were gone. "I figured I'd better get over here fast."

"Good thing you did. Bertie had me convinced the attacker was back."

"That's what I was afraid of. I was worried once you heard the license plate number, you'd start thinking *I* was the culprit."

She chuckled.

"What's so funny?"

"Only a guy in law enforcement would worry that anyone would recognize his license plate number. I don't even remember what my own was before I smashed my car to smithereens."

Bobby wasn't laughing with her. "This is no joke."

"No, it's not." She crossed her arms, trying to get her emotions under control. Being in the same room with Bobby made her lose her common sense. He'd been parked outside her house for two days, and he hadn't seen fit to tell her. Was he really being caring, or was he snooping? "And it's not very amusing that you chose to have a stakeout at my place without informing me."

"I didn't want to scare you, Jo."

"Why would having a Texas Ranger as my personal protector scare me?"

"Because I have to tell you, I think whoever it was who attacked you will be back."

She felt her whole body tense. Having someone confirm her worst fear wasn't exactly reassuring. "Why?"

"Because from what you told me, I don't think he was a thief."

She swallowed. She should have known Bobby wouldn't be fooled by the story she'd told the police.

"I think he might be a crackpot, maybe even a stalker," Bobby said.

"It's not a stalker," she answered quickly, not thinking.

He jumped on her assertion. "What makes you so sure?"

"Well...I haven't received any weird phone calls, or

letters, for one thing. You're the only one who's been sighted around here with any regularity."

"You seem awfully quick to dismiss the idea." The suspicion in his tone came through loud and clear.

"You think I *want* to believe there's a psycho after me?"

"I would think you'd want to be safe."

"I do."

"Then help me out here." The urgency in his voice made her feel guilty. He truly wanted to help her. "You haven't had any suspicions at all that this guy might be anything other than a hapless burglar?"

She shook her head, praying her act was believable. "None whatsoever."

Bobby sighed in frustration. "I just don't get it. A guy breaks in, carefully, as though he'd given the matter thought. And then he disappears into thin air, taking nothing, even though your purse was sitting right here. What did he want?"

"Maybe you're giving the guy too much credit, Bobby. Why can't you just accept it was a freakish thing—an amateur job? The police did."

He harrumphed.

"Have *you* seen anything suspicious?" she asked him. "You've had your eyes on the street all weekend. If anyone was up to no good, you would know, wouldn't you?"

He hesitated. "Maybe."

"And have you seen anyone?"

He didn't answer for a moment. "No." It sounded as if he were reluctant to admit it.

Sensing he was backing down from his police dog stance, she smiled—though it was hard to act nonchalant about the matter when in reality she was torn up inside with nerves. She would have given anything to be able to tell Bobby the truth, but she couldn't. She'd sworn she would never tell a soul, and she wouldn't, even when her life was at stake.

She forced herself to be casual. Collected. ''You want some coffee?''

In the silence that followed, she could feel him looking her over, and was suddenly aware of how her robe fell open at her chest, no doubt revealing her nightgown, which was low cut and a little too sheer for receiving casual guests.

She gathered the folds of her robe at her throat and lifted her chin, praying he couldn't see her embarrassment. But she held out little hope. Not much escaped Bobby.

''I've got a better idea,'' he suggested. ''Why don't you throw on some clothes and I'll treat you to breakfast.''

She didn't know what to say. Breakfast with Bobby?

They had tried getting together once, after Greg's funeral, and it had been a dismal experience. Neither had foreseen the many opportunities for missteps, the chances that a word or a simple shared phrase would send them spiraling back into the past, into that pit of guilt, grief and sadness they were both going to have to claw their way out of, separately.

''Oh, I don't—''

''Breakfast tacos at Pablo's?''

Her mouth watered at the suggestion. She realized suddenly that she hadn't eaten a square meal in days; she'd been too nervous to think about eating.

Right now her resistance to food wasn't strong. Her resistance to Bobby wasn't strong, either. It never had been.

Red flags waved frantically in her head; her common sense screamed out reasons why she should give him a simple refusal and send him on his way. Yet she felt herself relenting, thinking of feeble excuses to go along. It seemed like a million years since she'd been out with anybody who wasn't a musician...and what harm could there be in a cup of coffee and a breakfast taco?

She'd dreamed of Bobby too long. Dreamed of their having a second chance.

"Okay, you win." She smiled. "Pablo's. You and me. But promise to leave off with the Joe Friday stuff, all right? I'd like to forget the attacker incident for an hour or so."

"Your wish is my command. No questions, just fun. Like old times."

Like old times...

Once the words were hanging in the air between them, accompanied by images of Bobby and Greg and her, laughing together, she gave herself a mental slap. How could this possibly work? How could she even hope that it would?

Bobby released a ragged breath. "I wish Greg could go with us, Jo, but he can't. What are we supposed to do? Our lives can't stop. Haven't we both been trying to forget each other long enough? We've failed. At least, I have. We have to go on."

His words were so raw, so painful; somehow, though, she heard the truth in them. And she also heard him confess that he couldn't forget her. It was the bravest, most thrilling thing she'd heard in a long time.

She relented. After feeling lonely for so long she wanted just another hour with Bobby. "All right."

Wordlessly, she turned on her heel and headed for her bedroom before Bobby could see the tears in her eyes. More than anything in the world, she wanted to go on, too.

But she couldn't banish Greg from her thoughts.

It was impossible to say how much she missed her brother right now. If Greg were here, he would have known how to handle everything. The police, the attacker, Bobby... She could have confided in him. Greg, in fact, would have been the one individual in the world who would have understood her predicament. He hadn't been just her brother. He'd been her confidant.

If it weren't for Greg's help, she would never have been able to arrange Terry Monteverde's death.

CHAPTER FOUR

PABLO'S WAS the kind of casual, no-nonsense place Greg had loved. The restaurant was housed in an old diner. The decor hadn't changed much since the switch from American to Tex-Mex, except for the Christmas lights that hung year-round over a lunch counter that ran almost the entire length of the dining area. The counter was lined with high stools and dead-ended with an old black cash register near the door that had yellowing cartoons in Spanish taped all over it. And of course the Formica tables were now loaded down with *huevos rancheros* and breakfast tacos. The air was redolent with the smell of cilantro and grilling *fajita* meat.

Bobby and Greg had come here often to grab a lunch or dinner break when they were working cases together, and sometimes when they weren't. They had swapped stupid jokes, moaned about the dismal season the Astros were having, and stuffed themselves with Mexican food and Pablo's inky coffee.

During that time, Greg had voiced one constant refrain. "I've *got* to introduce you to my sister," he'd always say.

And Bobby, thickheaded idiot that he was, would smile politely and silently pray that Greg never got around to the introduction. Bobby had experienced a few situations where friends had set him up with female friends or relatives and they hadn't hit it off. It could really put a damper on a friendship.

Now when he thought of all those months he'd missed knowing Jo, he wanted to kick himself in the rear. After Greg had introduced Bobby to his sister, they had gathered here as a threesome for long weekend brunches when the place was packed. And they had all swapped jokes, talked about the Astros' bad season and stuffed themselves. It hadn't been awkward at all. In fact, those had been the best times of his life.

But the atmosphere at Pablo's was so steeped in personal history for both him and Jo that Bobby wondered suddenly if bringing her here this morning was such a bright idea after all. True, the suggestion had perked her right up—in fact, he'd suspected the idea of *where* she would be eating was more appealing than who she would be eating with. He prayed he was wrong, though.

He had two hopes for this outing. One, that it would be an icebreaker for them. Also, that she would open up a little about what had really happened at her house last Friday night. But if they were just going to be dragged into memories, into thinking about the past, they would never get anywhere.

But he needn't have worried. When they walked through the door into air full of the smell of fresh tortillas, Jo's face lit up. "I'm starving," she said.

For a moment her enthusiastic response hid the signs of stress he'd seen in her face. The dark circles under her eyes. The pinched, wary look that had him so worried.

He smiled. One of the things he loved about Greg and Jo was that they loved food as much as he did. The downside was, Greg had fancied himself the next Wolfgang Puck, but his cooking was awful. Spectacularly awful. Bobby couldn't count the number of meals he'd sat through at their house where the only edible things on the table were side dishes he and Jo had managed to sneak in from the grocery store. Or just bread.

They nabbed a booth by a window. Though she couldn't see out, Jo basked in the sunshine spilling through on her. The way the light played in her auburn hair wreaked havoc on Bobby's senses. He could have stared at her forever.

"Do you need help with the menu?" he asked her, remembering suddenly that she couldn't read the selections herself. He hadn't been around her since she'd lost her vision.

She shook her head. "Not if they still have the same number six breakfast special."

"Nothing changes here."

The restaurant stayed the same, he thought with a bite of regret. Only they had changed.

"Then I'm all set," Jo said.

The waitress scribbled down their orders and filled their coffee cups. Jo smiled at Bobby. "Thanks for bringing me here. It takes me back to better times."

"I was beginning to worry you wouldn't want the reminder."

"I wasn't sure I did," she said carefully. "But you know what? I've been trying so hard to forget, sometimes it seems all I've really forgotten are the good times. I dwell too much on the negative, I think. You know, the end."

He nodded in understanding. "I feel that way too, sometimes."

"But this is nice." Jo drew in a deep breath and flipped her hair over her shoulder. "Once I tank up on spicy chorizo, it'll be even nicer."

He laughed.

She leaned forward. "How is your family, Bobby? How's Denise?"

Denise was his youngest sister. Of his four siblings, she

was the one Jo had gotten to know best during the short time they were going out. Jo and Greg had stayed a few days last Christmas in his little cabin on his parents' ranch in East Texas.

"I've wanted to call her," Jo explained, "but..."

She didn't finish. She didn't have to. She had assumed that since she and Bobby weren't going out anymore, her sister wouldn't want to continue their budding friendship. But she was wrong.

"Denise would love to hear from you anytime. Especially now. She's eight months pregnant."

Jo brightened. "How terrific!"

Bobby shook his head. "Not exactly terrific at the moment. Her husband, Tom, works for a high-tech company and he's in Indonesia right now."

"Is Denise there, too?"

"No, because of their health insurance Denise can't be out of the country until she delivers the baby. So she's staying at the ranch with my parents. And she's going out of her mind."

"Isn't Tom going to come back for the birth?"

"He's going to try. But you know how these things go—they aren't exactly on schedule."

"Poor Denise!"

He laughed. "Poor nothing! My mother is fussing over her like Denise is a queen and the baby she's carrying is a little princess or prince. And you should see the amount of stuff she received at her baby shower. I never saw such a haul. She and Tom are going to have to move into a bigger house just so they'll have room to store all the baby's loot."

She smiled knowingly. "Uh-huh, and I bet you haven't bought a single thing for this new niece or nephew, have you?"

"Well..." As a matter of fact, he had gone a little overboard at the toy store one afternoon. "You know how close Denise and I are. I wanted to get something special."

Jo translated. "In other words, you bought the most gigantic teddy bear you could find, right?"

She knew him too well. "Technically it's a *panda* bear," he answered a little defensively. Then he shrugged helplessly, as if it were all beyond his control. And maybe it was. He loved kids. "After I bought that big Clifford dog for Lucia's boy I could hardly be a skinflint this time around."

"Oh, no, of course not." She chuckled. "These kids are going to grow up thinking of you as Uncle Pushover."

"That's okay by me," he said, smiling. "Being an uncle's the best job in the world. You can spoil a kid silly and then blame the parents if the little darling acts like a brat."

"You don't fool me. You'd spoil your own kids silly, too."

"Only for selfish reasons. Haven't I always said the best reason to have kids is so you can play with their toys?"

"That's right, I'd forgotten."

Her smile disappeared, followed by his.

Uncomfortable silence swamped them. The last time they had talked about children, they'd been assuming that parenthood might be a responsibility they might end up sharing someday. Now the mere mention of children ground their conversation to a halt.

Damn it. He hated that things had turned out this way. He wished they could just be honest with each other. But he still sensed Jo holding herself back, and not only when it came to the break-in. This formal, wary manner was nothing like the warm person he'd known last winter.

Or maybe she simply wasn't as nostalgic for the old days as he was.

"So you've been talking to Willie behind my back." She said this with a wry tone, but there was an undercurrent of accusation in the statement as well.

"We've had a beer together once or twice, that's all."

"Hmm. Strange that he wouldn't have mentioned it."

"Not so strange if you consider that I asked him not to."

"Why did you do that?"

"Because I didn't want you to think I was spying on you."

"But you were."

"I was checking up on you, not spying," Bobby said, though he feared she wouldn't differentiate between the two. "You can't blame me for wanting to find out if you're all right."

"You could have called me to find that out."

"Last time we talked it seemed like you didn't want me around."

Her lips twisted thoughtfully, and a look of genuine regret crossed her face. "I know. I'm sorry about that day at the hospital, Bobby. I acted like a real pill."

He shrugged, but inside he felt a pinpoint of hope. They were talking. It was a start. "Maybe it wasn't the best time for me to pay a visit."

"It was wonderful of you."

"Well, no one's at their best after they've had an accident."

"Especially after they've just discovered they might be blind for an indeterminate length of time," she said. "That really knocked the stuffing out of me."

He didn't say anything. What could he say besides the

fact that he was sorry? She was probably sick to death of hearing people's expressions of sympathy by now.

She surprised him by laughing. "Don't feel sorry for me, Bobby. I've stopped wallowing in self-pity. Going back to work after my forced vacation has been a real shot in the arm. I'm getting better."

He tilted his head and studied her as the waitress delivered their food. He noticed that Jo picked up her utensils and poked at her breakfast taco studiously, memorizing its placement in front of her. Other than her overly careful demeanor, he didn't suppose an unsuspecting person would have guessed that she couldn't see.

"Do you mean your eyesight's getting better?"

"The last time I went to the doctor they were very optimistic because they said I was receiving more light. And I can make out large objects better than before, I think, though most of the time things just seem bright and blurry instead of dark and blurry. But then sometimes..." She frowned.

"What?" he prompted.

She shook her head. "I'm not sure. Sometimes it almost seems that I can make things out. But that might just be my imagination filling in details."

He tried to imagine what she must be going through.

"It's all pretty strange," she said.

"But when you said you were getting better..."

"I meant in my head," she explained. "It took me several weeks to realize that the world hadn't come to an end because I couldn't see."

"For most people it would take much longer than that," Bobby observed.

"Most people aren't as lucky as I am. I was well insured—for a musician. Greg, Mr. Safety, insisted on my spending a lot to get good coverage. And while I was in the hospital, I learned how fortunate I was. Some there—little children, even—were totally blind, with no prayer of ever regaining their sight. But I have hope. The doctors say there's no reason why I shouldn't recover. And the most important thing is, whether I can see or not, I can still do what I love best.''

''Sing?'' he guessed.

She nodded. ''The people at Tumbleweeds have been great. I've done three shows there since the accident and we're going to be regulars there twice a week now. Plus we've got other gigs lined up around the city starting in a few weeks. So my disability isn't going to hurt me at all—unless I fall off a stage or something. But I'm such a klutz I could have done that back when my eyesight was twenty-twenty.''

''You're amazing,'' he couldn't help saying.

Her cheeks went rosy and she poked at her food. ''Remember Tammy?'' she asked after taking a few swallows.

He nodded. ''Of course. Who could forget her?''

''She's been a real help. She looks me over before I go on to make sure I haven't put on a pajama top by mistake or that I haven't applied eyeliner on my lips.''

''Have you ever?''

''Not so far, but I wouldn't put it past me.''

He laughed again. ''So you have another gig tonight?'' he asked. Willie had mentioned something about it.

''Yeah. Thank heavens. I like getting out of the house and doing things.''

If that were the case, she couldn't have had a very good weekend. From what Bobby had seen these last couple of days, she had been holed up inside her house like a hibernating bear. The only time he'd seen her go out was when she'd gone over to her next-door neighbor's house for a few minutes. Likewise, Bertie had visited Jo's place once. Jo was usually a much more active person. She loved outdoor activity. Yet she hadn't ventured outside her house even to water the pot of wilting begonias on her front step. True, she couldn't see the flowers. And yet they had apparently been well cared for before now.

She'd sworn that the break-in seemed just like juvenile mischief. A one-time deal. So what had her so scared she didn't want to step outside her front door?

Why didn't she just confide in him? "And you haven't noticed any suspicious activity at Tumbleweeds?"

Her face, which had been so animated just moments before, seemed to shut like a steel trap. Bobby knew he'd made a blunder. He'd have done anything to take back his question now. But he couldn't, any more than he could help seeking answers. Jo wanted him to think that she was shrugging off the attack, yet he could sense the fear lurking behind her eyes.

"I thought you were going to drop your Texas Ranger bit," she said stiffly.

"I'm not asking you as a Texas Ranger. I'm asking you as a friend. Someone who cares about you. God, Jo, it's obvious you know something's wrong. You're jumpy as a frog."

Her wide lips pursed. "*Now* I am. I was fine until you jogged my memory. Before that I was actually enjoying myself."

"Baloney. When I came to your house today you looked panicky."

"That's because someone had just told me there was a man watching my house!"

He stopped himself. She was right. A person would be freaked out if they'd just been told that.

Impulsively he reached out and took her hand, which

she reflexively jerked back. "Jo, I'm sorry. Can you blame me for worrying about you?"

She sighed in frustration. He didn't understand her—didn't understand what she had to hide from him. But he was trying. Lord knows he was trying.

"I don't need you to worry about me."

"I think you do."

"Well, we're at a stalemate then," she said.

"Don't you have any suspicions?" he asked. "The hair taken from the boot scraper was brown."

"Yes, I know. The police told me that. Unfortunately, about half the people I've ever known have had brown hair. For that matter, it could have been Greg's hair."

After six months? On a boot scraper that was sitting on a porch in the open air? Not likely. She knew that as well as he did. Why was she going out of her way to put him off like this? "Haven't you noticed anything strange at all?"

She crossed her arms stubbornly. "Just that suddenly you're hanging around again. You've made yourself scarce for a long time."

"That wasn't my choice. I told you it was pretty clear at the hospital that you didn't want me around."

"I didn't want your pity."

"That's not why I was there. I was there because I cared for you. I'd wanted to see you before then, to talk to you, but I couldn't face you, Jo. I felt I'd let you down. Most of all, I'd let Greg down."

She groaned. "Oh, Bobby! We went over this. It was my fault as much as yours. I wanted you to stay with me that night. I wasn't thinking about Greg at all."

"It wasn't your job to."

"I was his sister!"

"I was his partner," he muttered. It was an almost sacred bond between lawmen. Regardless of responsibility, having a partner killed was a scar men and women in law enforcement carried in their memories, in their souls, for as long as they lived.

"You caught the bastard who killed him, Bobby," Jo said, her voice full with emotion. "You couldn't have done anything more."

"Yes, I could have. I could have been there when Greg needed me and he might not have been killed at all."

"Or you might have been killed along with him."

Bobby fell into an anguished silence. It would be dishonest to say that he wished he had been killed along with Greg, because he didn't. He loved life. He just didn't like living with guilt. And besides, he knew in his heart that if he'd been there, things would have turned out differently that night. Criminals weren't brave; they were more likely to go after a lone officer. That night Greg had been alone, a vulnerable target, because Bobby wasn't there when he was supposed to be.

Jo sighed and tossed her napkin down on the table, obviously giving up on the idea of cleaning her plate. "Maybe you'd better take me home. This hasn't turned out the way I'd hoped."

As her words sank in, Bobby's heart seemed to stop. Across the table, Jo's face glowed.

The way she'd hoped?

"What had you hoped for, Jo?"

She shook her head. "Never mind."

But he had an answer. Even though she tried to make it look like her hide was tough as a walnut, even though she did her damnedest to act like it was all over between them, she still cared. She'd been hoping this outing would be an icebreaker, too.

And he'd spoiled it by bringing up the break-in.

Or maybe he'd just brought it up too soon.

HER BIG MOUTH. Greg had always told her it would get her in trouble. *Hadn't turned out the way she'd hoped?* She might as well have come out and admitted to Bobby that she had the hots for him. Her face was still burning.

She wished she could have seen how he reacted. Had he been embarrassed? Appalled? Had he wanted their meeting to turn out differently, too?

Disappointment coursed through her, though it was foolish of her to have hoped that she and Bobby could pick up where they left off. Not when where they left off was the night Greg died. They couldn't even have an hour-long breakfast without returning, inevitably and hopelessly, to Greg and the guilt they shared.

She sensed them approaching her house. Well, guess what? She'd lived without Bobby Garcia all these months and she'd been fine...if you didn't count the heartache, the aching loneliness, the traffic accident and the blindness. She was trying to be brave. If he dropped her off and she never heard from him again, that would be fine.

He stopped his car and let it idle. "Mind if I call you?"

She turned toward him. "To check up on me, you mean?"

As soon as the words were out of her mouth, she could have kicked herself. That wasn't what had been in her heart. Why did she have to be so churlish around him, so defensive?

He let out an impatient breath. "Yeah. To check up on how you're feeling and what you're thinking and what's going on in your life. You weren't the only one who had hopes for this morning, Jo. I've missed you. Maybe I didn't mention that before."

She smiled. His words lifted her from the depths of despair right up onto cloud nine. Was it any wonder she'd missed him? "Maybe I wasn't listening."

"Are you listening now?" he asked. "Because this isn't just about the break-in, Jo. I wish that hadn't happened. I'd like to catch the jerk who did it. But it happened and hopefully it's over and at least we're talking again. We were good friends, remember?"

They were a lot more than that, she wanted to say.

But maybe he was right. Maybe the thing to do was start back where they began—as friends. Could they manage that without Greg? He'd been their bond, their glue. Would they ever be able to be together without thinking about her brother? They had attempted to this morning, and look what happened.

She dismissed the nay-saying thoughts skimming through her head. It had taken weeks for her to have hope for her eyesight. Maybe it was time she reserved some hope for her and Bobby, too.

"Thanks, Bobby. I'd like it if we could be friends again."

"Maybe we should take baby steps."

She nodded. "Right, let's see. Brunch today. What comes next?"

"Maybe I could come hear you sing at Tumbleweeds sometime. Like tonight."

"Anytime," she agreed.

She could feel his smile. In fact, she would have sat there like a fool, forever basking in the warmth of the front seat and his friendship, if Bobby hadn't finally given her a verbal nudge.

"You want me to go inside with you?"

She shook her head. "No sense in that."

"Be careful, Jo."

"Friends," she warned Bobby. For a little while she

forgot that getting too close to Bobby and his inquiring mind could be dicey. "I don't need to be smothered. I'm not helpless, you know."

"Not as long as there's a boot scraper handy," he joked.

She laughed and got out of the car, then slowly made her way up the walk. She turned to him and waved when she was halfway to the door because she couldn't stand the thought of him watching her bumble up the sidewalk. She heard his car glide up the street—and then stop. She smiled to herself. Bobby was willing to let her think that he wasn't watching out for her...but not willing to actually leave her on her own. Try as she might, though, she couldn't resent his watchdog instinct. The attention was flattering—and when you came right down to it, wasn't too much Bobby better than too little?

After she had opened her door and shut it behind her, she listened closely and heard his car continue down the street.

She frowned; for all her bravado, now that she was inside her house again, the old worry returned. She needed to call Nina Monteverde. The calls she'd put in to Nina's home so far had only turned up the same answering machine message. Was she on vacation?

She tried to consider her options. Maybe if she worked with the operator, she could get the number for the Monteverde business in Rio, All That Glitters, and try her there. If nothing else, surely an employee would be able to inform her of Nina's whereabouts.

She crossed the living room to Greg's old chair. The phone sat on a table next to it. Halfway across the room, she tripped. Reaching down, she picked up the afghan that usually rested on the back of the couch. She must have knocked it over this morning.

"Klutz!" she scolded herself.

She replaced the throw and then went to the chair and sank down in it. And down. Her stomach lurched as she landed against the hard springs with a thud. Her legs jutted out awkwardly in front of her and her elbows were unnaturally high on the armrests. *Because the bottom cushion wasn't there,* she realized. Someone had removed it.

Someone had been in her house.

Might still be in her house.

It was as if all the air had been sucked out of her. She sat very still, looking, but not seeing.

Oh God, oh God, oh God... They were the only words that ran through her head. What was going on? Her heart was racing, hammering in her chest. It was so quiet in the house she could hear her pulse pounding in her temples.

She nudged her toe around in front of her and found the cushion on the ground. Someone had torn her house apart. The same someone, she was sure, who had been here before. Who might be here even now. He might be watching her. Waiting...for what?

Call the police, she thought. The phone was right there.

But if the man was still in the house, she wouldn't be able to utter a single word.

She had to get out of there. She could phone the police from Bertie's. Without conscious thought she counted to five. Then, with all the strength she had, she ran. She flew to the front door, threw it open and started yelling her head off. And with lungs like hers, screaming was one thing she could do very well.

Within seconds, not just the Winstons but half the neighborhood was standing around her. The police had been alerted. And Bertie Winston stood in the living room with Jo, marveling at the mess. Every drawer had been opened, she said, its contents dumped on the floor. Cushions had been not only pulled off the furniture, but sliced open. And it wasn't just the living room, Bertie said, but the kitchen, too. And her bedroom looked as if it had been completely upended—bed pulled apart, dresser drawers gone through, clothes turned inside out.

As each room's destruction was described to her, Jo felt increasingly nauseous. She clamped her hand around her stomach. Everything she owned had been pawed through. She'd never felt so scared, so violated. Her whole body was shaking.

"Oh, dear," Bertie said anxiously. "You'd better sit down."

"No," she said tightly, "I'll wait for the police."

Bertie tsked. "And we thought after all the work you'd had done this morning, this house would be safer than Fort Knox."

Jo tilted her head toward her neighbor. "Work? What are you talking about?"

"The locksmith that was here this morning," Bertie said. "His paneled truck was here till just about...oh, couldn't have been much more than fifteen minutes ago."

"You *saw* the locksmith, Bertie?"

"Yes, through the window. Not that I'm nosy or anything, but I heard the door slam outside. The van said A-Z Locksmiths. But of course you know that, since you called him."

She shook her head, feeling sick again. "That's just the trouble, Bertie. I didn't call a locksmith."

CHAPTER FIVE

HE'D PROMISED not to smother her. Okay. But he hadn't promised not to snoop.

Bobby made this rationalization to himself as he pored over old newspaper articles on the microfiche at the downtown police station. He would have gone to Ranger Company A headquarters, but his boss, Captain Doug Henderson, was already complaining they were overloaded. Right now Bobby was investigating a corruption case involving a real estate deal a developer had made with the city, and he had to testify next week against a killer they had just extradited from Mexico. And now, for better or worse, he was getting involved in Jo's problem. He didn't want his boss to know he was getting sucked into a personal investigation.

Maybe he should just ask for vacation, he thought. In fact, he would. He sure as hell wasn't going to be able to concentrate on real estate while Jo was acting so strangely.

An internet search on Jo had produced mostly local music reviews. But when he dug deeper, the results reminded him once again of what a dismal year she had been having. A year of accidents and funerals, it looked like. Jo's car accident had rated a snippet in the paper, but Greg's murder and the subsequent police funeral took up several articles. Bobby dug back a little further and discovered that last autumn a friend of Jo's had died in a boating accident; the picture accompanying the article showed Jo, face drawn—one of the crowd at the time the woman's missing boat had been found off Galveston Island.

Bobby combed his memory to see if he'd heard about the drowning at the time. He couldn't recall. If he had heard about it, he'd never realized that the woman had been such a good friend of Jo's—a college friend, it said in the paper. But then, he hadn't met Jo until later.

Poor Jo. A person shouldn't have to go through so much in such a short time. That she had, and still maintained her equilibrium, made her seem all the more amazing to him.

But he'd always known she was extraordinary. Never more so than this morning, when she'd described her blindness without a trace of self-pity. She'd been through so much, yet she still managed to cling to hope.

He still had hope, too. Hope that they could break down this terrible wall of anguish that had been erected between them. But before he could begin to break down the past, he needed to figure out the present. What was going on that made Jo so reluctant to really open up to him? What was happening in her life that she felt she couldn't share with him?

Unfortunately, none of the articles gave him a clue to why someone would have broken into Jo's house last Friday night. Or why Jo didn't want to talk to him about it.

Maybe he was being led astray by delving into the past. Maybe he should be looking into her life at Tumbleweeds. After all, nightclub life was notoriously seedy, and while Tumbleweeds wasn't exactly a dive, it wasn't the Mickey Mouse Club, either. Could someone there be blackmailing Jo for some reason? Could there be drugs going through the place?

He shook his head. Yeah, right. Jo involved with drugs? She was a sportswoman. The kind of person who felt guilty for only making it to the gym three times a week. Not to mention, her brother had been brutally murdered while sitting in front of a house with a meth lab. She wasn't likely to want to do anything to enrich the pockets of anyone who could be even remotely responsible for her brother's death.

Still, what else could it be? Whenever Bobby brought up the subject of the break-in, she became antsy and defensive, almost as if she were protecting someone. He decided to give Tumbleweeds a look-see tonight. Maybe something hinky would jump out at him. He'd told her he wanted to see her sing, so there would be no reason for her to be suspicious when she showed up at the bar.

And what the hell. It gave him another excuse to be with her for a few more hours today.

As he was leaving the station, Ed Taggart fell into lockstep beside him. "Sure is strange, isn't it?"

Bobby looked at the man, confused. "What is?"

"About Greg's sister, Jolene, and the burglary."

"Any leads?"

Ed stopped. His face blanched, as if he'd just blundered. "You haven't heard?"

Bobby's feet felt numb beneath him and his heart thumped heavily in his chest. "What's happened?"

"Her house was broken into again. Made a real mess this time, sounds like."

"Is Jo okay?" Bobby asked.

"I think so. I'm going over there right now to do a follow-up since I was the senior officer on the last call."

Bobby pushed him toward the door. "I'm right behind you, Ed."

MORE THAN ONE of the neighbors had seen the locksmith truck. They all had assumed Jo was home; she no longer owned a car so her empty driveway was no indication that she was away. No one had seen her leave with Bobby, apparently.

No one except the man who'd broken into her house.

Of all her neighbors, only Bertie could remember seeing the mysterious locksmith, but it was from a distance and she was unable to supply the police with a detailed description. Just that he was short, medium build, and wearing a navy-blue jumpsuit. The jumpsuit was stolen, no doubt, from the same person the van was stolen from. The man was also wearing a billed cap that had not only shaded his face but also covered his hair.

Jo's skin was still crawling at the idea of the man entering her house with apparent ease and pawing through all her things. He had even gone through her refrigerator—unscrewing pickle jars and scooping margarine out of its tub. It was the most peculiar thing she'd ever heard of. Some of the destruction would have seemed laughable if it weren't for the police saying that at first glance it looked as if the slashes in her furniture had been made with a serrated knife.

The idea of that creepy-voiced man from last Friday turning into a knife-wielding lunatic gave her chills.

Though doing so went against the grain, she continued to profess ignorance to the police. There was no way she could bring up the name Terry Monteverde. Especially not before she contacted Terry's sister, Nina. If only she could talk to Nina, maybe she could have some answers. But until then, and maybe not even after, there was no way she could utter a peep about her suspicions.

As she was standing outside, verbally tap-dancing around more police questions, a car screeched up to the curb. The sudden noise made her heart stop—but of course she was safe now. The police were here. She'd been safe all along, in fact. The man in the locksmith van had cleared out approximately fifteen minutes before she'd returned from breakfast. But of course there was no way she could have known that as she'd been frozen in that chair, her heart pounding in terror. Her blindness made her feel exposed, unsafe. She hated being so helpless. Most of all, she hated it that some crazy man out there knew that she was vulnerable.

A car door slammed and footsteps sprinted up the walk. "Jo!"

It was Bobby. Thank God.

They started speaking at once.

"I called your apartment—"

"I was at the police station—"

They faltered and he brought her into his arms for a strong bear hug. She liked it. Liked it far too much, in fact. It would be oh so easy to lose herself, and lose sight of her problems, in the comfort and protection of those strong arms of his. And she needed to remain on alert.

Again conflicting emotions flooded her. Although she felt safer having Bobby here, there was no doubt in her mind that this newest turn of events was going to throw his natural curiosity into overdrive. He might talk about not smothering her and simply being her friend, but the Texas Ranger in him would want answers. Answers she couldn't give him.

"What happened?" he asked.

She stepped back self-consciously and took a deep breath. No doubt there were several very interested policemen watching their reunion. "Ask these guys."

An officer filled Bobby in. "One of the neighbors saw a locksmith van in front of the house while Jo was out this morning."

"While she was..." Bobby let out a string of muttered curses. "Damn it!"

"What's the matter?" Jo asked.

"I'm a jerk," he said. "I should have come in with you."

"There was no way you could have known anything was wrong. The door didn't appear to be tampered with. I didn't figure out someone had broken in until I was already inside with the door bolted behind me."

"That's why I should have come in."

"It was the middle of the morning, for heaven's sake," she said. "Who would have thought the man would choose that moment to break into my house?"

"What about this locksmith disguise I heard about?" Bobby asked.

A cop replied, "We called A-Z Locksmiths and they're checking up on all their personnel now. The manager did mention that one of their men failed to show up for a ten o'clock job, though."

"So if the guy had the locksmith van and was here for a while, could be he made a set of keys to the house."

The thought sent a shudder through Jo. All the work she'd paid to have done this past weekend was for nothing. The man had found a way to completely undermine the thin shred of security she was clinging to.

But she knew now that her safety had been just an illusion all along. She wasn't safe here. "Oh, God!" she groaned without thinking—and immediately wished she could retract the exclamation.

"That's it," Bobby declared, obviously hearing the fear in her tone. "You're coming with me."

"Where?"

"To my apartment. You can't stay here."

She couldn't stay in Bobby's apartment, either. If she harbored mixed feelings about merely having Bobby around again, she certainly wasn't ready to start living with him. "I called Tammy. She's on her way and she's offered to let me stay with her." An offer that, given the circumstances, seemed unbelievably nice to Jo.

"Are you sure?" Bobby said. "I'd feel better if you stayed with me."

"*I'd* feel better with Tammy." At least she didn't lust after Tammy, or have to worry about talking too much. Tammy could gabble enough for both of them. "Besides, it'll be handier for work."

Bobby spluttered in disbelief. For a moment it sounded as if he were going into cardiac arrest. "You mean to tell me you still intend to work tonight?"

"Of course." Did he think she could simply drop everything because she'd become a target for some weirdo? "I have a job to do, Bobby. That hasn't changed."

"But, Jo, have you ever considered that maybe Tumbleweeds is where this crackpot first saw you?"

She tilted her head, recalling suddenly the uneasiness she'd felt singing Friday night. She'd about decided to chalk up those heebie-jeebies to her unfamiliarity with performing in front of an audience she couldn't see. "Why would you think that?"

"Because the attacks just started. Since your accident you've only been working there again for what—a week and a half? Maybe it's some sicko who gets his jollies from knowing you can't see. Some guy stalking you."

"Bobby," one of the officers interrupted, "you should go inside and look around. It might give you some different ideas."

"What happened?" Bobby asked.

"You'd better have a look-see yourself," the officer said, "but at first glance it doesn't appear to be the work of a stalker. Whoever went through that house was looking for something."

Jo felt her heart sink into her boots. She was hoping they wouldn't point out the damage in her place to Bobby. It was only going to make him more angry...and more suspicious. And more insistent that he watch over her like a hawk. But of course he probably would have wanted to check it out for himself anyway, and she couldn't refuse him entrance into her house. It was inevitable.

Following Bobby, they all traipsed inside again. Jo could feel his tension next to her as he surveyed the room. "What the hell...?"

Jo heard Ed Taggart's voice nearby. She hadn't even realized he was here. "Everything's been cut open or gone through or overturned. Bedroom, bathroom, kitchen, everything."

As they catalogued the damage again, Jo felt numb. What was she going to do? Besides getting the locks changed, she'd have to figure out a way to get the place put back together. But then it hardly seemed worth the effort if some maniac could just waltz in the minute her back was turned and tear it apart again. Even worse was the thought that he would come in while she *was* here. Would she ever be able to live here again?

"Forget going to Tammy's," Bobby said forcefully. "You're coming with me. We can go to the ranch."

"The ranch!" Jo exclaimed. The Garcia ranch in East Texas was about a two-hour drive north of Houston. "I can't go there."

"You can't stay here."

"What about my job?"

More important, how could she possibly call Nina in private from Bobby's place? It was imperative now that she contact Nina so that she could find out who was at the bottom of these attacks. Not to mention, she needed to make sure Nina herself was safe, which Jo was beginning to doubt.

"Forget singing, Jo," Bobby said. "There's a madman after you, and in case you haven't noticed, this attack was much more violent than the first. It's escalating."

His words weren't exactly comforting. Of course, he hadn't meant them to be. He was trying to scare the hell out of her—to make her see the wisdom of putting herself under his protection. She saw the wisdom of it, all right, but all the same, she couldn't.

She lifted her chin, putting on a brave face. "Not if you think about it logically. Friday night the man attacked me, but today he clearly waited until he saw me leave before he went through the house."

"What was he looking for?"

She swallowed. "I don't know." Never had she spoken truer words. The guy had really thrown her for a loop. "Maybe he *is* just a weirdo stalker. Could be he was trying to scare me or just wanted to go through all of my stuff. You know, those types like to collect mementos."

"Pillows and cushion fillings?" Bobby asked. "I doubt it. He was looking for something that he thought was hidden here."

"We can't know that for sure," Jo said. "Anyway, I can't just turn tail and leave the area, Bobby. If I do that, he wins."

"And if he manages to attack you again, you lose. It's ridiculous to put yourself in danger."

"I'm not going to stay here," she argued. "I told you, I'm going to Tammy's."

"Yeah, but—"

Just then, the door banged opened and somebody let out a long, deep whistle. "Holy Toledo, Jo!" Tammy exclaimed. "You always told me you were a crappy housekeeper, but this is something else!"

Leave it to Tammy to make her laugh when she was at her all-time lowest ebb. Jo wanted to hug the woman. She did, in fact, when Tammy came up to her and gave her a reassuring squeeze.

"You okay?" Tammy asked her.

"Oh, sure." She plastered on her brave face again, but it was wearing thin. The more she listened to Bobby, the more nervous she got. He was right; the man was looking for something. And it must be something pretty valuable to make him go to these extremes to find it. "I just don't know what I'm going to do."

"Pack your overnight bag right now. You're coming with me."

"I don't think that's wise," Bobby interjected. "I was telling Jo that I think she should leave town."

Tammy squeaked. "The girl can't leave town, Bobby. She's gotta sing tonight."

Thank you, Tammy, Jo thought as Bobby huffed in frustration.

"I'm not just being high-handed, Jo. I just want you to be safe."

"She'll be safe at my place," Tammy said.

"Besides," Jo added quickly, trying to diffuse the conflict between her two friends, "I wasn't even talking about where I was going to stay. I was worrying about what I'm going to do with the house. If it's as much of a wreck as everybody says, how will I ever make it livable again?"

"Don't worry," Tammy assured her. "Soon as the dust settles, we'll get some folks over here to do damage control. Buy a few pizzas and a six-pack of beer, you'll have volunteers galore among those cheapskate musicians. Of course, if you want quality you might have to hire a maid service.''

Bobby sighed again. ''Never mind all that, Jo. Until we find out who's at the bottom of this, your only thought should be trying to stay out of this lunatic's path. There must be some reason he keeps breaking into your house.''

Jo faced him, and she could imagine his dark, intense eyes pinned on her. ''I told you. I just don't know, Bobby.'' Squirming inwardly from the discomfort of telling more lies, she turned quickly back to Tammy. ''I guess I'll go pack.''

''I'll help you,'' Tammy offered.

Jo thought of one item that was absolutely essential. ''Oh...can you grab my address book? It's sitting next to the phone.'' Bertie had read Nina's phone number to her this weekend, but Jo wanted to make sure she had her address book in case she forgot it. She could always get Tammy to read it to her again if that happened.

''I'll get it,'' Bobby said.

Jo bit back a protest then followed Tammy into the bedroom. The last thing she wanted was for Bobby to start snooping into her address book, but if she made a stink about it he was bound to inspect it all the more carefully.

Once they were in the bedroom, she closed the door slightly.

''So the hunk's back, huh?'' Tammy whispered.

Jo heard her settling onto the bed's mattress. Or maybe the mattress was on the floor and Tammy was stepping on it. She made her way to the closet and nearly fell flat on her face after tripping over a dresser drawer. Her house, which had been hard enough for her to navigate before, was now a veritable obstacle course.

''Oh, hon, watch it!'' Tammy warned. ''Maybe you

oughta just tell me what you need and I'll see if I can pick it out of the debris.''

Jo ran a shaky hand through her hair. ''That big a mess, huh?''

''Looks like a cyclone's been through,'' Tammy observed. Then she added quickly, ''But don't worry your head about it. I guess you want a few bras, right? Underwear? They're over here somewhere....''

God, this was another indignity. She hadn't quite visualized her panties scattered to the wind for the cops to see. But the idea of her modesty being undermined was laughable. The police had also seen her quivering with fear when they'd arrived, so what was exposing a few stray foundation garments next to raw emotion and vulnerability? She felt around the closet floor until she found her small soft-sided suitcase. ''How about picking out some jeans and a few shirts?'' she asked Tammy. ''I don't need that much stuff.''

''Okeydoke.'' She heard the soft whisper of her little suitcase being loaded up. For the next few minutes, Tammy would ask if a certain garment was okay, and Jo would give her the go-ahead. Truly, she didn't care about any of this. She just wanted to get out of here.

Suddenly, Tammy stopped asking questions and Jo realized that they weren't alone in the room anymore.

''You been calling South America lately?'' Bobby asked with studied casualness.

Jo froze. ''What?''

She heard Bobby plop her address book into the suitcase. ''Your address book was opened to a number in Brazil. Seemed peculiar to me.''

''Oh!'' She shrugged as nonchalantly as her racing heart would allow. ''I called my friend Nina this weekend, that's all.''

"You can read the address book?" Bobby asked.

The skepticism in his tone rattled her. "Uh, no. I had Bertie read it out to me and I memorized it." That, at least, wasn't a lie.

"Must've been an important call if you went to all that trouble."

"As a matter of fact, it was important. I hadn't talked to Nina in a long time. Her sister died last year." She flashed an angry look in his direction. "Not that it's any of your business."

Tense silence seared the room, and for a moment she wished she hadn't said anything. She should have just laughed off his Bulldog Drummond act. Anything but offend Bobby, who, after all, was only trying to help her. There was no way for him to know that his helping could actually land her in more trouble than she could handle.

"You're right," Bobby said, and she winced at the anger in his voice. "It *is* none of my business. I guess the police have it all under control here. And you, too, Jo. You seem to know exactly what you're doing."

His words had a sinister echo, implying more than just anger. Did he think she was involved in something illegal? "What do you mean?"

He shut the door, closing them off from the inquiring minds of the police officers. "I mean I've seen places tossed in just this way before, Jo, and it's never just to scare somebody. If someone wanted to scare you he would have written on your walls, left some menacing message."

"I feel pretty menaced anyway," she assured him.

"I've seen this kind of break-and-enter before. Lots of times. Those rips in the cushions. Your mattress is in shreds. Hell, whoever went through here even tore up your old teddy bear."

Jo gulped in outrage. He'd torn up Fudge? She'd had

that toy since she was a toddler! Her parents had given it to her on her second birthday. The goofy little brown plush bear had practically been loved bald. It was one of the few relics she had left of her childhood.

But what did Bobby mean? "What do people usually rip up mattresses and childhood toys trying to find?"

"In my experience, drugs."

Jo gasped—if he'd slapped her she couldn't have been any more surprised. Did he think she was taking drugs? Or worse, dealing in them?

Tammy, who had been uncharacteristically silent through this exchange, gulped in outrage. "Wait just a cotton pickin' minute, Bobby! You might be a highfalutin Texas Ranger and think you have all the answers, but you're way off the mark if you're thinking Jo's involved in anything like that."

"I don't think it, but maybe someone else has reason to."

"There's no way," Jo said. "I hope you didn't say anything to the police about that."

"I won't have to. They weren't born yesterday. Sooner or later they'll start thinking the same thing, if they already haven't."

"Then sooner or later they'll be just as wrong as you are!" Tammy said.

"Maybe you'd better go, Bobby," Jo said, heaving a sigh. The truth was, she could be full of righteous indignation, but she couldn't be sure what the intruder had been looking for. Maybe it was drugs. Or something as valuable as drugs. "I don't think we're getting anywhere arguing about this."

There was a slight hesitation in the air. "You're right," Bobby said curtly. "I won't find any answers here, that's for sure."

The door opened and Jo heard his footsteps retreating down the tiled hallway. She felt a shiver of regret as he left. It killed her to have him think badly of her. Especially when they had just started making baby steps toward patching up their relationship.

"Men!" Tammy growled. "Here you are a nervous wreck and all he can think about is *answers.*"

Jo nodded numbly, half tempted to run after Bobby. To apologize. But she was afraid his quest for answers would lead him to some unsavory facts about her past. Facts that might not sit too well with a sworn officer of the law.

IF ANYBODY thought it was weird that he was sifting through the same police archives for the second time in one day, Bobby didn't care. He was a known workaholic around these parts anyway.

The first thing he'd done after leaving Jo's place was call Doug and tell him he needed a week off. It wasn't as if he was going to be able to get anything done on any other cases when he was so worried about Jo. His mind just wouldn't let go of it. What was going on? Why didn't she want to admit to the extent of the danger she was in and why didn't she want his help?

And he had no doubt that she was in serious danger now. They couldn't pretend it was just a one-shot burglary. Whoever it was menacing her was cleverer than Bobby had given him credit for after the first attack. That time he'd made a clean entry into her house and a quick escape, leaving few clues. But this time he'd walked into the house during broad daylight—in full view of the nosy neighbors. He'd planned and timed his break-in perfectly, and the missing locksmith hinted ominously that he was getting desperate enough now to resort to serious violence.

The thought that the bodily violence might soon be perpetrated against Jo herself made Bobby all the more frantic to find the man.

He stared at the legal pad he'd been scribbling notes on, trying to get his thoughts together. Trying to make heads or tails of any of this. The name of Jo's friend in Brazil, Nina Monteverde, was at the top of the page. What was it about that entry in Jo's address book, apart from its being in Rio de Janeiro, that had caught his eye?

Going on instinct, he went through the same material on Jo that he'd covered this morning. Working backward chronologically, he flipped past the article on her accident, past Greg's funeral, then his murder. Finally he came up with something that clicked. What he'd been looking for. The article on her friend who had drowned. Her name was Terry Monteverde. That, at least, was squaring up with what Jo had told him. Terry was Nina's sister, and she had died last September, a little less than a year ago. So possibly Jo *had* felt bad about neglecting Nina.

But would she really have been worried about neglecting a friend on another continent when she herself had just been attacked and her house broken into? Jo was a thoughtful, caring person, but even so, the timing didn't ring true. Unless she wanted to call Nina specifically for the purpose of telling her about the accident.

He frowned. Jo wasn't the type to unload her problems on someone like that. He especially couldn't imagine her doing it long-distance.

It rang even less true the more he read about this friend who had died in a boating accident off Galveston. Terry Monteverde apparently wasn't the most savory character. A jet-setting party girl with more looks than sense was the description he gleaned from between the lines of the article. As beautiful and rich and spoiled as they came. And the real topper: she was a fugitive from justice in Brazil, accused of embezzling and smuggling precious jewels. Now that was interesting.

He discovered other peculiarities as well. For instance, at the time of her death in a tropical storm in the Gulf of Mexico near Galveston Island, Terry had been visiting an old friend from college, Jolene Daniels. What the paper hadn't reported was that Jo was an excellent sailor. Her father had run a boat rental operation on the island, and Jo had practically been raised on the water. Bobby had been out with her on a lake last December, and she'd made them head in when the winds kicked up a little too strong. Just from that one instance he knew that she wouldn't mess around in a tropical storm. She wouldn't let a visiting friend do so, either.

Stranger still, the first officer on the scene at the time Terry was found was Greg Daniels, Jo's brother.

Bobby racked his brain to remember the events of last year. He'd known Greg at the time of the boating accident, had worked on a few cases with him, but hadn't yet met Jo. They hadn't met until Thanksgiving, when Greg had invited Bobby to have dinner with him and his sister because Bobby and Greg were working together on Thursday night and Bobby wouldn't be able to make it to the ranch to visit his family for the holiday. He remembered stepping through the door of Greg's house and seeing Jo standing there wearing a ridiculous apron with a cartoon lobster on it.

The moment their eyes had met, it was like someone had knocked him upside the head. He'd felt dazed, almost goofy. He'd spent the whole afternoon just staring at her, hardly able to make conversation. And he certainly couldn't eat the poor bird that had been sacrificed to Greg's meager culinary skills. But his lack of social graces hadn't mattered because Jo and Greg were more like best friends than brother and sister. They could have talked and laughed the whole afternoon away all by themselves.

November would have been two months after Terry's death. In the time he and Jo had spent together, he was sure Jo had never mentioned the accident or even her friend. He did remember Greg being gone for a few days sometime early in the fall and someone saying a friend of his had died, but Bobby and Greg had never specifically talked about the incident.

Nothing strange about that, though. Greg didn't like to talk about work. He'd been the kind of cop who was able to leave the job when he was off duty. He enjoyed movies and country music and trolling for junk at garage sales. He was always telling jokes or humming some song—completely off-key—or describing the plot of the latest TV show or movie he'd seen. His unbounded enthusiasm for the world around him was more like a little kid's than an adult's. But maybe he was able to keep that enthusiasm by not dwelling on the bad stuff. Like work. Like beautiful friends who died tragically young in accidents. He'd kept the negative stuff close to the vest.

What had gone on that weekend Terry Monteverde had drowned? Something told Bobby that it wasn't nearly as simple as it sounded. A woman, a fugitive, accused of smuggling...a boating accident...Jo. How did she fit into all this?

And did any of it tie in with the attacks on Jo now?

Maybe he was completely off track, but there was only one way to find out. And that was by talking to Jo again.

Only how could he talk to her when she got so defensive around him the moment he tried to ask a few questions? There was something she didn't want him to know.

And predictably, that just made him want to know all the more.

CHAPTER SIX

JACK PIKE WAS a man with problems. Luckily, he was also a man with a job that allowed him plenty of time to think through those problems. That was one thing to say for driving a cab. Maybe it would never make him a millionaire, but it gave him time to think. And people to talk to. Jack liked to talk.

He picked up his latest fare on Main Street near the medical center. He usually had good luck in this area. The middleaged man who got into the back seat was wearing a tailored gray herringbone suit and carrying a small black suitcase. He was probably a doctor or a medical supply salesman. Something like that. Jack tried to be careful who he picked up. You couldn't be too cautious in this business.

In an even, quiet voice—so quiet Jack slid open the window in the Plexiglas partition separating the front and back seats to hear him—the man gave him an address for a motel out by Hobby Airport.

Jack frowned. "Believe that place closed, mister."

The man shook his head. "That's impossible. I just called over there." Jack repeated the Gulf Freeway address and the guy nodded. "That's what I said. I've got a reservation over there. You don't think they'd give me a reservation if the place was out of business, do you?"

The man had a point. Maybe the motel had reopened. And if it hadn't... Well, it was the fare's dollar. *Mine is not to reason why,* Jack thought philosophically. Back in the good old days when he was a kid, businesses had one slogan: The customer is always right. He missed those days, so in his cab the passenger was always right.

As long as he paid, he amended. But this guy looked like he had plenty of cash.

Besides, Jack had his own problems to think about. He cut a glance into the rearview mirror. "You married?"

The guy sure looked married. He had that harassed, nervous look about him that in Jack's experience was usually the result of living too long around those of the female persuasion. Also, his clothes were very neat. Like there was some woman sending his duds out to the dry cleaners regular.

But to his surprise, the man shook his head.

"Lucky!" Jack drawled.

He pulled a watermelon candy out of his pocket and popped it in his mouth. He used to smoke cigarettes, but he'd given them up when fares had started complaining about secondhand smoke. "I was married. Now I'm divorced."

He waited for his passenger to interject a little something. An "Is that so?" or even a grunt. But there wasn't a peep from the back seat.

Jack sighed. "Now I've got child-care payments for a kid I hardly ever get to see. She's practically grown now. You got kids?"

When he checked the rearview, the man shook his head.

"Lucky again! You'd think once it got older the kid would get easier to handle. But you know, it don't seem to work that way. You think when they're babies that nothing can be worse than all the crying and colic and the dirty diapers, but no sooner do they stop cryin' than they start screamin'. That's bad, too, but when they stop screaming they start sulking, then rebelling. I tell you, the things my kid does, my daddy would have taken off his belt and really whupped the tar out of me.''

''Like I said,'' the man said stiffly, ''I don't have kids.''

Jack nodded. ''The thing is, if I so much as laid a hand on my kid, my ex would have child protective services on me. She's always telling me what a bad parent I am, but let me tell you, mister, *she's* the one. Spoils that kid silly.''

There was a weird noise coming from the back seat—a clicking sound. He glanced into the rearview but couldn't see anything amiss. The guy was just looking absently out the window now as if he couldn't be bothered to listen to Jack's problems. Probably hadn't been listening to him for a while now. That's the way fares were sometimes.

He should have known by the suit. Those types were always a little aloof.

He shook his head and sucked on his candy. ''This last week my ex was tellin' me that she needed money because Sara—that's my girl—wants to go on a camping trip. A coed camping trip down on the coast. Have you ever heard of such a thing? The kid's twelve. I said no way was I going to contribute to that kind of a situation. You know kids. These days even at that age they're just itchin' to experiment with booze and sex. They'll get down to that coast and no telling what all will happen.''

The clicking sound grew louder. The guy must have something in his pockets, Jack decided. Pebbles or marbles or something. People had all sorts of nervous tics.

''But of course Sara is sayin' she's going to be an outcast if she doesn't go on this thing. She's making all kinds of a stink about it. Everything at that age is about *popularity.*''

When Jack pulled into the motel, it was empty. He even drove around to the office to make sure. Completely deserted, just as he had predicted. He clucked his tongue. "Looks like you need to find yourself another place to stay."

The man frowned and pulled out his wallet. He shoved way more money than necessary through the window in the partition. "Wait here a second, will you?"

Jack turned to the guy in amazement. "You getting out here?" What for? The empty lot with the debris of old newspapers and cola cans blowing around it was enough proof the place hadn't seen a paying guest in over a year.

Nevertheless, his passenger jumped out of the car, walked three steps and stared at the empty building as if wishing could make it open. It hadn't been much of a motel to begin with, to tell the truth. Surely the fellow could afford better than a fleabag place like this. Jack was beginning to wonder if the guy wasn't a little cracked.

He rolled down his window. "There's plenty of other hotels nearer the airport, mister."

"But this one suits me," he said.

Jack's face contorted in puzzlement just as the man turned, pulling something out from under the jacket of his suit. That something was a Ruger Mini 14.

LEO STARED DOWN in distaste at the cabdriver's body, which was bleeding from the head all over the front seat. He didn't relish cleaning up the mess, but at least he'd be working in silence. Blessed silence. He couldn't abide cabdrivers who never shut up.

MAYBE BOBBY WAS right about not going to work, Jo thought. Not just because the man who had attacked her could be in the audience watching—though God knows she couldn't get that eerie possibility out of her mind. But also because she was so nervous she wasn't giving the audience their money's worth. Every time she remembered sitting in that armchair and realizing that someone had been in her house, she started shaking like a leaf.

The trick, she supposed, was not to think about it. But how could she avoid it? As she looked sightlessly out into the shadowy gray in front of her, she was reminded that *he could be out there. Right now. He could be watching her.* Maybe he was the type of sick creep who enjoyed seeing how close she was to cracking up. One look and he could probably tell he was getting to her.

Anyone could. The police had finally found the missing locksmith, who had been hit over the head, stripped of his uniform, trussed and hidden behind an empty warehouse building not far from Tumbleweeds. The man had suffered a massive skull fracture from the blow to his head and was in the hospital. The moment he'd been conscious, he'd told the police that he hadn't seen his attacker.

So the man behind the assault and her break-ins, whoever he was, was crafty. He wasn't just blundering around. He had been watching her closely, tracking her movements without her knowledge—or the knowledge of Bobby, who had been looking after her. And somehow, he must have known that she and Bobby were going to be gone for a certain amount of time that morning. How could he have known that he would have just enough time to get into her house, tear everything apart, and get out before she came back?

Or had he waited for her to come back and given up?

The more she mulled the problem over, the more antsy she became. And she couldn't stop thinking about it. She stumbled over lyrics. She sang the last half of "Crazy" first. "Crazy"—the song *everyone in the world* knew backward and forward. Her guitar player and drummer had wobbled when she'd made the mistake. She couldn't blame them. She was acting more like a nervous amateur at karaoke night than a seasoned performer.

When she stepped down after her second terrible set of the night, her legs rubbery with relief to have the wretched performance over with, Tammy slapped her on the back. "Kid, you done great."

Jo laughed. "You liar. I wouldn't have paid five cents to hear me."

"Well, you've had a rough day," Tammy admitted. "Why don't you have a beer? Loosen up?"

It would take more than a beer to get the troubles out of her head. Nevertheless, Jo nodded. Even liquid courage was better than no courage at all. "Sure, that sounds great." If nothing else, maybe it would deaden her disappointment over having given less than her best tonight. She liked to think of herself as a trouper.

Tammy hesitated. "Now I know I should be worried about you."

"Why?"

"Because you *never* drink at work."

Tammy gently led her over to the bar. It was a weeknight, so the place wasn't as packed as usual. Jo usually liked these nights because they were a little more intimate. But tonight she felt as if she should visit each table and personally apologize for what she'd put them through. Tonight nothing felt right.

"Bobby didn't show up here while I was singing, did he?" Jo asked.

"Nah, I didn't see him," Tammy replied.

Jo twisted her lips. "He'd mentioned coming to hear me sing sometime, but I imagine after today he probably never wants to see me again."

Tammy laughed. "I wasn't exactly Miss Manners to

him myself. But then, he wasn't being very nice, either, what with that talk about drugs.''

Jo nodded. Right now she couldn't think about losing Bobby yet again. It was too depressing. ''Has anyone heard from Willie yet?'' she asked Tammy.

That was another thing that had gone wrong. She'd had to sing without a bass player because Willie hadn't shown up. His absence had made her uneasy. Not that Willie had never missed a gig before. In fact, he had a reputation for being undependable—which was probably why Jo had been able to convince him to work with her on a regular basis when he was such a seasoned performer. Jo knew that Willie's reputation came from the days when he was drinking heavily...not recently. He'd been doing great since they'd teamed up.

''Don't you worry about old Willie,'' Tammy told her. ''He's probably curled up with a bottle or a card deck somewhere.''

''That's not like him.''

Tammy snorted. ''You didn't know him when. And this wouldn't be the first time he's toppled off the wagon.''

''You called his apartment?''

''Sure did. Several times.'' A glass of beer landed on the bar in front of Jo. ''Listen, Jo. When we called him this afternoon and told him I was takin' you to work, he probably saw that as a freedom from responsibility and started on a toot. He's been pretty careful since he's been drivin' you, you know. Probably he views your stayin' with me as a kind of holiday.''

''I shouldn't be staying with you,'' Jo said. This was another thing that had been bothering her all day. Tammy was generosity itself, but Jo didn't want to repay her friend's kindness by putting her in the path of a violent madman.

Tammy scoffed. "Now don't start that."

"I'm trouble. This guy, this maniac, whoever he is, is obviously watching me. Sooner or later he'll figure out I'm at your place."

"Let him!" Tammy leaned into Jo's shoulder and whispered conspiratorially, "Just between you and me and the four walls here, I've got me an automatic pistol that's never seen action outside a shooting range. Some nut steps into my apartment, he's toast."

The knowledge that Tammy had an itchy trigger finger failed to comfort Jo. She didn't want Tammy to get involved in all this. That afternoon, when she'd agreed to stay at Tammy's, she'd just been desperate for somewhere to go. Anything to get her away from her house. Away from Bobby. But now that she knew the locksmith had been beaten and could have been killed, and realized that the attacker must have been watching her movements carefully and possibly eavesdropping on her, it was all too clear that Tammy's wouldn't be a safe place for her, either. Nowhere would be for long. He would figure out where she was.

And he obviously wasn't averse to using violence against anybody—no matter how unrelated—to get at her.

She needed to keep moving. A moving target was more difficult than a stationary one. The trouble was, Tammy was too nice by half. She wouldn't hear of Jo going to stay anywhere else. But it just didn't seem right.

Tammy really was a tough, brave bird. Jo had no doubt, no doubt at all, that she would lay down her life for a friend. And that was the very thing she was most afraid of. Somehow, she had to get out of Tammy's apartment without Tammy finding out and trying to talk her into staying.

"If it's okay with you, I think I'll go back to the apartment now." She took a sip of beer.

"Why don't you hang around awhile, Jo? Then I can take you home myself." She still had a couple of hours to go on her shift.

"I would, but to tell you the truth, I'm beat. I'll just get one of the guys to take me to your place. You gave me your spare key, so I assume you don't mind my being there alone."

"Hell, no—make yourself comfortable. Plenty of soft drinks in the fridge, or hootch in the cabinets if you're interested in something harder."

"Thanks. I'll never forget how nice you've been, Tammy."

She could just imagine Tammy rolling her eyes and waving her painted fingernails in dismissal. "Quit, you're embarrassing me. Sorry, Jo, but I gotta get back to work now. I got several tables of guys who look like they're going to evaporate if I don't give them more beer pronto."

Jo nodded. "Okay. See you later."

Lying was getting easier. She'd been lying to Bobby, and now she was lying to Tammy. She had no intention of being at the apartment when Tammy returned home.

She got up and made her way to the door. Halfway there she was joined by Jim Stevens, her drummer. He was twenty, twitchy, and just itching to play in a rock band. Jim considered the material Jo performed to be pokey old-time stuff. Crowd-pleasing geezer music. But he was happy enough to be a working musician even if he was a round peg in a square hole. *Square* being the operative word. At least, it would do until INXS called him up.

"Hey, Jo! There you are. I've been wanting to talk to you about some stuff. You know, about our act?"

She tilted her head toward him. Jim was always full of

bad ideas, but he might be able to help her out tonight. She either needed a ride or help calling a cab. "What about it?"

"Well, for instance, do you know the singer Britney Spears?"

Jo coughed to cover a guffaw. "I guess I've heard the name bandied about…the few times I've pulled my head out from under my rock."

Jim chuckled uncomfortably. "Okay, it's just that I thought maybe you could consider doing a few covers of her stuff."

Jo couldn't help it. She chortled.

"I'm not kidding," Jim said, obviously disappointed by her reaction. "You shouldn't sell yourself short. If you dressed a little differently you could really be hot."

"Thanks."

"It might widen your appeal and bring in a younger crowd. You know, like get us noticed a little more. 'Oops I Did It Again' is practically a standard now."

"Mmm, right up there with 'Your Cheatin' Heart.'"

Jim hesitated. "What's that? It's got a catchy title."

Jo had to keep from sputtering in surprise. She shook her head. This boy wonder of the music world had a new idea every week, but his Britney Spears brainstorm was his worst yet. "I'd love to talk this all over sometime, Jim, but…"

"Oh, I know. You're probably in a hurry to catch your cab."

Had Jim suddenly become clairvoyant? She tilted her head suspiciously. "What cab?"

"You know. The one Willie sent over. It's waitin' right outside. The driver sent me in to tell you." He frowned. "Didn't I tell you?"

"No, you didn't." She let out a breath of relief. God

bless Willie! Even when he was on a toot he was as good as gold.

Jim took her arm and led her out to the cab. She was grateful for the assistance even if she did feel like somebody's granny. She needed to hurry if she was going to go to Tammy's place and then clear out to a hotel before Tammy got home. She'd leave a note telling her that it would be for the best if she holed up by herself for a while. A different hotel every night, so whoever was menacing her couldn't discover a pattern. Maybe she would be able to shake the attacker this way. At any rate, it was better than luring him into the lives of her friends.

After Jim handed her into the cab and shut the door, she slipped across the slippery vinyl seat to the center. She rested her hands against the glass partition dividing the front from the back seat as she gave the driver Tammy's address. As she leaned forward, she got a blast of disinfectant from the front seat.

Well, at least she knew the cab was clean.

The driver didn't say anything, but he had probably nodded. Jo was getting used to that. People sometimes forgot that blind people couldn't see their gestures.

When the car moved forward, Jo slid back and expelled a breath of relief. She was sure now that she was doing the right thing. So many people had been put out on her behalf already. The police were investigating two break-ins without having the information necessary to solve them. The locksmith, a man she didn't even know, had been beaten up. She'd lied to Bobby and then was rude to him this afternoon.

But honestly! How could Bobby even entertain the notion that she was involved in drugs after what had happened to Greg? Her own brother had been killed by drug dealers. That was the last type of person she would want to do business with! Bobby had to be crazy or majorly confused if he thought even for a moment that she would have anything to do with drugs.

Of course, considering the half-truths and evasions she'd been doling out to him, why shouldn't he be confused?

She sank further into her seat, wondering at the mess her life had turned into. It had been so good to be with Bobby this morning. For a little while in Pablo's while they discussed his family and reminisced, everything had seemed so easy between them. She'd been able to forget the worries hanging over her head and had allowed herself to wonder if things could really work out between them. Then he'd started in with the questions. But what would it have been like if they'd gotten together without all this other stuff hanging over them? Would they have gone on laughing, maybe had some more good times together? Would they have been able to overcome the shadow of the past?

Maybe she'd never know. Bobby had sounded so angry when he left her house that afternoon that she feared he might never come back. That possibility nearly made her sick with sadness.

She rested her head against the warm glass of the window, then frowned thoughtfully. It was taking a while to get to Tammy's. The cab seemed to be going fast, so she doubted they were on a city road. She leaned forward again. "Are you taking the interstate?" she asked the driver through the partition. "It's a lot faster just to cut through town."

The driver didn't answer.

"I said you shouldn't have to get on the interstate," she said more insistently. She'd heard of cabs taking advantage of blind people by taking roundabout routes. It was infuriating.

She still received no answer.

She stewed for a moment before a terrifying possibility crept up on her. Then suddenly it was as if she were back in Greg's chair again, realizing she was sitting in the middle of a ransacked house. Only this time she wasn't in her own home. She was in a vehicle flying down the highway in God only knows which direction.

Her body went rigid with fear and cold. And her heart beat with the sickening heavy timbre of a bass drum inside her chest.

Willie had not sent this cab.

Oh, God. Oh, God. She was being…

Kidnapped. That was the word. But it was a moment before she could actually accept that was what was going on. She'd been scared all day. But when she'd pictured what could happen to her, she'd imagined being beaten senseless like the locksmith. She hadn't imagined being snatched right from work—after being helped into the cab by Jim!

Think. She needed to think, not panic. But how could she help panicking when her mind was a jumble of terrified thoughts and her body didn't seem to be functioning? Aside from her sweat glands. She was drenched in perspiration. She even smelled of fear, if such a thing was possible.

She'd always assumed that violence was noisy, messy. But what scared her most now was the silence. Just the sound of the car's motor, her own uneven breathing…and something else. From up front, she heard a rattle or a clicking—sort of like the sounds ice cubes made. What the hell was that?

It didn't matter. She had to think.

She tried to recall what she knew about kidnappings, but what snatches she could remember from reading in the papers or seeing on television were not encouraging. She remembered a self-defense class Greg had insisted she take. *Don't get in a car with a stranger,* the instructor had told them, as if this were worth thirty dollars an hour. *Fight like hell to keep from getting in that vehicle.*

Well, it was too damn late for that bit of advice now, wasn't it?

The clicking continued, driving her to the brink. Why didn't he say anything? Was he watching her in the rear-view mirror? Did he know that she knew she was in trouble? She was certain the panic showed in her face.

Thoughts scrabbled around her brain like mice in a maze. What should she do? What could she do? She didn't know where she was or where she was going.

The car slowed and she felt the driver swerve onto an off ramp. They were leaving the interstate. Where were they? She couldn't even gauge how long she'd been in the back seat. Fear had confounded her sense of time.

She rolled down the window and poked her head out, leaning against the gust of air like a dog. What she could sense was all bad. She smelled cut grass—not lawn grass. Hay. They weren't even in the city anymore!

It didn't take a detective to know that this was terrible news. He probably had somewhere isolated in mind. Oh, God.

She tried to focus her thoughts. Every once in a while her brother had erupted with unasked-for advice. She remembered once watching television with him and seeing a story about a little girl who had been abducted from her home. The kidnapper had told the girl not to make any noise—and she hadn't, not even when they'd been stopped by a policeman.

"Poor kid," Greg had said. "She should've screamed her head off."

"But she didn't know that," Jo had argued. "She was just trying to pacify the guy, probably."

Greg had gaped at her. "That's women's thinking, Jo. The guy's not going to reward the kid for doing what she's told. He's just trying to get away with murder."

Murder. She gulped. But Greg had been right. Being quiet wasn't going to help her. She stuck her head further out the window and let out a blood-curdling scream.

The car swerved again and she heard a string of curses from the front seat. She screamed all the louder.

"Christ's sake, shut up!" the man yelled.

It was the same voice from Friday. But she'd known it would be.

She screamed some more. She screamed her head off.

"Nobody can hear you!" the guy shouted back at her. "We're in the middle of nowhere."

If he thought that was going to shut her up, he was nuts. She pulled on the door handle and her door cracked open.

"Jesus!"

The cab lurched and then braked. It was still moving, but she didn't care. Dying from jumping out of a moving car was better than dying at the hands of a lunatic. She'd take her chances with the pavement.

Saying a quick prayer, she threw the door open. She hadn't expected the resistance from the wind. She had to keep it open with her left arm as she pushed herself out. The next thing she knew, she was on the ground, rolling against grass and gravel and sticker burrs. She felt a sharp flash of pain, but she didn't care. She just kept rolling until she could get to her feet. Then she started running. She didn't even know where she was going. She just ran blind, stumbling. Expecting at any moment to have the guy catch up with her.

Behind her, she heard the car door closing. Then another. That made her stop, turn. Two cars? Had someone stopped to help, or did her kidnapper have an accomplice?

Just run! a voice in her head screamed. But her feet remained rooted to the spot. She couldn't move. She squinted through the darkness and could make out two sets of headlights and the silhouettes of two figures. Two.

They were fighting. She could hear them. Mutters and struggling. They must be on the ground, or... Who was helping her? She stumbled back toward the commotion and fell. She must have been eye level to the kidnapper's headlights, because a beam hit her eyes straight on. She blinked, and angled her head slightly. When she opened her eyes again, she saw someone.

She saw Bobby. He was leaning over the kidnapper.

"Bobby!" she said.

He looked up at her. It was a mistake. While he was momentarily distracted, the man threw him off and started running. She ran toward him, then tripped over a rock and went tumbling down into the ditch at the side of the asphalt road. She bit her lip and tasted blood. Before she had even stopped rolling, Bobby was at her side, picking her up.

She couldn't help it. She was weeping. She didn't know whether it was from pain or relief. "Don't stop for me, Bobby." But the moment the words were out, she became equally panicked at the idea of him running after the kidnapper. The man who had attacked the locksmith. He'd kill Bobby if he could, she was sure of that.

Bobby left her side and ran back toward the cars. She heard a door slamming, keys jangling, and footsteps running. In the distance, barely audible, Bobby cursed. Then he came back toward the spot where she was standing on trembly legs. She gripped her arm to her side. Her face burned, and her shirtsleeve had been shredded from her tumble from the car.

Bobby held her and she sucked in her breath. "Are you all right?" he asked.

"Yes, just some scrapes, I think."

"C'mon and get in the car," he said, tugging her. "We'll find him. I got a good look at him this time, at least."

Jo wasn't even sure if she *wanted* to find him. She would have been happy to get into the car with Bobby and drive forever and never look back. "How did you ever happen to show up?" she asked as he slid into the seat next to her and the car lurched forward.

"I followed you."

"Followed me?" She heard her own voice arc up practically an octave. "From where?"

"Tumbleweeds. I was waiting outside to follow you to make sure you made it home okay. I didn't expect you to be getting into the cab." He braked, then sped forward again. "Damn it! Where did he go?"

Jo looked out but saw only darkness. Unlike a few minutes ago.

The sudden, stark memory of Bobby in the beam of those headlights brought her up short. Her heart raced. "Bobby!" She turned to him. "I saw you!"

"What?" His voice sounded distracted as well as confused. "Saw me when?"

"Back there, when you were fighting. I *saw* you."

He braked the car. "Damn it! It's like he disappeared!" He reached out and took her hand. "You're probably just thinking you saw me. Maybe you heard my voice."

She frowned, surprised by the leap of her pulse when his hand touched hers. She'd been so consumed by fear she wouldn't have thought herself capable of feeling desire right now. "No, I—"

"Did you see the other guy?"

"No." She let out a sigh of disappointment. She'd only seen Bobby. But maybe she'd been so surprised to see him, she hadn't looked further. Or maybe… "No." Bobby was probably right.

"Well, I don't see him now, either."

"Where are we?"

"To our right there's pine trees and nothing but. To our left there's a plowed field. My guess is he headed for the trees. I need to call for more people. Plus we need to get you to a hospital."

"I'm fine," she said automatically.

"Like hell. You jumped out of a moving vehicle. It nearly gave me a heart attack."

"I preferred jumping to being escorted wherever Mr. Wacko felt like taking me."

A horrible thought occurred to her and she gripped the armrest. Fear sliced through her. "Bobby, I need to go back."

"Back where?"

"Back to the city. Now."

"Why? We need to wait for the police, Jo."

But she felt so awful suddenly that she knew she couldn't wait for another minute, let alone the time it would take for the cops to arrive and start searching the woods for her abductor.

"Jim told me that cab was sent for me by Willie, but it wasn't. But somehow the cabdriver knew that Willie wasn't going to be able to take me back to my house." Jo swallowed. "Willie didn't show up for the gig tonight, Bobby. Tammy called and called his apartment, but he never picked up the phone."

Bobby didn't wait for any more explanation. He headed back toward the city.

CHAPTER SEVEN

THE DOOR WAS locked so they broke a window to get into Willie's apartment. Bobby stood in the middle of the living room with his hand poised on his department issue SIG-Sauer. A cursory glance around the one-bedroom unit revealed nothing. He'd been so sure they would find some sign of foul play.

"I don't get it," he said.

"Did you see his truck out in the parking lot?"

"Yeah. It was right in front of the apartment complex."

Jo remained rooted to the spot where she stood in the apartment's kitchenette. She was still ghostly white from her abduction, and he knew what must be going through her head. If Willie wasn't here, then where was he? Maybe he'd been kidnapped, too.

"What now?" she asked.

"I'm calling the police," Bobby said. "I'm sorry, Jo, but it looks like we've got a long night ahead of us."

"Not like I was about to go to sleep anyway."

He gazed at her over the receiver. Her face was scraped and smudged with dust, and her shirt was torn and stained with dirt and blood. She was holding her arm strangely, which made him suspect that she wasn't as okay as she had declared herself to be. "We still need to get you to an emergency room."

Her lips were parted to reply when Bobby was distracted by two things at once. First, someone on the phone was answering his call. But more important, there was a thump coming from the direction of the bedroom.

He and Jo pivoted as one toward the noise.

Then, as Jo moved forward, he stopped her by bracing his hands against her shoulders. She was shivering; the skin beneath her shirt felt like ice. A wave of protectiveness surged through him. He wanted to wrap her up in warm blankets and tell her that everything would be okay. That she was safe. But now…

He looked toward the bedroom. He shouldn't have even let Jo come into this apartment with him. Of course, she hadn't wanted to stay out in his car alone in the parking lot and he hadn't wanted to let her out of his sight.

Damn it! Why couldn't he ever seem to do right when it came to Jo?

"Stay here," he told her, handing her the phone, "and keep the police dispatcher company until I figure out what's in there." He frowned. "Does Willie have any pets?"

She shook her head. "His dog, Burt, died two years ago."

The thumping continued.

"This sure as hell isn't Burt's ghost."

He strode into the bedroom and flipped on the lights. The thumps were coming from a closet he hadn't even noticed in his first pass through the apartment.

In the next room, he could hear Jo whispering their address to the dispatcher. Smart woman, he thought. First things first—a cop's sister would know that.

He drew his gun as a precaution before opening the closet door. And when he did, he opened it quickly—so quickly he nearly scared Willie half to death.

The old guy was trussed up like a Thanksgiving turkey. His hands were tied behind his back, his legs were bound tightly at the ankles, and there was a gag in his mouth. Bobby quickly undid the gag.

Reflexively, Willie inhaled a deep breath. "Hellzapoppin!" he drawled in a voice that was half excitement, half exhaustion. "I thought I'd never see daylight again!"

"It's still night," Bobby told him as he undid the ropes around his hands and feet. "How long have you been tied up?"

"Since around six, I guess. I remember I was just on my way out for dinner before the gig."

Hearing Willie's voice, Jo slammed down the phone and ran in. "Willie! Willie, are you okay?" She felt her way along the wall until she could kneel down next to him.

Willie chuckled hoarsely. "I'm not sure yet. I'm a little stiff. And my head feels like someone clubbed me with a baseball bat."

"What happened?"

He winced as he gingerly touched an ugly-looking bump that showed through the bald spot on his head. "Someone clubbed me with a baseball bat."

"Tammy was calling you all night," Jo said, holding fast to Willie's arm. Her face was etched with concern and something that looked like remorse.

"I heard the phone," he said, flapping his newly freed wrists. "But as you can see, I was otherwise engaged. Tied up, you might say. Damn!" He sat up straighter and rubbed his head again. "Whoever it was who got me gave me quite a thump."

Bobby looked at the angry bluish-red lump on Willie's head. This made two people they needed to get to the emergency room. But he also hoped Willie would be joining him at the police station. "Did you get a look at the guy?" It would help if there could be two of them going through mug shots instead of just one.

Willie shook his head. "Nope, 'fraid not. What happened was, I was walking out the door. I forgot something so I went back inside to get it. That's when I heard a noise. Next thing I know I was out colder than yesterday's gazpacho."

"Then you didn't see whoever it was who hit you at all."

Willie shook his head. "Sorry, Bobby."

"Thank God he didn't kill you!"

At Jo's exclamation, Willie looked alarmed. "Huh? Who'd want to kill an old leathery bird like me?"

"The same person who wanted to kidnap me, we suspect. It's been quite an evening." Jo filled Willie in on the unpleasant details of the night. "I feel so guilty," she said when she had finished relating the story of her kidnapping. "So many people are getting hurt. First that locksmith, and I'm sure the kidnapper stole that cab from someone. And now you. If he'd done anything worse to you, Willie, I'd never have been able to live with myself."

"It's not your fault, Jo. Stop talkin' like it is."

Jo just looked frustrated.

"Who'd be wantin' to do all this?" Willie asked. "It doesn't make sense."

"Not to me, either," Bobby said.

But he noticed Jo was conspicuously silent on the subject. They'd get to that later.

"He *could* have killed you. You must have been terrified," she said, "locked in the dark for so long."

"Tell you the truth, it was a more sobering experience than my first trip to AA." Willie rubbed his whiskery chin. "I had plenty of time to think about what matters and what doesn't. And I decided that if I ever got out of that closet, first thing I was gonna do was call up Lena and ask her if she'd like to get hitched."

Jo smiled. "That's great! I'm so glad. Typical, though, that it would take a clunk on the head to make you propose, Willie."

"That's just what Lena will say," he agreed with a rueful smile.

Bobby looked at Jo. "Are the police on their way?"

She nodded.

"Good. We'll have a lot to tell them before we head out."

Jo's brow furrowed. "Head out where?"

"First, we're going to an emergency room to have you two looked over," he told her. "Then we're driving out to the ranch."

She shook her head. "I can't go there, Bobby."

He had predicted an argument. She was as headstrong as they came. "You can't *not* go there, as far as I can tell. Staying here you're just putting yourself and everyone else you know in danger."

The last half of the statement seemed to affect her reasoning as nothing before had. Slowly, she nodded. "But what about you? I can't put you in danger. And your family..."

"Your mysterious attacker is still running around in the woods, I imagine."

"How do you know?"

He held up a set of keys that he'd pulled out of the cab's ignition before making chase. "Unless he's an expert at hot-wiring, he won't be able to start up his cab. Besides, he's bound to know there'll be police all around. He won't want to go back to that vehicle anyway."

She nodded. "So he can't get back here to follow us anytime soon."

"We should be able to make a clean escape without

anyone seeing us. There's no way he'll be able to trace us."

She let out a long breath. "I guess you're right then. The only way for me to try to stop all of this craziness is to get out of town."

Willie laughed. "Don't worry, Jo. Even the best of us have had to get out of town at one time or another."

WILLIE REFUSED to go to the hospital with them. The stubborn old goat insisted that he had survived wickeder bumps on the head than the one he had received tonight. In the end, they hadn't been able to persuade him otherwise.

Later, Jo had reason to wish she'd held out against Bobby's insistence for emergency care. She'd felt okay until the doctor had started trying to make her feel better. Now the antibiotic a nurse applied to her many scrapes and deeper cuts stung like a hundred little needles pricking into her skin and made her eyes tear.

But that was nothing next to the shooting pain when the doctor tried to rotate her arm.

"This is just a sprain, not a break," the doctor announced.

Whatever it was, it hurt like hell now.

After the doctor had fitted her with a sling and she'd swallowed down several aspirin, a nurse helped her back out to the waiting room. Jo had left Tammy there a half hour before, nodding over yesterday's newspaper and a cup of cold coffee. Jo knew Tammy would be worried when she got home to an empty apartment, so Bobby had called her from the hospital to assure her that Jo hadn't disappeared. After she'd heard the abbreviated version of the night's events, Tammy had insisted on coming down to the ER, which worked out well because she could bring Jo's suitcase, which was still at her house.

Tammy had also generously volunteered to sit in the waiting room while Jo checked in and waited to see the doctor. During that time, Bobby was off at the police station looking through mug shots to see if the man he'd fought off was one of the three hundred most wanted in the Houston area.

Now Tammy met the nurse halfway through the waiting room and guided Jo over to a chair. Time to wait for paperwork, and for Bobby. "What's the diagnosis?" Tammy asked her.

"Just a sprained arm and some cuts."

"You look like someone ran a rake over you."

Jo laughed. "Thanks, Tams, you're great for my ego."

"Does it hurt much?"

"Only when I breathe," she answered, then she chuckled. "Actually, I'm exaggerating. It's not that bad."

"No need to be stoic," Tammy admonished her. She sighed in frustration. "I hope somebody catches that son of a bitch! The man is obviously some sort of lunatic obsessed with you, Jo. You hear about these things all the time, but you never think you'll come any closer to them yourself than a movie on TV."

Jo nodded.

"I wish you'd followed my advice, hon, and waited for me."

"He would have gotten us both, probably."

"Humph! Maybe I would have got *him,*" Tammy said. "But what I don't understand is, why did you take a cab in the first place? You told me that one of the guys in the band was taking you home."

Jo could only hope that Tammy couldn't see the panic in her eyes as she thought of a suitable excuse. "I figured

I'd get Jim to take me home.'' She tried to think fast, to remember events that now seemed as if they'd happened years ago instead of mere hours. ''But then he started pestering me about singing bubblegum songs and I just couldn't deal with it. So when he told me there was a cab waiting, I took it. It was a stupid decision on my part, I know...''

Tammy was immediately remorseful. Which of course only made Jo feel worse. ''That Jim! I'm sorry, hon, I'm sure everything will be okay.''

But would it? Despite Bobby's assurances, Jo still had her doubts. This person they were dealing with—the slight brown-haired man—seemed to know just when to attack. He was either very keen or very lucky.

''I hope everything works out for you and Bobby, Jo.''

Jo stiffened. ''Bobby's just trying to look after me.''

''Right. Because he's in love with you.''

She faltered in response. ''Oh, sure. So in love he was accusing me of illegal activity this afternoon.''

''He was just trying to come up with an answer and he hit on a boneheaded one.''

Jo shrugged. The idea of Bobby being in love with her should have made her off-the-charts happy. Instead, it sent a numb pang of regret through her. Bobby was being so good to her, and how was she repaying him? Not with honesty, that was for sure. He'd risked his life tonight to help her, and yet she still was hesitant to reveal all she knew.

''Bobby's just a friend. The main reason he's here at all is that he made a promise to my brother to look after me if anything happened to Greg.''

''Oh, for Pete's sake. Believe me, Jo, I saw the way that man was looking at you when I came in here, and it was not like you were his cross to bear, if you get my meaning.

The last time I saw a look like that on a man's face, I ended up eloping to Mexico within six hours."

"Well, I'm not eloping. I'm just going to a safe house. Though I hope hiding out on his family's ranch isn't a mistake."

Tammy patted her leg. "Maybe we were too hard on him this afternoon at your place. He's right. You need to be somewhere far away from here."

But was anywhere safe? Jo was beginning to wonder if there was anywhere she could go where this man wouldn't find her. But perhaps Bobby was right. If there was no chance the guy could follow them out to Bobby's ranch tonight, how would he ever be able to locate her? There was no way for him to know Bobby's name, much less where he lived.

She clung to that thought.

"Here comes Galahad now," Tammy said. She hopped to her feet. "And my cue to exit." She bent down and hugged Jo. "Good luck, Jo. Give me a buzz sometime and let me know you're okay."

"I'll be back soon."

She could feel Tammy's smile. "In a secluded cabin with the hunk in boots? Don't be a nitwit. Take your time, girl."

Bobby walked Tammy out to her car and returned just as Jo was checking out. The bill for the ER visit was staggering. Not for the first time, she thanked heaven for Greg's insistence she carry comprehensive insurance.

"Where now?" she asked him as he steered her out of the hospital. It felt like it must be six or seven in the morning, yet the nurse had told her it was only two-thirty. "Could we swing back by my place to get more stuff? I'm not sure what I've got in my suitcase."

Also, she was curious to see if she'd received a message from Nina Monteverde.

"That's not a good idea, Jo. I don't think you should go back there for a while."

She tilted her head, catching the ominous note in his tone. "Why?"

"I've been thinking. There has to be some kind of surveillance device in your house."

"A bug?"

"Right. He could have planted one in your house before you got home Friday night."

All this time, she'd been worrying about being watched. She hadn't given a thought to someone *listening* to her. Here was a whole new reason to be spooked. Her mind raced back. If there was a bug in her house, the man would have heard all her conversations with the police, with Bobby, with Bertie. He would know that she had been calling Nina.

That last thought made her feel sick with uncertainty. But Bobby was right. She didn't want to go back home now.

When they were finally headed north, Jo sank down into the seat and focused straight ahead. She hated being in the dark, feeling as if she were rushing forward. The sensation reminded her of when she was a kid and would close her eyes on a roller coaster. Movement would catch her by surprise, and she would lurch unexpectedly in one direction or another. Her stomach turned over at bumps she had no way of anticipating. And tonight, when she'd been in the cab and had suddenly realized she was being taken God-only-knows where, it had been more terrifying than anything a thrill-ride designer could come up with.

Bobby's car didn't have the comforting smells of Willie's truck. It wasn't open with a rattly feeling. Instead, she felt as if she were locked inside with memories. And she was. The light scent of Bobby's cologne permeated the air, reminding her of the times when just a whiff of it would make her heart trip with happiness. Obsession. It was amazing to her that she could even recall those moments in the midst of the nightmare that was this evening.

They didn't say anything for miles and miles. Bobby just drove—slightly too fast, she guessed. It was late and they were both dead tired.

"Did you find the kidnapper in the mug shots?"

"No. Could be the guy's not from this state, even. Or maybe he doesn't have a criminal record."

"Wouldn't that be unusual?"

"Yeah, it would. But frankly, nothing about this guy would surprise me from now on. He's a real piece of work."

She crossed her arms. Earlier tonight, when Bobby had saved her, she had just wanted to get as far away from her kidnapper as possible. Now she began to see how terrible it was that they hadn't caught him. He was still out there. He would still want to find her, so he could get his hands on whatever it was he thought she had.

"Jo, you can relax, I swear it."

She turned toward the driver's seat. Bobby was very observant. She realized that she was clenching her hands into tight fists, and even the skin on her face felt taut with tension. Her temples throbbed with the beginnings of a headache. "I don't think I'll ever relax again. I can't believe this is happening to me. It's terrifying."

"It's natural for you to feel that way after what you've been through. But you've got to try to get some rest. Why don't you lean back and take a nap? We won't be home for another half hour."

His voice, with its ever-so-slight drawl, was like a caress

against her skin. But she was too antsy to truly unwind. And the thought of closing her eyes didn't have much appeal right now. She was afraid of dreaming—afraid her subconscious would take her back to those moments when she was being kidnapped.

"What if they pick up somebody and they need us in Houston to identify him?"

"*Could* you identify him?" Bobby asked.

"Maybe his voice..."

"It's okay. If they pick up somebody, we'll go back into town. It's not *that* far a drive."

It certainly seemed like it tonight.

But part of the problem was that she felt both exhausted and keyed up. At the same time her body felt sapped of all energy, a rush of nervous adrenaline kept sweeping through her, making her heart race. Every time she closed her eyes and took a deep breath to expel some tension, she was back in that cab again, rushing toward an unknown destination she knew in the marrow of her bones she didn't want to reach. She'd never been so scared, so helpless. So close, she was certain, to dying.

Horrible, gruesome thoughts paraded relentlessly through her mind. Thoughts of what might have happened if Bobby hadn't shown up. What might have happened if the kidnapper had hurt Bobby. Bobby himself seemed cool, calm. Too calm. But of course he'd been through things like this before. He knew how to handle pressure. He'd faced up to worse. After all, he'd found Greg.

She turned to him again and felt hot tears in her eyes. Remembering her brother threatened to undo her composure as nothing else tonight had. He, too, had been some lunatic's victim.

"What is it, Jo?"

"Do you think Greg was afraid, Bobby?" She remembered the heart-in-her-throat terror she'd felt and prayed her beloved big brother had been spared that.

"Jo..."

"Do you think he knew what was happening to him?"

"It was a dark night. He was caught by surprise," Bobby said in a soft voice. "It had to have happened in a split second."

She tried to pull herself together. What was the matter with her? It was selfish of her to make Bobby relive that night. "Like Willie said happened to him?"

"Yes."

They drove along in silence for at least ten minutes more, each lost in their own thoughts. She was wondering if they would finish the drive to the ranch that way when Bobby's voice cut through the darkness.

"You were trying to ditch Tammy, weren't you?"

She let out a sigh to cover the curse on her lips. Damn! The man was a bloodhound. "Why do you think that?"

"Because you would have just waited for her and caught a ride home that way."

"Maybe I wanted a little time to myself."

"Uh-huh. A little time to pack and clear out, maybe."

She crossed her arms, unable to help being a bit annoyed. Was it possible to get away with anything around Bobby? "It was all pointless anyway, since you were snooping."

"So you were trying to sneak away from Tammy's."

"Yes," she admitted. "I *couldn't* stay there, Bobby. Not after what had happened to that locksmith. And look what happened to Willie! I was right to try to steer the guy away from Tammy."

"Where were you going to go?"

"To a hotel." She thought about her scheme and realized how foolish it sounded now. "I had some sort of cockeyed idea that I could stay at a different hotel every night and the guy wouldn't be able to catch up with me."

"Sounds like something you'd get from a bad detective novel."

She tossed her hands up in frustration. "That's what my life feels like."

"You should have told me where you were going."

"I couldn't."

"Why?"

"Because I didn't want you to get involved."

"Why not?"

"For the same reason I didn't want Tammy involved."

"But I was already involved, Jo. When it comes to you, I always will be."

She swallowed. Hard. These were the words she'd wanted to hear for so long. Nearly the words. Bobby hadn't told her he loved her, but then again he didn't have to. It was there in his voice. It was crackling in the very air between them.

I saw the way he looked at you, Tammy had said. Jo wished she could see Bobby, to witness that look for herself. She would have paid any amount of money to be able to gaze into those dark eyes of his again and have that certainty that he loved her reaffirmed with every glance.

"But, Jo, for heaven's sake, how can I help you if you're not telling me the truth?"

She was glad the darkness inside the car covered the blush that she could feel sweep across her face. How did he know?

"What are you hiding?" he pressed on persistently.

She kept facing forward, torn by conflict. By her deep, abiding affection for Bobby on one hand, and fear that he could make her reveal more than she should on the other. But maybe she had to stop being afraid of telling him. She had no one else to turn to. And if she couldn't trust the man who had saved her life tonight, who could she trust?

The trouble was, her silence was a habit now. One not easy to break.

He waited for her response and then released a ragged sigh when it didn't come. "All right, I'll drop it," he said. "We're both tired right now."

Right now, he'd said. Which indicated he would be returning to the topic sometime in the near future. But of course he would. Once Bobby sank his teeth into a problem he was like a dog with a bone.

And tonight, she realized, she had become his problem.

CHAPTER EIGHT

SHE WOKE WITH a start to the enticing smell of strong coffee brewing and the sound of breakfast being prepared. It took a moment to make the warm comforting smells jibe with the terrifying events of the night before that rushed through her mind like a horrifying spectre.

Then she remembered. She was at Bobby's. Safe. Lying snug and sound in a soft bed.

She rolled onto her back and opened her eyes. She saw enough light to know that Bobby had let her sleep late.

She'd been in Bobby's cabin once before, last Christmas, when she and Greg had come up for a visit. It only had two bedrooms, and from the smell of Obsession embedded in her pillow, she could tell that Bobby had given her his room. She'd been so tired last night she hadn't questioned which sleeping quarters she was getting, or worried that she was probably putting Bobby out. She'd simply fallen into bed as soon as she'd wiggled into a nightshirt. But Bobby had given her the best bedroom.

Of course. Always the gentleman.

Bobby. She still remembered that flash of vision she'd had in the glare of the cab's headlights. It was tantalizing to think about now, even though it had occurred under frightening circumstances. But it was also frustrating. She didn't want glimpses of him—a brief look at his muscular silhouette. She wanted the luxury of looking her fill into those dark brooding eyes and seeing what she had last winter: boundless love reflected back at her.

Maybe that love wasn't so boundless after all, though. After last night Bobby could surely see that she wasn't the safest person to hang around these days. Or even the nicest. Yesterday at her house in an attempt to get him off her scent, she'd snapped at him. Last night she had evaded his questions.

How much longer would he be willing to put up with her?

How much longer could she accept his help, and now his hospitality, without being able to tell him what was going on? She was weary of lying to him.

Mindful of her sore arm, she got out of bed and dressed carefully from the bag Tammy had brought to her at the hospital. She pulled out an oversize T-shirt and a fresh pair of jeans. There wasn't anything formal about Bobby's family's ranch. That was one of the things she loved about it. It was Bobby's hideaway for just kicking back and relaxing.

She wondered if any of his family had come over. Did they even know Bobby was here yet?

She moved her arm gingerly and decided to forgo the awkward sling. If she was careful, she wouldn't need it. She felt her way out to the hall and followed her nose to the kitchen. She heard the sounds of eggs crackling in a pan and had to hold back a smile. *Huevos rancheros* made with fresh salsa from his mother's recipe. Actually the recipe went as far back as the Garcia clan itself, and the family guarded it as closely as if it were the formula for Coca-Cola.

"Morning!" Bobby greeted her when she reached the door. He walked over to her and clasped his hand on her good arm. His touch had the effect that two cups of coffee would have had. She felt wide-awake.

"Sorry I slept so late."

"That's okay. Have a seat, I'm almost done with breakfast." He dropped her off at the table and she sat down obediently. A quick investigation revealed that the table was already set. She smelled sage in the air and she tilted her head curiously. "Have you been picking flowers?"

"Can you see them?"

She shook her head. "I can smell them."

"Oh..." He sounded disappointed. After she'd seen him last night, perhaps he, too, had gotten his hopes up. "It's just a little bouquet of sage, cosmos and lantana from the yard."

She nodded. They were hardy flowers that could hold up unattended in the Texas July heat. It amused her to think of Bobby out picking flowers, much less having the foresight to plant them. And it touched her that on this of all mornings, he would think of adding a small decorative touch to the cabin. He was obviously trying to make her feel welcome.

He banged a few pans around, then filled up a cup with coffee and placed it in front of her. "No sense letting them just die outside, unappreciated. They perk the place up."

She remembered Bobby's cabin—the kitchen was painted yellow, she recalled. Bright and cheerful. The summer flowers would look pretty there. "I like the fresh smell. The coffee smells good, too."

"Maybe it will revive you."

"Do I look that bad?" She touched the raw scrapes on her cheek and winced.

He chuckled. "You look fine. I just figured you were bound to feel a little draggy. We didn't get in until after four last night, and it's just ten-thirty now. You always did say you were a mess unless you had your eight solid hours.''

It was hard for her to believe that yesterday had been such a nightmare and today she was here with Bobby making breakfast for her *and* making jokes. ''How long have you been up?'' Obviously long enough to lay in some provisions.

''Since about nine. That's when my mother called. She said she was out early and saw my car from the main road.'' Bobby's parents lived at the other side of the ranch, about a half mile away.

''I didn't even hear the phone ring.''

''I almost didn't, either. But you were really out. You didn't hear the knock at the door when she brought the eggs and stuff over.''

''That was nice of her.''

''I didn't want to leave the cabin,'' Bobby said.

He didn't want to leave *her,* was the implication. Warmth rushed through her. Suddenly she was very glad she'd come here. This was the first time in five days she'd actually felt safe. She had Bobby to thank for that. After last night, she had Bobby to thank for her life.

''I didn't tell Mama what happened last night, but she picked up on something, I think. She seemed worried about you.''

Or maybe she was just worried about her son bringing a woman home to his cabin. Abruptly, Jo pictured Bobby's mother coming to the cabin while she was conked out in Bobby's bedroom, and realized how that must have appeared to an inquiring parental mind. She groaned. ''Your mother probably thinks we're living in sin!''

''I told Mama you were just here for some R and R,'' Bobby explained.

Jo laughed. ''I'm sure she believed you.''

"Probably not, but don't worry about that just yet, Jo." He walked over from the stove and she heard him ladling eggs onto the plates. The delicious smell made her stomach rumble hungrily. "Eat first. Then we'll talk."

The implication of his words left her poised nervously over her eggs. *Talk about what?*

She'd been so relieved to be here, with Bobby, feeling coddled and protected, that she wasn't sure she wanted to be dragged back into her personal nightmare. But of course she had to be. She had to figure some way to get out of it, too.

Maybe Bobby could help her. But to enlist his aid, she would have to confess the truth to him, and in doing so she would be reneging on a promise she'd made to someone else.

Despite her trepidation, they ate companionably. Bobby informed her that he'd called Company A headquarters and asked for the week off, which the captain had agreed to. So Bobby was free through the weekend. They had five whole days ahead of them.

They discussed whether they should go horseback riding or canoeing and decided on canoeing. Jo wasn't the best horsewoman anyway—she was adventurous, but not being able to see might be too much of a challenge. As it was, she would be nervous enough being on a boat on a lake. She hadn't been on a boat since losing her vision, and only a few times since Terry's last boat ride on the Gulf of Mexico.

She quickly flitted across that memory, dismissing it. She again focused on what Bobby was saying. Dinner at his parents' house one night, he said. And his sister Denise was dying to see her.

It was surreal. They were chatting as if this was just a holiday. As if they hadn't spent the past six months apart.

As if yesterday had never happened. As if there wasn't actually a maniac out there trying to find her.

It was disturbing, and yet she wished it could go on. It was the first moment of normalcy she'd had since last Friday night. She owed this little window of security to Bobby. Letting her guard down was dangerous, though. Because it left her completely vulnerable when he suddenly changed the subject. "So what does your friend in Brazil have to do with the man who tried to kidnap you last night, Jo?"

The change in topic blindsided her. "What?"

In the following moment of silence she imagined that he could read every guilty thought reeling through her mind. She could feel him studying her with those dark, penetrating eyes of his. Bobby wasn't a crack detective for nothing. He'd already put together far more than she'd imagined. And from what? An address book she'd left open.

"The woman in Brazil is Nina Monteverde," she answered carefully. "She's the sister of a woman I went to college with."

"Terry Monteverde," Bobby said. "The woman who died."

"How did you find out about that?" That had all happened months before Greg introduced her to Bobby.

"I did a little research. But I don't think I got all the facts."

"You mean you looked it up in the newspaper?" She couldn't help feeling spooked. Not only had he been following her, he apparently had been investigating her past. "When?"

"Yesterday. I thought it was strange that you would be calling Brazil."

"I explained that."

"That's right. You said you'd felt bad because Terry had been dead for almost a year and you hadn't called Nina. But why would you feel guilty about not calling someone who sounds like a mere acquaintance?"

Defensive anger flashed through her. "Is this an interrogation?"

"An informal one," he said. "Believe me, Jo, I'm only trying to help. You can't tell me that there's not something fishy about what happened to your friend."

Her heart thumped so loudly in her chest she was almost sure he could hear it. "Why? She drowned."

"In a squall off Galveston Island while she was visiting you and your brother?"

"I wasn't with her at the time. She'd rented a boat...."

He sputtered. "Come off it, Jo. Do you think I was born yesterday? She was in your hometown, sailing. You're a sailor. Are you telling me that you of all people would let your friend go out on the Gulf of Mexico in tropical storm force winds?"

Oh, God. She felt like a bug pinned to a board. After a few mere minutes of questioning, Bobby already had her flustered.

The trouble was, she wasn't a good liar. Especially when she was nervous. Especially when, logically, she could use Bobby's help. But could she trust him? Then again, could she afford *not* to trust him?

"For God's sake, Jo," he pleaded with her, his voice raw with emotion. "What's wrong?"

She sighed. "I wish I could tell you."

"You can!"

She shook her head. "You don't understand. I'm the only person..." She thought about her unanswered call to Nina and shivered. "Maybe the only person alive who knows."

"Who knows what?"

She hesitated. She couldn't speak. Keeping her own counsel on this matter had become a way of life with her.

Bobby expelled a long breath. "You need to tell me, Jo. If you don't tell me what you know, I'll have to take you back to Houston and you can tell the police."

The threat sent pure panic racing through her. "Why?"

"Because this isn't just about you anymore. It's not only a curious case of a house being broken into. Like I said, it's escalating. In the past twenty-four hours, whoever is after you has resorted to assault and kidnapping and murder."

She felt the blood drain out of her face. "Murder?" She repeated the word numbly.

Bobby swore. "I'm sorry, I didn't want to tell you this right away this morning, but you'd have to find out eventually. The driver of the cab your kidnapper stole—the police found him last night, dead."

"Where?"

"In the doorway of a defunct motel near Hobby Airport. An anonymous tip led the cops to the body. They think a bunch of kids were fooling around there and called in after they found him. The man had been shot in the head."

The words sucked the breath out of her. She lifted a hand to her mouth; she felt sick and had to swallow several times, rapidly, for fear of losing her breakfast. Fear burned her throat, and sadness for the man and his family tore at her heart. *Why? Why was this happening?*

Bobby's voice softened. "This is no joke, Jo. The guy's a murderer. Maybe some kind of psychopath. He would have killed you, too."

Her heart was racing; her thoughts were panicked. Right now it was her life versus someone else's. And yet…

Maybe if she told Bobby they could figure out a way to stop this killer before he got any closer to the truth.

"We need to do anything we can to get this guy off the streets. At least tell me what you think he's after."

"I'm not sure I know," Jo finally confessed. "At least not everything."

"Well, what's your hunch? Obviously there's something illegal involved?"

Reluctantly, she nodded.

Bobby paused. "And does it have to do with you?"

She lowered her head. She was glad she couldn't see the disappointment in his eyes. But she could feel it. Bobby lived by the law; in his mind, she had probably crossed to the other side.

More quietly, he asked, "Does it have to do with you and this Monteverde woman? Are you trying to protect her memory, is that it? Did she confess what she'd done while she was visiting you and then commit suicide by taking that boat out? Is that it?"

She was surprised that he would have thought of something like that. Surprised and even a little offended. "Oh, no. Terry would never kill herself."

"Then what?"

She hesitated. Then she remembered Nina, whom she had never been able to find. And then the cabdriver, dead by a gunshot to the head. Bobby was right. The important thing now was to stop the violence before more innocent people got hurt.

Oh, Terry, forgive me.

"It's not her memory I'm protecting, Bobby," she confessed. "It's her."

"Who?"

"Terry."

"But she died."

"No, she didn't, Bobby. I believe—I hope—my friend Terry Monteverde is still very much alive."

THIS WASN'T WHAT Bobby had expected. Worst case, he figured that this Terry Monteverde woman had planted something on her unsuspecting friend. Or maybe, just maybe, she'd actually asked Jo to hold on to some of the contraband she'd reputedly smuggled.

But alive? How could she be alive?

"The newspaper said she died in a boating accident."

Jo nodded. "That's what we wanted. Documentation."

Bobby squinted at her. "Wait—who's *we?*"

"Terry and me...and Greg."

Incredulity made him falter. "You mean the three of you, you..."

Her head kept bobbing as he slowly began to piece it together. "We faked her death, Bobby," she told him. "We only wanted to make it look as if she were dead."

"How?" he asked. "And why? Why on earth would you—would Greg—do such a thing?"

Greg, a policeman. He'd known Greg so well. Last year Bobby would have said Greg was the most honest person on earth. No way would he be involved in something shady. Faking the death of a woman who was probably a felon? A fugitive from justice in her own country? He had a difficult time wrapping his mind around the idea.

"You don't know Terry," Jo said. "When I heard all that stuff about her being caught smuggling—it was beyond ludicrous, Bobby. It was nuts."

Bobby tilted his head. "Who first told you about her legal troubles?"

"Terry told me."

Naturally, he thought with irritation. The woman had bamboozled her best friend and her best friend's cop brother into believing her. "I guess she was able to put a pretty rosy spin on things."

"Not at all," Jo said. "In fact, I'd never seen her so scared as that day when she knocked on our door. That's how Greg first got involved. He was there the night Terry found me at our house in Houston."

"She just showed up?"

"She'd called from Rio, days before, and talked to me on the phone. About how the police believed that she had smuggled jewels into Brazil. How she was afraid she'd be found guilty and sent to jail. I couldn't believe it. I hadn't spoken to her in months—it just came out of the blue. I was worried sick."

"And then she showed up at your house?"

"She was frantic. Really scared. She said she needed help. She wanted to disappear."

"Because she was guilty," Bobby guessed.

Jo shook her head. "No." The simple word was an adamant proclamation of belief in her friend.

"I read in the newspaper that millions in rocks had been found in her possession, Jo."

She nodded. "Terry said it was all a setup, and I believed her."

"Why?"

"Because I knew her."

Yes, and five minutes ago he thought he'd known Greg and Jolene Daniels pretty well. But apparently he'd been wrong about them. Hadn't he?

What were the boundaries of right and wrong when it came to loyalty and friendship?

"I knew she was innocent," Jo repeated. "I wanted her to go back and try to clear her name, but she was so certain she didn't stand a chance."

He had a hard time swallowing that. But he decided to

skip over it for now. "Okay, she wanted to disappear. And so you cooked up some kind of drowning scheme."

"The timing was right because it was September and there was a tropical storm in the Gulf," Jo explained. "We went down to Galveston and Terry rented a boat in her name, and Greg and I took out the small boat that we kept down there after Dad died. Then we sailed pretty far out, capsized Terry's boat, and abandoned it. Afterward, we drove Terry back to Houston and dropped her at the bus station. We waited several days before alerting anyone that she was missing, in order to give her time to get far away."

"Didn't the authorities in Galveston wonder why you didn't report her missing earlier?"

"Why would they? We never told them we had been in Galveston at the same time she was. We just said that she had called us in Houston days before and told us she was going out sailing to think through her problems. We told them that when we didn't hear from her again, we started to worry and Greg snooped around and discovered the boat rental record. The rental guy had already reported his boat missing, but he'd assumed it had been stolen. Hours after we got there, the Coast Guard finally found the boat. Terry had left some of her clothes and her wallet in the hold to make it look like she must have drowned. She wouldn't need her old driver's license or credit cards anyway, because she intended to assume a whole new identity."

Bobby frowned. This was more twisted than he ever could have imagined. What had they been thinking? "What happened after that?"

"Well, our problem was there was no body. Terry had wanted to make sure that the people hunting her in Brazil knew she was dead. Greg knew a doctor in South Texas—retired under questionable circumstances, you might say.

He'd met this doctor in the course of a criminal investigation years before."

Bobby understood. He had contacts that weren't always on the up-and-up, people who gave him tips thinking it would help them down the line if they ever tripped up. Most cops did have little black books of shady characters they could call on in a pinch.

"Greg convinced the good doctor to sign a death certificate for us. And for good measure, we shipped a casket back to Brazil. Nina even came to pick it up."

"An empty casket?"

"It had one hundred and twenty pounds of sandbags."

"Why?"

"Because we thought it would be more convincing if there was a funeral in Brazil."

"The newspaper reported she hadn't been found, though."

"But in Brazil no one would read the Galveston papers, or even the Houston papers. So we were banking on the fact that whoever had set her up would hear about the accident through rumor, and then when the casket arrived with a death certificate they would just assume that her body had been found."

Never assume, Bobby thought automatically. Then he frowned in thought. "You gave evidence...you lied to the authorities."

Two stains of red appeared in her cheeks. "I know, Bobby. But I did it for Terry. You have to understand."

He doubted he would ever understand. Most of all, he couldn't imagine the magnetism of a woman who could go so wrong and yet inspire such loyalty. Jo had obviously been willing to keep silent forever to protect her friend.

He leaned forward and rubbed his temples. He imagined beautiful, rich Terry Monteverde as he'd seen her in the insert photo of the paper. Was she out in the world continuing her spoiled rich girl life while people like Jo covered her tracks for her, and completely innocent people like the cabdriver paid with their lives for hers?

"I can't imagine Greg doing something so wrong," he said.

She shook her head. "No one who had seen Terry the night she arrived at my house would have said helping her was wrong. It went beyond being afraid to go to jail, Bobby. She didn't say so in so many words, but I got the feeling she was protecting someone."

Bobby straightened. "Who? Her sister? A lover?"

"I don't know. But I'm sure there was more to it than what she told me."

He let out a bitter laugh. "That's good, because it doesn't sound like she told you a whole hell of a lot."

"I didn't pester her for answers. That's not the kind of friendship we had."

"Great," Bobby said. "So she was protecting somebody and now you're protecting her. And now somebody's after you."

"But doesn't that just prove that we were right to cover for her?"

"I'm not following you," Bobby said.

She raised her hands, which drew his attention to her scraped and bruised arm, reminding him of how much she'd already risked for Terry Monteverde's sake. "Whoever is after me is after something he thinks Terry left behind. But the only person who would do that would be someone who had planted something on Terry, right?"

Bobby shook his head doubtfully. "It might not be so simple. Maybe Terry had an accomplice."

She huffed in frustration. "You don't know her."

"You said yourself she seemed to be protecting someone."

Jo's face tensed in concentration. "Maybe I was wrong about that, but I wasn't wrong about Terry. She's innocent."

Sometimes there was no arguing with blind loyalty. He'd seen it time and again. Mothers who couldn't believe their sons were killers. Wives who couldn't believe their husbands would beat them again. Love was an effective blinker. "Does Terry know what's going on now?"

"I don't know."

Her answer made him uneasy. Or maybe it was her tone. "We're going to have to find her and get to the bottom of this."

Jo shook her head. "I can't. I don't know where she is."

"You *what?*"

"When Terry said she wanted to disappear, she wasn't kidding. I've only heard from her once since that night we arranged her death. She called me from a pay phone in a café. And the only other person who's aware that she's alive is her sister Nina in Brazil."

"What did Nina tell you?"

She released a long sigh. "After the break-in to my house, I tried calling her but all I've gotten so far is her answering machine. I've left three messages for her to call me, but she never has."

"So you knew right away that the intruder was looking for Terry."

"Yes."

"How?"

"Because all he said to me was, 'Where are they? Where did she hide them?' For some reason this person thinks Terry left whatever he's looking for in my possession."

"How did he get your name?"

"That's what really worries me. Unless he read that same newspaper article that you found and somehow pieced it all together, the most obvious source for the truth would be Nina. I'm really scared something's happened to her, Bobby. Especially after you told me that there must be a bug in my house. If the attacker wasn't wise to the connection between Nina and me before, he is now."

Bobby also felt anxious for Nina's safety. Jo's not being able to reach Nina could be just a coincidence, but he doubted it. They would have to try again to hunt her down. He could use Ranger contacts. In the course of extradition work and some drug investigations, Texas Rangers sometimes dealt with international agencies and foreign governments and police. He would have to call Doug again and see what they could arrange.

"Nina would have died before she told anyone about her sister's whereabouts," Jo said. Her voice was almost a whisper.

"So Nina knew where Terry's hiding?"

Jo twisted her napkin nervously. "I'm not even sure, to tell you the truth. Terry told me that she would send messages to Nina through a middleman. But I'm positive they wouldn't be very specific. She was trying to protect us by giving us as little information as possible."

"Some protection!" Bobby couldn't help muttering.

"Even when Terry called me last Christmas, she didn't tell me where she was. She wouldn't even say what state or even what country she was in. And when I started asking too many questions, she hung up pretty quickly. She was skittish about it." She wiped a tear that fell from her eye. "I'm so worried, Bobby. What should I do?"

"You're doing all you can now," he told her. "But honestly, Jo, I'm not sure how much longer we can keep this story from the police. It's wrong. Especially if bodies start piling up."

She shuddered. "I feel so sorry for that poor cabdriver. Did he have a family?"

"The Houston police are still trying to notify next of kin." He tapped his fork handle, thinking. "First things first, Jo. We'll call Nina again, and then start trying to figure out where Terry is. She's the only person who can help us find out who might be after you."

Jo's lips twisted into a rueful expression. "To think Greg and I were worried our plan to help Terry hide wouldn't work. Now it looks like we were a little too successful."

So successful that they had convinced the world Terry was dead and drawn a maniac's attention to Jo.

CHAPTER NINE

"HERE," Bobby said, taking Jo's hand. "I brought you something."

Jo smiled tentatively, hoping she could smother the jolt that was a reaction to the pressure of Bobby's skin against hers. She'd been standing in the sunshine for several glorious minutes, just listening to the birds chirping and cicadas sawing away. The bucolic peacefulness of it all, the sensation of being able to stand in the open and not feel vulnerable, was something she couldn't take for granted now.

Unfortunately, she found it difficult to trust, as well. Could she really be out of the woods, danger-wise? It was still so hard to believe, here in this quiet, rural idyll, that not twelve hours before she had been rocketing from one end of Houston to the other in a nightmare come to life. After that, this rural hideaway hardly seemed real.

But having Bobby's hand on hers made her believe that perhaps she actually could be safe. "What is it?"

He placed the object in her hand—a walking stick, obviously culled from nature, but sanded and smooth. No doubt he'd sensed her need for aid from the way she'd been fumbling around his house all morning.

"Thank you. God only knows where my own cane disappeared to last night."

As she mentally retraced the frantic hours after she left Tumbleweeds, she couldn't even remember the last time she'd used it. Just the fleeting thought of last night made a cloud descend over her.

"What's the matter?" Bobby asked her.

"This doesn't seem right."

"What doesn't?"

"Me, being here. About to take a walk as if I didn't have a care in the world. Someone died last night because of me."

"Not because of you. You can't blame yourself for the acts of a murderer."

They made their way to the path that led to the small pond on the property. It was slow going. Jo had a hard enough time getting around on hardwood floors and smooth concrete sidewalks; the ruts and little rocks in the dirt path posed a whole new challenge that her brief rehab at the hospital hadn't prepared her for. Fortunately Bobby had more patience for her disability than she herself did.

"Maybe we should try Nina again," she suggested, partly because she couldn't get Nina out of her mind, and partly because she wasn't sure a nature walk with Bobby was the best idea. She felt a strange stirring inside, a prick of desire that didn't seem appropriate under the circumstances.

Of course, given that this was the first day in so many long months she'd spent in Bobby's company, maybe that prick of desire was inevitable.

"When we get back," he said.

They'd already called Brazil once that morning. But it was clear from the length of the beep they were getting on the other end that Nina was receiving a lot of messages that she wasn't picking up. They had also tried Nina at All That Glitters, but the only thing the woman Bobby had spoken to there would tell them was that Nina would not be in the office for a few days. When they questioned the employee for more specifics, she didn't seem able to enlighten them on where her boss had gone. Either that or she didn't trust them enough to tell them.

On the other hand, the employee didn't indicate any nervousness about Nina's safety, either. It didn't sound as though anything were amiss. But Jo still felt, deep in her bones, that there was something wrong.

She tripped over a tree root and Bobby grabbed her arm. Once she was upright again, she expected him to let her go. He didn't.

She didn't tell him to.

The truth was, she loved the feeling of his hand on her arm. Guiding her. Protecting her. It seemed like so long since she'd had anyone to lean on. She'd gone through so much alone, she was more than ready to have someone help her now. That the person was Bobby brought a swell of feeling inside her that she wasn't sure she was ready to examine fully.

She still wished to heaven that necessity hadn't forced her to tell him Terry's secret. But it had, and now that she'd spilled the story she'd been carrying with her for so long she was relieved, as if a thousand-pound weight had been lifted off her shoulders. She'd dumped her burdens into Bobby's lap, of course, which wasn't entirely fair. But he'd asked for it. And she was so grateful to him for wanting to help her. And so glad not to have to keep hiding behind evasions and half-truths. Lying to Bobby had never felt right because she knew with certainty that he would never lie to her.

"Tell me about Terry," Bobby said.

"About her disappearance?" She raised her shoulders and took a deep breath. The air here smelled of pine and the sharp weedy scent of the summer flowers around them. It was a rich, rustic smell she hadn't experienced since she'd lost her sight. She liked the country. "I've told you everything I know."

"But what about before Terry disappeared? If we're going to have any hope of finding her, I need to know more about her. Frankly, on paper at least, you two seem an odd match."

"You mean how did a hick like me ever come to be hanging around a rich Brazilian playgirl?" She tipped her head slightly and laughed. "I met her at college. At Northwestern."

"Did you meet in class?"

"No, we were roommates when I was a freshman there, and we stayed friends until I had to leave during my last year."

"So you were probably thrown together by a computer in a college residence office. Did you have a lot of interests in common?"

She laughed. "It was more a Mutt-and-Jeff kind of thing...with me being Mutt, of course. I'd barely ever been out of South Texas when I went up to Chicago. I was like Little Nell from the country, and Terry...well, she was *always* Terry. Sophisticated even at eighteen. Did you see a picture of her?"

Bobby grunted. "She was a looker."

"*Is,*" she reminded him. She clung to the fact that Terry was still alive with every fiber of her being. Besides, if Terry wasn't alive, would Jo have been able to feel a very mild but real stab of jealousy to hear Bobby call her a looker?

"She was the first person I'd ever met who seemed glamorous," Jo continued. "She could have been a model, and she certainly dressed like one. You should have seen her closet—it was packed."

He interjected wryly, "Sorry I missed it."

She chuckled. "Maybe you'd have to be female and eighteen to appreciate a closet full of designer wear. I'd never known anyone with so many clothes—to me it seemed she dressed like a movie star even to go to English comp."

"I would think you'd find her a little intimidating."

"I did," she admitted frankly. She smiled, remembering those sobering first days of being a little fish in the big pond of college. "Especially at first. After all, I was just a scholarship kid from Galveston, Texas. I didn't really know how to talk to her. But then one night Terry asked me to go out with her, and we went to a bar—another first for me. She got me to talk about all the stuff I had done, which wasn't much, believe me. Singing at a county fair and doing the lead in *Oklahoma* in high school, that kind of thing. I'd certainly never traveled or met the kind of people Terry seemed to know. I felt silly even discussing my own life, but she encouraged me.

"And then she did the most brazen thing. There was a piano player and guitar combo playing at the bar, and she suddenly went up to them and asked them if they'd let me sing a song with them."

Bobby laughed. "What did you do?"

"I howled in protest, first of all. I couldn't believe what she was doing. Those poor musicians. They must've thought she was a lunatic. But she told them that I was a really good singer but she'd never heard me and that she wanted to listen to me sing. And the guys said that if I knew the next song they were playing they'd let me sing it. The next song was 'St. Louis Blues.' *Everybody* knows that."

"Not everybody," Bobby said with amusement. "So what happened?"

"Well, there wasn't a Nashville talent scout in the audience, if that's what you're wondering. There was no MGM musical plot twist of the coed being discovered. I just sang the song. But forever after, Terry was my biggest fan. She treated me like *I* was something special."

"You are," Bobby said in a deep voice that made her knees feel just the slightest bit rubbery. "Maybe your friend Terry isn't such a birdbrain after all."

"She's not." Jo ducked her head at how conceited that comment could be construed. "I mean, not just because she liked my singing. She was really smart—a good student. She was so passionate about so many subjects, and when she took an interest in someone, watch out. She would tell everyone we met that I was a good singer. She could have been my manager."

"The newspaper described her as being a party girl."

Jo frowned, shaking her head. "I know they did, but that always puzzled me. When we were at Northwestern, she partied like any other college kid, but she wasn't excessive. She didn't drink too much or even have that many boyfriends. I think that was something she started when she went back home. I got the feeling there were some family conflicts. You know, her sister was always the good one and so maybe she felt she had to compensate by being wild." She shrugged. "That's just an armchair psychologist's view, though."

"Do you think anyone in her family would want to set her up?"

She shook her head violently. "No way. Terry loved her family. Nina, especially."

"Did you ever see her outside college?"

She could see what he was doing now. He was trying to find out where Terry might have settled after she disappeared. "For spring break our freshman year, I invited Terry down to Galveston. I was so shocked when she said yes—I thought for sure she'd be going to the Bahamas or somewhere glamorous. But it was so much fun! My dad thought she was great, and Greg, who was just starting in the police force, came home to visit one weekend and fell under Terry's spell.''

''Do you think he could have fallen in love with her?''

She laughed. ''I think it would be hard for a man *not* to fall in love with her.''

''Did she like Texas?''

''She loved it. She said everybody was really outspoken and friendly. Especially the men.'' Jo grinned at the memory of exotic Terry, in a flirty skirt and halter top that showed off her midriff, as the center of attention in an old honky-tonk bar outside Beaumont. ''She never seemed to realize that the reason all those men were so friendly was because she was a knockout.''

''You mean she didn't realize how attractive she was?''

She shook her head. ''She was surprisingly modest in a lot of ways. And she was a good, good friend. When my dad died and I had to leave Northwestern before graduating, she came down for the funeral. It was such a help to have her there. I was so depressed about leaving college, but I wanted to be close to Greg and help take care of things down here. And Terry was very supportive. Once I made up my mind, she said that I was doing the right thing and tried to help me sort out my conflicted feelings. She was the one who convinced me that I should stop procrastinating and try to start a singing career.''

''Do you think she would have stayed in Texas?''

Jo had thought about this and thought about this. ''I just don't know, Bobby. She liked it here, I'm sure of that. But she liked Chicago, too. And that's a bigger city. Easier to get lost in. So maybe she went back there.''

''But if she spent four years in that area, there's also

more chance she'd be spotted by someone she knew.'' He let out a considering sigh. ''And she'd know it would be easier to trace her there. People who knew anything about her would know she'd gone to Northwestern.''

''Yeah, that's true,'' Jo admitted. ''On the other hand, it obviously wasn't hard for someone to find out her connection to me.'' They stood in silence for a moment. A mockingbird called from a tree nearby. ''It's strange. You hear about people who are missing, and yet I always wondered how people could just vanish. We have so little privacy, it hardly seems that anyone could hide anymore.''

''Well, let's hope that's not true.''

Jo turned toward him questioningly. ''Why? I thought you wanted to find Terry.''

He squeezed her arm more tightly. ''I do. But I don't want whoever else is looking for Terry to find *you.*''

She looked toward him and felt his gaze on her. A blush suffused her cheeks, and for a moment she wondered whether he was going to kiss her. The world seemed to close in, cloistering them in balmy warmth and serenading them with the beautiful rustling and singing of nature. Her whole body tensed, waiting. In that moment she knew absolutely that she wanted him to kiss her. Yet she stood still, waiting for him to make the first move.

After a few moments, however, Bobby clucked his tongue. ''Well, I guess we should get back. Make some more phone calls.''

She stepped back, flustered. Had she only been imagining the moment between them? Disappointment shot through her, though she knew it was wrong. Bobby was just trying to help her.

''Okay,'' she said, more brightly than she actually felt. After all, romance should have been the farthest thing from her mind right now.

Should have been. But it obviously wasn't.

DENISE WAS COMING OVER. So far, Bobby had managed to keep most of his family at bay by telling them that Jo had had her house broken into and was so shaken up she needed some peace and quiet. And of course if anyone could have seen her, they would have agreed. Not only did the scrapes on her face and arms tell the story of last night, Jo's skin seemed to have been blanched by fear. She'd lost a little weight in the past week, and sometimes when he glanced at her when she didn't know she was being watched, she looked like she was straddling the edge of her last nerve.

But it didn't matter because Denise, who had liked Jo from the moment they had met last year, was not to be put off merely by the need for peace and quiet—words that barely registered in his little sister's vocabulary. Denise had been holed up at the ranch for a month and she was dying for some new company. If they wouldn't come to the big house, she declared over the phone to Bobby, then she was simply going to pay them a visit.

"I'm giving you fair warning so you can clean up the love nest, brother."

"Right now this is more a safe house than a love nest."

"Right," Denise said skeptically.

Denise more than anyone knew that he'd been running at half-speed since Greg's death. Among his family, only she seemed to sense how much he missed his old friend and the guilt he harbored because of his murder; and she knew that he was in love with Jo. She knew it without his ever having had to confess it in so many words. Denise was four years younger than him, but she'd always been the sibling he'd felt closest to.

For all his honorable talk about safe houses, the truth of the matter was that his real thoughts about Jo weren't quite so lofty. During their walk this afternoon he might have been asking dutifully after Terry Monteverde, but all his thoughts were focused on Jo. For the first time he felt fiercely jealous of the past, of the people who'd been lucky enough to be around Jo before he had. He wished he'd known Jo back in college—wished they'd met sooner and had had longer together before they were broken apart. Standing by the pond, he'd wanted nothing more than to take her in his arms and make up for all the lost time.

What stopped him was the knowledge that she had agreed to come to his ranch out of desperation. He didn't want to scare her away from this secure hideaway by his inability to control his passions. He didn't want to take advantage of her when she was vulnerable.

So he'd turned away from her when every cell in his body wanted her. And he still wanted her. But he was trying to be patient. He had to believe this trouble would end. He would find whoever had attacked her and killed the cabbie Jack Pike, and once he did, he and Jo would have the rest of their lives to work out their relationship.

After talking to Denise, he got on the phone to Doug Henderson at Ranger Company A headquarters. Doug was not happy to hear from him.

"Damn it, Bobby, you're supposed to be on vacation. You'd better have a good reason for pestering me."

"I do. I need to find someone in Brazil."

"Brazil!" His long-suffering commander repeated the name of the country as if it were in outer space. "Who?"

"A woman named Nina Monteverde. She seems to have disappeared."

Doug sighed. "This have to do with a case?"

"It has to do with a Houston murder," Bobby said, trying to skirt carefully around the issue of Terry. Jo hadn't asked him to keep mum about Terry around the police, but he knew she wanted him to. He was willing to try to keep Terry out of it...for as long as possible.

He just wasn't sure how long that would be. He still wasn't entirely convinced that Terry hadn't brought all this trouble down on herself.

"This Nina Monteverde might be able to give us the name of the suspect the Houston police should be looking for," Bobby continued. "Think our contacts in Rio could hunt her down?"

Doug grunted. "Sounds like you're going on a hunch."

"It's a pretty strong hunch."

"Uh-huh." There were more mutters and grunts and long considering slurps of coffee over the line before Doug capitulated. "Well, okay. You usually have your saddle on the right horse. Tell you what I'll do. I'll give our police contact in Rio a buzz and see if he can sniff around a little for us."

"Thanks, Doug." He gave the captain what information he had on Nina Monteverde—her phone number and address and the name of her business.

"Okeydoke, Bobby. Don't call us, we'll call you. Enjoy your vacation, if that's what you call what you're doing. Frankly, it sounds as if you've just picked up and moved operations to a more rustic setting."

Bobby hung up the phone feeling a little more optimistic. At least they weren't just spinning their wheels now. They would have someone in Rio checking on Nina's whereabouts for them. He was getting pretty tired of listening to the message on the woman's answering machine.

Jo had been standing in the doorway, apparently listening intently to his side of the conversation. "What do we do now?"

"I'll get back to Doug tomorrow to see if he's got anything for us.'' He tried to inject some confidence into his tone, because Jo looked like she was losing heart. And he secretly had to agree that Nina's absence from both home and business seemed ominous, despite her employee's assurances to the contrary.

''And after that?'' Jo asked.

''If she's there, then we'll probably have all the answers we need.''

''And if she isn't?'' Jo lifted a hand to her brow. She looked sick. ''Oh, God.''

He couldn't help himself. He went over and hugged her. Tight. ''Don't worry about the ifs until they crop up, okay?''

She nestled against his chest, her arms lightly touching his shoulders. It felt good to have her body against his. It felt right. He also realized he was beginning to think thoughts he shouldn't, like how good it would be to press his lips against hers, to taste the warmth of her mouth.

As if sensing his thoughts, she pushed away from him. ''Thank you, Bobby,'' she said, as if he'd just been doing her a favor by hugging her. She stood about a foot away from him, her hands clasped primly in front of her as if to prove that she was all better now.

He was a wreck. He took out a handkerchief and mopped it across his brow. He felt an ache of longing and told himself to grow up. ''We need to figure out why someone is trying to find Terry, Jo. What are they after?''

She lifted her arms so that her shoulder blades protruded, making her seem small and vulnerable. Not how he usually thought of Jo at all. ''Whatever they think Terry took with her out of Brazil.''

''She was accused of smuggling jewels, so I'd lay money that's what our man is looking for. Did you remember seeing anything like that on her?''

"No, as a matter of fact I don't even remember her wearing any jewelry at all when she was with me—sort of odd for Terry. She'd always accessorized herself liberally, if you know what I mean. But when she was at my place, she wasn't wearing any jewelry that I can remember. She didn't look so hot, to tell you the truth."

"But she'd obviously been under a lot of stress."

"Right. That's part of the reason I was so worried about her. She looked out of shape and she was wearing dowdier clothes than I was used to seeing her in."

"She probably didn't want to draw attention to herself. People are more apt to remember seeing a pretty woman than a drab one."

"Right. Also, she was trying to travel light. She just had her one suitcase. I saw it open in her room. It contained odds and ends—just clothes and maybe a few personal-looking mementos. And her makeup bag held her usual assortment of cosmetics and stuff. She must have known that the stress was sapping her, because she was taking vitamins as big as horse pills."

He released a puff of frustration. Terry could have smuggled anything out of Brazil. Even large diamonds or emeralds weren't difficult to hide in vitamin bottles or garment hems. She could have taken enough stuff out of Rio to move herself to Europe and whoop it up until doomsday. But of course Terry wasn't going to show Jo evidence of her crime.

If she'd even committed a crime. Bobby was trying to keep an open mind, though given the position Terry had left Jo in, it was difficult. "You said she called you once last year. Christmas, wasn't it?"

Jo looked toward him. Her hazel eyes narrowed in memory. "Yes—just before Christmas."

"Was it a collect call?"

"No. I just picked up the phone and she started talking. Said she just wanted me to know that she was okay." Her lips turned down in puzzlement. "But maybe she really wanted to make sure *I* was okay."

"What did the line sound like? Clear, or tinny, like she was calling from a foreign country?"

"Clear," Jo answered with assurance. "So clear she could have been calling from right across town."

"And that's all she said? That she was okay?"

Jo concentrated. "No. First I asked her if she was all right, if she needed anything. She said she was fine. She said she had a job."

He jumped on the detail. "As what?"

"That's what I wanted to know! As far as I knew she'd only ever worked at her family's business, so I wondered what she could be doing to earn a living. I asked, but she just repeated that she was getting along. And then there was an interruption or something and she hung up."

"Interruption? Did you hear people talking?"

She shook her head. "Not really. It seemed loud in the background, though. I could hear a little traffic noise in the distance, and a baby crying. I asked what all the commotion was and she told me she was calling from a pay phone in a café. And then she said she had to go and hung up really quickly."

He rubbed his chin, thinking it over. He had to hand it to Terry; she was wily. "It would make sense that she would call from somewhere public. Less likely to be traced. But of course she wouldn't want someone to overhear you."

Jo crossed her arms. "Nothing from that phone call helps us, does it?"

"Not much. Except for one thing."

"What's that?"

"It confirms what we suspected—Terry didn't think she was safe even after she faked her death."

"But that doesn't make sense. She was innocent. I assumed once she took on her new identity, she would be safe. I thought that was the whole point."

"Unless she wasn't innocent," he couldn't help saying. But he immediately wished he had kept silent.

Jo's eyes snapped with fire. "She told me she was, and I believe her."

"Jo, I realize she was your friend, but innocent people don't usually skip the country."

Yet Jo continued to shake her head back and forth. "She wasn't a smuggler. Why would Terry smuggle jewels? It's ludicrous! Her family is dripping in money. They have their own jewelry business."

He raised a brow. "How did they come by them?"

"Honestly!"

"Maybe it wasn't jewels she was involved in, then...."

Jo crossed her arms and directed a sharp look toward him. "Is this another drug theory? If you think that, you don't know jack. And you certainly don't know Terry."

"You're right, I don't. But I do know this. Prison is pretty terrible, but an innocent person doesn't give up everything—including her home, her business, her very identity—to avoid it. An innocent person hopes to fight the system and appeal."

"But the papers are littered with stories about innocent people who have spent years and years in jail—some of them on death row," Jo said. "And that's in this country. It's probably even worse in South America. You hear stories about people languishing for years under horrible conditions on little or no evidence."

Maybe she was right. But Bobby still wasn't quite ready to join the Terry Monteverde cheerleading squad. "It doesn't change the fact that by skipping the country and faking her death, Terry was acting like a woman with something to hide.''

She lifted her hands, as if she were out of answers.

''When was the last time you saw her?''

''The night we staged the boating accident, I dropped her off outside the Greyhound bus station in Houston.''

''Why did you drive back to Houston? Why not Galveston?''

''Houston's bigger. We were worried that in Galveston she might have to wait longer for a bus and someone might remember seeing her if her picture was ever in the newspaper later. Terry didn't even let me go into the station with her because she didn't want to risk anyone seeing us together.''

''Where was she buying a ticket for?''

''She wouldn't tell me. She didn't want me to know.''

''Damn!'' he muttered. ''She had it all planned out, didn't she?''

She put a hand on his arm that was meant to be soothing but had the exact opposite effect. ''I know it's frustrating, Bobby, but I can't blame Terry. There was a good reason why she kept me in the dark.''

''Why?''

Her mouth turned up in an ironic smile. ''She thought she was protecting me.''

CHAPTER TEN

"SO WHEN DID you and Bobby decide to get back together?"

Jo loved Bobby's sister, but Denise had a habit of interpreting events the way she wanted, regardless of reality. "We're not together," she insisted. She had a feeling Bobby had already told Denise this, and obviously his assertions had gone in one ear and out the other. "My house was broken into twice this week. Bobby thought I needed to get out of Houston for a while."

Denise's voice was concerned. "I guess those scratches on your face are the souvenirs."

Jo's lips twisted into a rueful smile. "They probably look worse than they feel."

"Do you think some kind of stalker's after you?" Denise asked.

"We're not sure," she said, carefully evading the question.

Lord, she didn't want to drag Bobby's whole family into her mess. They had been so welcoming to her last Christmas, and they had been incredibly supportive when her brother died. The last time she'd seen Denise had been at Greg's funeral. Even though Denise had only met Greg once and didn't know Jo all that well, she'd been there, showing her support to her new friend.

Jo steered the conversation back to Bobby. "Your

brother was kind enough to make me the offer of his cabin.''

She was jolted when Denise let out one of her gusty laughs. ''Oh, Jo, listen to yourself! *My brother? He was so kind?*'' Jo heard her slap the table and was glad Bobby had gone to the store for cold drinks and wasn't here to listen to this. ''Puh-lease! *My brother* has been pining for you for months! He probably jumped at the opportunity to play knight in shining armor.''

''He knew I needed a place to unwind, that's all.''

''Sure,'' Denise quipped, ''but I notice he's not sleeping in the barn.''

''He's not sleeping in my bed, either,'' Jo told her. ''He's been very helpful.''

Denise let out a strangled cry of frustration. ''For Pete's sake, what's the matter with you two? One minute last winter you looked like you wanted to jump all over each other. The swoony gazes you kept exchanging during Christmas dinner made all of us old marrieds squirm with embarrassment. And envy, I might add. I can't remember the last time I got a steamy gaze from Tom!'' She released a sigh. ''Anyway, the next thing I know, Bobby was talking about you as if you were out of his grasp. He's been moping for six months.''

''Moping?''

''It's obvious—to me at least—that he's missed you like crazy. He's hardly been the same man since you two parted ways.''

The idea that Bobby had missed her as much as she'd missed him tore her in two directions. She wanted to believe he'd missed her, but she didn't like to think of him as unhappy for any reason. ''He's probably been more upset over what happened to my brother. He took Greg's death hard.''

Mention of her brother might have caused a more sensitive soul to clam up, but Denise was a veritable freight train when it came to conversation. She just kept chugging along no matter what debris was lying on the tracks. "Oh, Jo! Greg wouldn't have wanted his death to bust you two up!"

Jo froze as a suspicion that had been in the back of her mind on more than one occasion was shouted at her full blast.

"Last Christmas when ya'll were here, I had a long conversation with him and he told me that he hoped you two would get together," Denise said.

It had been a while since she'd had anyone tell her a story about Greg. Most people tried to avoid talking about him now. "Did he really tell you that?" Jo blinked back tears.

"Swear to God," Denise declared. "He was so proud of having done a little matchmaking. He also said he hoped you two would get married because he had all sorts of plans for the house once you moved out."

Jo laughed. That sounded like Greg, all right. "He always wanted to put in a pool table and have a real swinging bachelor pad. Unfortunately, the only place for a pool table was my bedroom, and I refused to vacate so he could have the dissolute life of his dreams."

"Isn't that like a guy?" Denise cracked. "I bet Bobby wouldn't mind swapping me for a pool table, either."

"No, he wouldn't. Bobby loves his family. You most of all."

"Ha! He's sick to death of us all, I'll bet, and you know why?" Typically, she didn't wait for Jo's answer. "Says all we do is pester him about getting married. And he's right—that's what we do! He's the baby boy of the family and everybody wants to see him happy."

The statement made Jo wonder. ''Isn't he happy?''

''He used to be. But this last year has squished the filling out of him.''

''That makes me feel terrible.''

''Well, maybe it's not *all* you, Jo. You're right, it's also Greg, and that job of his. He's so proud to be a Texas Ranger, but...''

Jo knew what Denise was getting at. She'd seen the same dichotomy in Greg, especially after he'd been present at a particularly gruesome crime scene. Her brother had liked the idea of helping people, but unfortunately police work put him in situations where it was often beyond his power to give anyone assistance. Disastrous car accidents. Murder scenes. Domestic violence that would shake the firmest belief in the basic goodness of humanity. He'd wanted to help people, but he'd found it distressing to see people suffer.

And of course, Bobby had had to deal with Greg's death and his feelings of guilt. It couldn't have been easy for a man who was used to being a law-enforcement hotshot to have made a mistake, even an innocent one that might not have changed the outcome. Bobby would always wonder about those ten minutes.

So would she.

''He'll work through it,'' Jo assured Denise.

''I think he's reached the point where he's tired of working through his problems alone. He needs a partner in life. I guess he thought he'd found her.''

Jo ducked her head. Denise's meaning was obvious. *She* was supposed to be that partner. Which was what she had wanted, too.

''Bobby and I are just friends now,'' she insisted.

Denise tsked loudly. ''That's a shame. It really is.'' She

sucked in her breath as if she'd just been shocked by a punch. "Jeez!"

Jo frowned. "What's wrong?"

Denise took Jo's hand and placed it over her belly. "Feel that?"

Jo was startled by a sharp movement under her hand. She retracted her arm and laughed in surprise. "It kicked me!"

"It, nothing. I've got Muhammad Ali in here."

Jo laughed again, almost giddy with her contact with that new life stirring. She loved babies. "You must be so excited. Pretty soon you'll be able to hold him or her in your arms."

"Frankly, I'm too tired to think about it most of the time," Denise answered in a comical deadpan. "Everybody keeps telling me since it's my first baby, the little monster'll probably be weeks late. That's what I've been having nightmares about lately. I keep worrying that I'll be the first female in the history of humankind to gestate for ninety months instead of nine."

Despite her silly words, Jo could detect the anticipation and genuine love in her friend's voice. She felt a rush of happiness for her. Tom and Denise had been trying to have a child for several years. The last time she'd spoken to Denise she'd mentioned that she might be pregnant—and now the baby was almost here. It was heartening to think that this long year had brought good things, too. For someone.

"I hope Tom makes it back in time," Denise said.

"He will," Jo assured her.

"See?" Denise exclaimed. "*This* is why you need Bobby! I'll bet that brother of mine would never skip off to Indonesia if you were about to have a baby."

Jo didn't require a sales pitch. But the thought of Bobby

and babies was too much for her to absorb right now. She'd tried so hard to put dreams like that aside. More than anything she wanted a family. In the old days, she'd thought what really mattered was a singing career. But as the years passed and it became clear that she was never going to be Wynonna Judd, and maybe it was better for her that she wasn't, she'd begun to yearn for a family of her own. Now that she'd lost both parents, and her brother, it seemed more important to her than ever. She missed having a blood bond with someone else.

"Maybe someday..."

"Someday!" Denise squeaked disapprovingly. "When? When you and Bobby are wheeling around together in the old folks' home? Don't you want to enjoy life now, while you're both young? Why are you both looking for reasons to stay apart when it's obvious you belong together?"

The words struck a chord, and for a moment Jo was reminded of something Willie had said to her. *You can always find reasons to stay apart....*he'd told her in his truck one day last week.

That had been right before all the trouble started. Right before Bobby had arrived at her house to help her. And now she'd unloaded her whole passel of troubles on him. And she couldn't forget that added to all their other problems was her blindness.

Oh, she tried to be optimistic about it. But she worried.

"We've got so many hurdles to overcome," she said.

Denise gave an understanding grunt. "Join the club. But you'll work it out. I know you will. It was meant to be."

Unfortunately, fate was something Jo was used to singing about, but she wasn't a big believer.

As her conversation with Denise was grinding to a halt, Bobby came back with a bag full of caffeine-free sodas and beer. They ate the sandwiches that Bobby's mother had sent over with Denise.

"Does your mother provide all your meals while you're here?" Jo asked Bobby curiously.

Denise laughed. "Why? Did the weekend squire lead you to believe you'd be roughing it out here?"

The cabin could hardly be described as roughing it. There was air-conditioning—thank God. The July heat would be nigh on unbearable without it. There was running water and plumbing and even a washing machine. The one modern convenience Bobby's cabin lacked was a dishwasher. Outside, there was an old rustic woodshed where he kept horse feed and all the power tools necessary to keep his acreage reasonably manicured. Jo knew this from her previous visits. She and Bobby had shared a long searing kiss in that shed, in fact.

Remembering their kiss made her blush, and she dipped her head to take a sip of soda, hoping no one would notice. "Last time I was here no one catered the meals."

Denise snickered. "That's because no one thought you two were too busy to cook."

"Too busy?" Jo asked, clueless.

Bobby groaned. "My mother obviously thinks we're having a little honeymoon."

Jo felt her face go scarlet.

"But she's having dinner tomorrow night and definitely wants you two to be there," Denise said. "It's a command performance, in fact."

After what Bobby had just announced, Jo feared she would be too embarrassed to face his parents. Hadn't he told them why she was here? Surely his whole family knew it was all over between them....

They knew it like Denise knew it, a voice in her head

answered. When it came to her and Bobby, she was beginning to think these Garcias just wouldn't take no for an answer.

"HERE'S WHAT we got so far, Bobby," Ed Taggart said over the phone. "We got one vehicle with fingerprints galore. That cab glowed when we sprayed it. Unfortunately, most of the prints in the front belonged to Jack Pike, the driver. So nothing there."

"Any word on who Jack Pike was?" Bobby asked. There was always the chance that he had known his killer, in which case he might himself be a clue to the identity of the man they were searching for. "Did he have a record?"

"Nah, not a thing on the guy. By all accounts, he was honest. He was divorced, had a kid. Never been in trouble with the law. Hardworking."

Bobby sighed. The more Ed went on, the more depressing it seemed. "Then it sounds like we still don't have much to go on."

"That's a fact. One curious thing, though. On the ground outside the cab, we found something weird—a marble."

"A marble?"

"Yeah. This is one of the big ones. A shooter. Remember those?"

Bobby frowned, curious. "You think that had something to do with the guy I was fighting with?"

"Could be. There's a possibility it fell out of the cab or the guy's pocket. Thing is, we got a print off it—a ninety percent partial. It matched up to some fellow in San Antonio name of Leo Hayes."

Bobby's brow furrowed. "When was he arrested?" If the cops had his prints on file, then the man sure as heck wasn't a Boy Scout. "Is he on parole?"

"Nope—the only thing this guy has is a conviction from way back. White-collar all the way. He was convicted of doctoring the books at a business he worked at. Had some kind of money-shifting scam going on."

Embezzling. "You got a picture?"

"Sure—it's twelve years old, though. The man fulfilled his parole and hasn't had so much as a parking ticket since. Runs a successful little business in San Antonio called Old Tyme Toys."

"Could you fax the photo to me here at this number?" Bobby kept a printer-fax-telephone at the cabin in case trouble came up on weekends he was staying here. He also usually brought his department-issue computer notebook with him, just in case.

No wonder Doug called him a workaholic.

"Sure thing," Ed said. "I'll have it to you in ten minutes or so."

When he hung up the phone, Jo was hovering nearby. "What's the news?"

"We might have a suspect. His name's Leo Hayes. Did you ever hear Terry mention that name?"

Jo's face tensed in concentration for a few minutes and then she shook her head. "No, but that doesn't mean she never did. I might have just forgotten. Who is this man?"

"Well, I'm not too sure. He's never been charged with a violent crime. Just embezzling."

She pursed her lips. "What makes the police think he could be a suspect?"

"They found his fingerprint on a marble that was picked up where I tussled with the guy last night."

"A marble? That's weird."

"Maybe not so weird. The guy runs a little toy company in San Antonio. They're faxing me the picture they have on file for him."

"Do you think it's him? Really?"

"We can't jump to any conclusions, Jo. This could be a complete dead end. Maybe this Hayes fellow was a passenger in the cab days before and dropped the marble then. You might have kicked it out when you made your leap." It still gave him chills to remember her jumping out of that moving car. He couldn't believe how brave she was.

Despite his warning, however, Jo was practically quivering with excitement at their having a suspect.

"I don't want you to get your hopes up," Bobby warned her. But he was feeling the same buzz of anticipation himself. By the time Ed's fax of Leo Hayes's picture came through, he was practically ready to rip it out of the paper tray before the transmission had finished printing. As the image appeared, Bobby felt the thrill of recognition. Short lank brown hair—albeit not as short as he wore it now. Wide-set eyes. Pasty looking. "That's the guy, all right."

He was on the horn before Jo had made it to the fax to feel the piece of paper and squint at it, trying to make out the face. As if she could force herself to see by concentrating hard enough.

"Ed? Yeah, that's the guy."

"Hot dog!" Ed said.

"Something tells me we gotta move on this guy fast. He's been pretty clever so far. He might have guessed already that we're on to him."

Ed chuckled. "You think a guy would notice a missing marble?"

"You never know."

"Okay, Bobby, I'll get the captain to put out an APB, and we'll have San Antonio search Hayes's business ASAP."

Jo was smiling at him when he hung up. "This is good news, isn't it? They'll probably be able to catch him now."

Bobby knew better than to be overly optimistic. He'd seen too many good leads fray into a hundred dead ends. "This is a starting point. We know who we're after. The police are going to be checking out his business in San Antonio."

"When?"

"It'll probably be tomorrow morning before they can get the search warrant and the manpower to check it out. And when they do, I want to be there. We need to go through his things and see if there's a connection between Old Tyme Toys and All That Glitters. Or anything that would give us a connection between him and Terry."

"Good. Won't we have to check out his house or apartment, too?"

Her question stopped him cold. "Not we, Jo. You need to stay here."

"Alone?"

"No, I'll drop you off at the main house and you can visit the folks tomorrow. There's bound to be a lot going on over there with the big dinner for tomorrow night."

Her face flushed. "Drop me off, nothing. I'm not going to spend tomorrow snapping beans and setting the table while you're out hunting down a murderer."

"You can't go with me."

"Why not?"

Because I want you here, safe. He sighed. "What good would it do?"

She crossed her arms stubbornly; he could see the muscles in her cheek working as she ground her teeth. "You mean because I'm blind? You think that's why I wouldn't be any use to you?"

"It's not that I don't think you'd be any use, Jo. It's just I don't want you involved in chasing this guy."

"I'm already involved," she argued. "Besides, if

there's a clue anywhere in that man's possession that might exonerate Terry, I want to be the first to get my hands on it. Don't you see, Bobby? If we catch this person, it's not only going to free me from danger, it might also free Terry from her life in exile. I might be able to get my friend back!"

It was wrong, he knew. The cops wouldn't want her there. Heck, they probably wouldn't even want *him* there. For the most part the Rangers had good working relationships with all branches of law enforcement, but there were still some police who saw Rangers coming into a case as an encroachment on their territory. In this case Bobby didn't particularly care what they thought. He was personally involved now, and he was going to make damn sure he stuck his nose into every aspect of the investigation.

Maybe that's what swayed him to Jo's point of view. If he felt personally involved, imagine how she felt. Plus, the expression on her face told him she wasn't going to budge. She was determined.

And though he hated to admit it, part of him admired her for her will.

"If you don't let me go along with you," she warned him, "then I'll just stay right here. Alone."

"Damn it, Jo, you're stubborn."

She smiled. A radiant, triumphant smile. She knew she'd worn him down.

JO HAD NEVER ridden in a plane as small as the chartered jet that took them from the tiny airfield near Lufkin to San Antonio. She wasn't sure she liked it. Every time they hit so much as a whisper of turbulence, she couldn't help imagining they were twenty thousand feet in the air in a craft made of tinfoil and bubble gum. She wished they could have driven, but that would have taken too long. Like Bobby, she felt the need to hurry. To find Leo Hayes.

Something told her he wouldn't be in San Antonio, though.

When they arrived at Old Tyme Toys, a little store in a strip mall near the wealthy Alamo Heights neighborhood, the place was just opening its doors. April Smith, the young female clerk who worked there selling simple wood and metal toys to the well-heeled, seemed surprised that her first customers of the day were two uniformed policemen, a Texas Ranger and a blind woman.

"You won't find Mr. Hayes here," the young woman declared. "I haven't seen him myself for over a week."

"Do you know where he's been?"

"He *said* he was going out of the country on business."

Jo jumped on the news and blurted out a question even before the police could. "Where?"

She heard gum snapping and wished she could read the woman's expression. "Who knows? Mr. Hayes has business all over the world. Africa, Asia, South America..."

"Brazil?" Bobby asked.

"Oh, sure," April said. "He goes there a lot. But he doesn't tell me details. Says I'm just here to stock the shelves and work the cash register."

"How do you manage things when he's not around?"

"I do okay, and Mr. Hayes is a real pest with the telephone. That's another weird thing. This week he hasn't even called in. It's been kind of nice, honestly."

One officer sat down to interview the clerk about her boss's disappearance in more detail while Bobby, Jo and the other cop headed straight for the tiny office in the back of the store. Jo felt strange just walking into someone's private space and tearing the place apart for clues, but then she remembered that Leo Hayes had felt no compunction about ripping her whole house to shreds to find whatever he was looking for. She didn't normally consider herself a vengeful person, but when she recalled all Hayes had done, it sapped every ounce of human consideration out of her.

In the office, they sifted through papers. Right away, Bobby found something very interesting. Leo Hayes had jotted a phone number on a business card by his phone. It was for a number in Brazil. "It can't be a coincidence," Bobby said.

Jo's heart felt as if it were beating double time. The possibility of finding Leo Hayes and clearing Terry's name was too wonderful to quit thinking about. Even if they didn't find Hayes today, it felt as if they were getting close.

Since Jo couldn't read and therefore wasn't much help sifting through the business papers, she wandered back out to the store and listened to more of April Smith's interview with the cop.

The young woman was clearly worried now. "Has something happened to Mr. Hayes?" she asked. "Is he... dead?"

"No, ma'am, not that we know of. We're just trying to locate him."

"Because when he left so quickly last week and didn't show up Monday with no explanation, then yesterday and today..." The girl sighed. "Well, that's just not like him. Mr. Hayes usually wants to know *everything* that's going on here. He doesn't trust me to run the store all by myself. Even when he's out of town he'll call in at least twice a day."

"Would you consider him a good boss?"

"Oh, sure. Very professional. Especially when you consider it's mostly just me and him here on weekdays. He's never put the moves on me once. You wouldn't believe how rare a thing that is. The pervs I've worked for! Mr. Hayes is a little icky, but at least he's not a perv."

The cop cleared his throat, apparently trying to think of a way to subtly get April back on track. "Right. So when Mr. Hayes goes on business trips, you're in charge?"

"Like I said, he still calls in all the time. He thinks I'm an idiot."

"I thought you said he was a good boss." Confusion was evident in the cop's voice.

"Oh, sure. He is. He gives me raises pretty regular, too. But he thinks I'm an idiot. He thinks everyone is an idiot but him. He has another employee part-time on weekends and he thinks she's an even bigger idiot than I am. Her name's Hannah."

The cop took down the other employee's full name and asked for her address.

"But I've talked to Hannah already," April said after she'd given the street address for her co-worker's apartment. "I did that first thing when Mr. Hayes didn't show up Monday morning. She said she hadn't seen him, either. He didn't call Saturday, apparently. That's really weird."

"What about Sunday?" the cop asked.

"We're closed Sundays."

Jo puffed out a breath of irritation and turned away from the interview. It would have been so much more gratifying if April had told them that her boss was a complete scumbag. She eased around some of the tables and shelves, touching the toys. There was a whole display of plastic and metal windup toys. She also made out several wood pull toys with wheels and lots of dolls. The items here really did seem old-fashioned. No electronic toys among them.

It seemed a strange business for a criminal to be involved in, actually. She moved along and discovered a bowl full of slick round objects. Marbles. She grabbed up three and felt them in her hand. They clacked together.

All at once, she went completely still and tilted her head as if some memory were scratching the farthest reaches of her consciousness. She rolled them again and felt cold flash deep in the marrow of her bones. It was the sound she'd heard in the cab. She'd thought it was like the clicking of ice cubes...but it wasn't. It was the sound marbles made when they hit each other.

Behind her, April giggled uncomfortably. "Gosh, for a second there I expected to see Mr. Hayes."

Jo turned sharply. "Why?"

"Because that's what he always does," April responded. "You know, like a nervous tic. He rolls these marbles in his hands. It's kind of creepy to hear it sometimes."

No kidding.

Jo hurried to the back to tell Bobby. She held three marbles in her hand and demonstrated the sound for him. "That's exactly what I heard. He must have had them in his pockets and they fell out while you were fighting."

Bobby hugged her. "Good—that's another connection. Unfortunately, it and the discovery of the phone number in Rio are probably the only ones we'll glean from this search. There's nothing here that looks illegitimate. It doesn't look like he's cooked the books, even."

"Leo Hayes is apparently very adept at leading a double life," Jo said. "You should have heard the praise April was giving him. Apart from the fact that he's a misanthrope, he's apparently a good boss."

A paper fell on the floor and the cop who had been sorting through files in one corner let out a muttered curse. "It *would* fall behind the heaviest-looking piece of furniture in the place!"

"Here," Bobby offered, "I'll give you a hand moving the cabinet."

The two of them grunted in their efforts to budge the heavy piece of furniture, then Bobby let out a long, low whistle. "Okay, we've hit pay dirt. It's a safe."

It took them a half hour to crack the safe because they had to call in a specialist from the station. And when they did finally get in the safe, the results were disappointingly meager. All the safe contained was a box of kaleidoscopes.

"What the hell?"

April cleared her throat from the doorway. "Those are Mr. Hayes's latest favorite. Kaleidoscopes. We sell a lot."

"Why would he have them in a safe?"

She giggled. "You don't know Mr. Hayes. Sometimes Hannah and I joke about how obsessive he is about these toys of his. Every once in a while he'll just develop a sort of…fetish…for a certain kind of toy. Anyways, he won't let us near his office. I didn't even know he had a safe in here, but it makes sense. He's a real private-type person."

Jo heard Bobby scoop up the box. "Well, as of now his privacy has been invaded. I'll take these along with me."

Jo couldn't tell what good that would do.

From Old Tyme Toys they went to the police station to see what had turned up at Leo Hayes's house. Apparently that search had been just as disappointing as the one of his office. By the time she and Bobby were on the plane flying back to East Texas, Jo felt thoroughly frustrated. The trip today had yielded nothing. She'd thought for sure that when they found the safe it would all become clear. She fingered one of the kaleidoscopes now and had to stifle the urge to toss it across the plane in irritation.

"How could there be *nothing?*"

Bobby was much more philosophical about the day's shortcomings. But he was more accustomed to being thwarted by the criminal mind than she was. Because they were wedged so close together in the small plane seats, she could feel his shoulder lift in a negligent shrug. "Could be one of several things. There's a possibility that we're mixed up. We've either got the wrong Leo Hayes, or Old Tyme Toys is just a front operation. Or it could be that we passed over evidence without realizing its significance."

Jo shook her head adamantly. "Hayes is the guy. The marbles, remember? I heard the sound and April confirmed it."

"You convinced me, but I doubt the sound of marbles clicking would convince a jury."

She bit her lower lip. "What was the other possibility you were talking about? About the toy store being a front?"

"Maybe Hayes rents a place where he handles all his illegal activities. It might be another office he rents under a different name, or it might be just a rental storage unit. It would make sense that he'd do something like that. The man got caught embezzling when he was younger. He learned early the importance of covering his tracks."

"How do we find out whether there is such a place?"

Bobby grunted. "That's the tricky part. It could take forever. Let's hope we find Leo Hayes first."

"But if the police are looking for him..."

Bobby laughed mirthlessly.

She frowned. "What's the joke?"

"It's not funny. But, Jo, you of all people should know how thoroughly a person can disappear when he, or she, wants to."

CHAPTER ELEVEN

"I THINK I've discovered something," Jo said after nearly an hour of tense silence.

When they returned to his cabin that afternoon, Bobby and Jo had tried to settle in for the hour or so left before they needed to be at his parents' house for dinner. But how could they relax when they had the name of the person causing all their troubles and yet no information on his whereabouts?

The Houston police inquiries into Leo Hayes's driver's license and credit cards had led to dead ends. The Rio number they'd found at Old Tyme Toys had led them to a Brazilian man named Gilberto Ruiz, who swore up and down in several languages that he had never met Leo Hayes, never even heard of him. Bobby doubted the man's story, but it was hard to bust a lie over the phone.

The man named Leo Hayes seemed to have dropped off the face of the earth.

Now Bobby was sitting by the phone, waiting to hear from his boss or Ed or the San Antonio police, while Jo was lying on the couch, where she'd been popping wintergreen candies she'd bought at the airport and squinting into one of those damn kaleidoscopes. Watching her fiddle with the thing was driving Bobby to distraction.

Or maybe it was just watching her that was making him nuts. She looked so sexy curled up on his couch. Like a cooped-up house cat with a new toy. Her long legs were crossed, and she lay upright against a mound of pillows. Her curly auburn hair spilled over her shoulders.

He leaned forward. "Discovered what?"

She resumed peering at an angle into the small opening of the toy and turned it to him so that it looked like the aluminum end of the tube was talking to him. "If I turn my head just so and close my eyes, then open them just enough to look into the small circle here, I can focus enough to see the kaleidoscope design."

"Are you sure?"

She glanced over the tube, her lips turned up in amusement. "Of course I'm sure. I've been doing nothing but staring into this thing for forty-five minutes."

His heart lightened. "Jo, that's great!"

She responded with a wry nod. "It would be great if all the world could be looked at through a half-inch hole. Unfortunately, as long as I keep my eyes open all the time, it doesn't work so well."

"Yes, but if you can see even a little…"

She shook her head. "I've been getting occasional flashes now for a while. Like when I saw you in the headlight of the car." She paused, thinking. "Maybe that was it. You were backlit, and I was squinting." She squinted again now, but didn't seem to have any luck with it. "Oh, heck. I could just be going insane."

"No, Jo." He crossed to the couch, plopped down, and gathered her into his arms. He might have expected a protest, but she didn't seem to mind. "It's a beginning. Don't be frustrated. You saw something two nights ago, and now today."

She nodded. "I guess."

"The doctors have never given you any reason not to hope, have they?"

"No." She buried her face in his shirt. God, it felt good

to feel her against him. Too good. He could feel his blood heat. Feel his groin tighten. He shouldn't have these feeling for Jo right now; he'd brought her here to protect her and make her feel secure, not to take advantage of her.

"The doctors are all cockeyed optimists," she said. "But I don't think any of them know what it's like to wake up and not be able to see the ceiling over your head."

Bobby nodded, understanding. "They're professionals. They have to be sympathetic, but they don't know what you're going through. They can't. It's the same way with police. We have to go to all sorts of situations and try to tell people that everything will be all right, but half the time we can't be sure that it will. I don't know what a woman who's had all her money stolen by her own husband really feels like, for instance. But it's my duty to try to make her see beyond the present."

"You're right," Jo said. "I get so angry with doctors sometimes, but I know it's not their fault I can't see. They weren't responsible for me hitting that truck. It's just the human urge to place blame away from ourselves."

"Accidents happen, Jo," he said. He knew from long months of blaming himself for Greg's death. You had to let go of the guilt a little or the torment could drive you crazy. "You can't blame yourself too much. At least you didn't hurt anyone else."

A shudder racked her body. "Yes, I'm so thankful for that. I don't think I would have held up at all if something had happened to the person I hit."

He believed her. At times Jo could seem brash and tough, but she was one of the most caring people he'd ever known. And she was so vulnerable. It pained him that all this had happened to her. Life hadn't been fair to Jo. She'd lost her mama when she was just a little girl, her father when she was twenty-one, and her brother. Now who did she have?

Me, his heart answered as he looked into her hazel eyes. He lifted his hands and touched the coils of springy auburn hair at her temples. As he did, her mouth parted.

"Oh, Jo, I'd do anything to change what happened. You know that, don't you?"

Wordlessly, she nodded. Her cheeks flushed and he bent down and touched his lips to the soft skin there. He felt her intake of breath. His heart was pounding.

It was oh so easy to shift just slightly, to brush his lips against hers. Once. Twice. Momentarily, Jo dipped her head back, then sought his mouth more forcefully. After that, it was as if something between them had snapped. He'd thought of this moment for too long, had yearned for the warm pressure of those lips for six long months. He'd ached for the taste of her—a taste of coffee and wintergreen and sweetness. The smell of that freesia stuff in her hair hit him, too—all the things he remembered about Jo were just the same. As were the fundamental qualities he'd always admired in her. Her humor. Her loyalty. Her goodness.

He grasped her more tightly into his embrace and they fell against the pillows in a tangle. She felt so good. Every inch of her. Her breasts pressed gently against his chest, stirring his blood. He nearly groaned, then plundered her mouth with his tongue. She curled her hands at his nape. It was a give-and-take he remembered well from last winter. Stolen moments in his car, or while they were alone in her house together before Greg finished his shift. They'd acted like teenagers then, kids with a delectable secret they weren't yet ready to share with the rest of the world.

Neither of them had been ready to admit how much they loved each other. They had been friends first, and were loath to take the leap that would turn their relationship into something else. So they had laughed and kissed and longed for more. They'd known there was something special between them, and neither had wanted to move too fast. They'd thought they had all the time in the world.

Now it occurred to Bobby that all these long months he had mostly been thinking of himself, of his own loss. Of how much he'd wanted her. To touch her now and know from her response that she'd missed him too, had longed for him as much as he had for her, was almost as gratifying as it was heartbreaking.

He kissed her chin, then worked his way down her long neck, savoring the soft sweet flesh, so pale and vulnerable there. She tipped her head back, letting out a little moan, yet inviting him to explore more. Gently, he worked the buttons free on her blouse until the soft pink satin of her bra was exposed to him. The fabric was delicate, enticing. He traced the lacy edge of the garment with his fingertip, then rubbed his palm across her breast. Underneath the satin, he felt the bud of her nipple tighten at his touch. He teased it into a peak, then became impatient with the barrier between him. He undid the closure at the front of her bra and pushed aside the fabric.

She was so beautiful. Her creamy breasts were perfect. Bending down, he coaxed a nipple into a tight knot with his tongue before taking it into his mouth.

She let out a soft moan and instinctively pressed her hips against his thigh. Bobby felt his last thread of restraint start to fray. His hands brushed down her body, skimming over the smooth skin of her midriff and down onto the stiff fabric of her jeans.

Her hands on his shoulders tensed and he felt her nails through his shirt. She, too, was losing control. His hands massaged along her thigh up to the V where her legs met, and she turned, pushing slightly upward.

The movement dislodged the kaleidoscope that had been resting on her lap. The toy rolled off the couch and fell with a crash onto the gray stone tile.

Both he and Jo straightened up, startled by the noise. When he saw the broken toy roll across the room and come to a stop against the fireplace in the corner, he assured her, "It's just that stupid kaleidoscope."

They exchanged anxious, relieved smiles.

Smiles that faded as soon as they took in what had happened. As quickly as it had materialized minutes before, the rushed feeling of intimacy between them now vanished.

Blushing, Jo resnapped her bra. As he watched that one action, it was all Bobby could do not to knock his forehead against the coffee table in frustration. And recrimination. What had he been doing?

Well, he knew what he'd been doing. He'd been on the verge of making love to her right then and there on the couch, when just moments before he'd been patting himself on the back for showing such restraint. For not taking advantage of the situation.

So much for good intentions.

"Bobby, I'm sorry," she said. "I got carried away."

She got carried away? Did she think that she had instigated that incident? That she had somehow enticed him?

She *had* enticed him. But he hardly blamed her for his own desires. "It's okay, Jo." He held her hand, rubbing it gently. He wondered if there would ever be a time when they felt so unguarded with each other again. "It's never been a secret that I want you, has it?"

The two bright stains were back in her cheeks as she shook her head. She not so subtly changed the subject. "It must be late, right? I guess I'd better get ready to go over to your parents'...."

Now that was a sobering thought. He sat up and repressed a long-suffering sigh. Right now the last place he wanted to be was a half mile away under the eagle eyes of his mother and father. Not to mention his siblings! They were sure to make insinuations and wisecracks to show their impatience with his single status, which would no doubt cause Jo as much discomfort as it would him.

She smiled. "It's all right, Bobby. I love your parents. It'll be fun. And I didn't really have long enough to talk to Denise yesterday."

Resigned to the fact that the moment between them was truly over, Bobby slithered off the couch and got to his feet, picking up the broken end of the kaleidoscope as he did so. It didn't escape his notice that Jo said she loved his parents but wouldn't say that she loved *him*.

"I hope they won't be offended if I show up in jeans," she added.

"They won't." Anyway, in his own biased opinion, Jo in jeans was equal to any other woman in a Christian Dior suit.

He crossed the room to gather up the rest of the kaleidoscope and discovered that the guts of the thing had spilled out onto the tiles. Little chips of colored glass fanned out across the gray, sparkling up at him as if to wink in mockery. This was a job for the whisk broom.

He strode to the kitchen, fetched the little broom and dustpan and set about cleaning the stuff up. As he was standing to carry the colorful debris to the garbage pail in the kitchen, a glint from the dustpan suddenly stopped him cold. Amid the colored glass were several pieces of clear stone, thicker and more lustrous than glass. In fact, several were the size of small rocks and were cut in geometrical shapes.

"Jo!"

She jumped off the couch and hurried to the fireplace. "What is it?"

"The silly kaleidoscope you were playing with—"

"I'm sorry. It was evidence. Did I do something wrong?"

"No, you did something very right. It had diamonds in it!"

Her mouth dropped open and she gazed up at him in astonishment. "You mean Leo Hayes—"

"His little toy-import business that seems so on the up-and-up is just a front for smuggling diamonds. I guess I can see now why he had the box of kaleidoscopes in the safe. There are probably hundreds of thousands of dollars in rocks in them."

"April said he seemed to have a fetish for certain toys. No wonder!"

"Right. His toy store was probably completely legit. It's just he was using the toys themselves as conduits for some sort of smuggling operation."

She sucked in her breath. "That's it then!" she said excitedly. "Leo Hayes is a smuggler, we know that now. And we know he has some connection to Rio, too. He has to, in spite of what that Gilberto person says. Leo Hayes has to be the one who set Terry up. Once the police snag him, Terry will be cleared."

"Not so fast," Bobby said. He hated to disappoint her, but things rarely were as simple as they seemed. "You said that Terry seemed as if she were trying to protect someone. What if the person she was protecting was Leo? Or maybe she double-crossed Leo Hayes and was on the run from him."

Jo puffed up at his words. She looked as if he had betrayed her. "How could you think that?"

"Jo, my suspicion of Terry has nothing to do with how I feel about you. I admire your loyalty. I want to believe that Terry is innocent almost as much as you do. For your sake."

She crossed her arms. "What will it take to convince you she's innocent?"

He hated to be the wet blanket, but he couldn't just drop his skepticism, either. "Maybe some proof that she had reason to protect someone other than a criminal or her own hide."

DOUG HENDERSON hung up his phone and sighed. This had been a long day and it wasn't even close to being over yet. The workload was overwhelming. Company A was already trying to track down a serial rapist operating around the Montrose area. Sergeant Seals was in Mexico City negotiating an extradition. The men had two different drug cases they were working on day and night, a corruption case and a Conroe lawyer's wife had just been kidnapped.

In other words, it was business as usual.

And now Bobby Garcia—who, last Doug heard, was supposed to be on vacation—was pestering him every hour on the hour for information about the whereabouts of this Brazilian dame. But their police contact in Rio hadn't called him back and he didn't have anything to report to Bobby yet.

Doug leaned back and stared at his coffee cup and tried to remember the last time he'd drunk something that didn't have caffeine in it. This morning maybe? He remembered pausing next to the juice machine briefly and considering a can of grapefruit juice. But then the smell of freshly brewed coffee from the break room had beckoned. He'd drunk coffee for breakfast, a Pepsi around eleven, black coffee with his sandwich at lunch, and two cups through the afternoon to keep himself awake. Maybe he wouldn't need so much of the stuff if he could just get a decent night's rest. But he'd been having such a hard time sleeping lately.

He leaned back in his chair. If he kept up this level of coffee consumption, his kidneys were probably going to be like two walnuts by the time he retired. He was going to have to ease up. Maybe start drinking some water one of these days.

His nose wrinkled at the thought. He'd never been a big fan of water. It just didn't taste like anything.

There was a knock at the door and Doug looked up at the guy standing there. The pale man's smallish frame was swallowed by blue coveralls and a hard hat with the phone company logo on it. The massive utility belt around his waist looked like it probably weighed more than he did.

"Can I help you?" Doug asked.

The worker held up a new beige phone that made Doug groan. It had a million buttons all over it. "We're replacing all the phones in your department, sir."

Doug shook his head. That was DPS efficiency for you. They couldn't get a copier that worked worth a damn and it took forever to pry the smallest expense reimbursement out of the government, but the department seemed to be getting newer, fancier phones every three months. No sooner had he figured out one system than they switched to something else—always something more complicated. Funny how they never seemed to actually make things simpler in this world.

Oh, well. It wasn't the phone guy's fault. He rolled back

from his desk and gestured generously at his phone. "It's all yours."

He stood and looked at his watch—4:35. Still a ways to go yet before the end of the day. He needed to call Brazil again for Bobby, see if they had anything yet. The man had seemed desperate for new information. That murder case he was looking into for the police must be heating up.

He grabbed his coffee cup and headed for the break room. If he didn't get some more caffeine in him, he just wasn't going to make it to quitting time.

AFTER THE CAPTAIN had gone, Leo worked quickly. *Like taking candy from babies,* he thought with disgust. No wonder the world was such a dangerous mess these days! You couldn't count on the police for anything. They couldn't even catch a murderer walking through their offices. It was just another example of shocking incompetence.

He shook his head. Oh, he was clever all right. More clever than these morons. The hard part had been making a plan. He'd known the man he'd fought with Monday night was a Texas Ranger. Leo made it his business to spot uniforms, and the unofficial Ranger attire was pretty obvious, even in a state where half the population seemed to be dressed in boots, white shirts and Stetsons. Plus the guy he'd fought had worn the silver badge of a sergeant in the Rangers. There was no mistaking that.

Just his luck that Jolene Daniels would have a guardian angel in law enforcement.

After that night Leo had checked out of his hotel and taken up his alias, Ben Blythe, just in case the police were catching on to him somehow. There had to be some reason that Ranger had followed him. Had they found the cabdriver that quickly? Had he left a clue behind somewhere? Leo found that hard to believe. He was not sloppy.

Well, it was all a damned nuisance. Until he got this cleared up he wouldn't be able to go home or check on the store. He supposed that idiot April could handle things until he figured out what was what, but he hated to leave her alone too long.

Forget the toy store, he remonstrated himself. The diamonds. They were the important things. He needed to keep his eye on that prize. All these trials would be worth it in the end if he finally got his hands on the diamonds Terry Monteverde had spirited out of Brazil. Of course, the possibility that they had been lost in that damned boating accident occurred to him. But what about the Daniels woman? Why would she be hiding if she didn't have what he was looking for?

The key thing now was to find where Jolene Daniels had gotten herself off to. A bug in the phone of her guardian angel's boss should handle that problem quite nicely. A little research on the web at the public library had revealed that the Rangers' Company A was headquartered right in Houston. Very handy. One site even listed all the Rangers' names beneath photos. The Ranger he was looking for was named Robert Garcia. Unfortunately, the man didn't appear to be at his home.

But sooner or later he would check in at work, Leo was pretty sure of that. And when he did, clever Leo would be listening.

BY THE TIME they reached Bobby's parents' house that night, Jo felt as if she'd been up for twenty-four hours. But the energetic hum of the Garcia home soon took the weariness out of her bones. And the smells wafting through the air alerted her stomach to the fact that she hadn't eaten anything since the half a sandwich she'd had in San Antonio. When she walked into the kitchen she discovered enough food to feed an army. There was a cauldron of her favorite, tortilla soup, on the stove and a long platter of enchiladas ready to be popped into the oven. Additionally, there were bowls of salad and plates of little *empanadas,* which Marisol Garcia, Bobby's mother, pressed on Jo the minute she walked in the door.

Jo didn't turn down the offer. She was starved, and she realized it wasn't just for food. Ever since Bobby's kiss she'd felt edgy, ravenous, unsated. All the enchiladas in the world wouldn't fulfill the need she really felt, but the Garcia bounty was a start. Besides, it was something to distract her from thinking of Bobby being just across the room from her.

Every time she thought of those brief, incredible moments they'd spent on his couch this afternoon, she wanted to weep in frustration. Maybe the timing was all wrong, but she wanted him so much. Wanted him, and was irritated with him, too. Bobby had seemed put out with her for believing in Terry's innocence, but how could she doubt one of her oldest friends? Terry wouldn't be in cahoots with a scumbag like Leo Hayes.

By the time she sat down next to Bobby's father at the dinner table, Jo was practically full already just from nibbling. Which naturally didn't stop her from chowing down more. She stuffed herself from the tortilla soup right down to the last drop of *cajeta* sauce on the apple pie for dessert.

Dinner at the Garcias' was a multilingual affair Jo could barely keep up with. Her Spanish was broken at best, but then, so was theirs. Bobby and his four siblings spoke English almost exclusively at the table, while their father, Raul, who'd emigrated from Mexico in his twenties, slipped Spanish into the conversation whenever possible.

Marisol, a second-generation Mexican, alternated English and Spanish. And Bobby's nieces and nephews seemed to have no difficulty keeping up with any language and sometimes spoke something that could only be called Spanglish.

The conversation around the table was rapid-fire and heated at times, with discussions and even arguments erupting over politics, the ranch, Denise's husband and whether Bobby should take vacations more often. His mother was for it; Raul understood that a man needed to work hard.

Jo was always amazed by this. When she was growing up, meals had been the quietest of times. Her father, after a day in the heat chartering boats, usually liked his quiet. And though he enjoyed Greg's sense of humor, he never would have put up with loud and rowdy discussions at the dinner table.

But Jo preferred the atmosphere at the Garcia house—it felt lively and free. And fun. For a few hours she was part of a tight-knit, boisterous clan, and she liked the sensation of inclusion. The closest thing she'd experienced like it was her group at Tumbleweeds, but this felt even better. This felt like a home.

After dinner, when they were all stuffed and tired, Raul got out his guitar and picked several tunes before Denise piped up, "Sing a Spanish song, Jo."

The call was echoed by several others. Jo shook her head. "The only Spanish song I know besides 'La Cucaracha' is 'Malaguena.'"

Raul knew that one, too, and Jo didn't have a difficult time putting all her heart and soul into the song. All she had to do was think of Bobby, and how much it had hurt her to lose him for all those months, to make her fully realize the longing in the words.

"Why don't you and Bobby dance?" Marisol suggested when she was finished singing.

Surprised, they both faltered.

"Oh, I couldn't—"

"No, that—"

"Well, *I* want to dance!" Bobby's sister Lucia declared. As Raul started the strains of "The West Texas Waltz," Jo heard Lucia and her husband get up and start to glide around the room. Their dance was met by a running commentary of laughter and jeers from the peanut gallery of siblings, sons and daughters. This was another big family occurrence that Jo had never experienced. Spontaneous ballroom dancing.

Bobby came up to her and took her hand. "Want to join them?"

Was he crazy? Here he was supposedly paranoid about his family trying to get him married off, and now he was dumping fuel on the fire. Still, she had a hard time resisting the upward inflection in that deep voice. As his hand tugged gently on hers, she silently acquiesced by standing and walking right into his waiting arms. It would have been difficult to do otherwise, given the way she was feeling. After their kiss that afternoon, her resistance was low.

And now, as they swayed easily together, she felt her cheeks heat in a telltale blush. She could just imagine the heads that would be bumping together after they left tonight, but surprisingly she didn't particularly care. Bobby's family had been so nice to her. Amazingly nice. They didn't seem to have any prejudice against her as a match for Bobby, even though she wasn't Hispanic or Catholic and she made a living—barely—from singing in urban honky-tonks. They either truly liked her or were really desperate to marry off their son.

Bobby's hands touched her softly at her waist, and their

bodies swayed together in a loose waltz rhythm. Their feet weren't actually moving very much, for which Jo was grateful. The last thing she wanted during this intimate moment was to trip publicly over Bobby's feet. They were barely touching, but the dance felt almost as intimate as their kiss this afternoon had. And when one mouthy niece called out, "Hold her closer, Uncle Bobby!" she was in agonies of embarrassment and longing.

Then, just as suddenly as it had begun, the dance was over. Raul put his guitar away and scurried to the television to watch his favorite game show. Everyone else gravitated toward the kitchen for the big cleanup.

Bobby and Jo were still standing in the living room. She could feel his eyes blazing down at her, and when she turned away and closed her own, then opened them again, she could see his deep-brown eyes with amber flecks. She gasped.

"What is it?" he asked.

"I saw you! Your eyes."

She could hear the smile in his voice. "Really?"

She nodded excitedly. "Just as well as I could see that kaleidoscope image this afternoon. Maybe the doctors really are right," she said.

"Occasionally they are."

She laughed, and he scooped her into a hug and swung her around in a circle.

"What's all this?" Denise asked, clearing the table.

"Jo said she saw my face," Bobby replied, putting her down.

His sister clucked her tongue. "Imagine! What a thing to see after all these months!" Despite her joking tone, she walked over to Jo excitedly and put a hand on her arm. "Did you really just see my brother's scary mug?"

"Gorgeous mug," Jo corrected. "I think my sight's

coming back a little. I can see images now that I couldn't just days ago.''

Denise put her hand on her arm. ''That's great.''

Jo tried to keep it all in perspective, though it was difficult. Seeing Bobby's eyes was the greatest gift she could have asked for. In fact, if there had been one thing she could have asked to see, that would have been it. ''I guess that doesn't exempt me from clearing the table, though, does it?''

Denise and Bobby were quick to tell her not to bother, but she *wanted* to bother. For the first time in weeks, she felt upbeat. Part of a family again. She wanted to help.

Afterward, Denise pulled her into her old bedroom where she was waiting out her pregnancy, and where all her baby shower loot was assembled. She nudged her toward the giant panda Bobby had bought. ''We're going to have to get the kid mountain climbing gear just so he can hug his teddy bear.''

Jo laughed. ''Bobby loves kid stuff.'' She did, too. She couldn't wait to get back to Houston and go shopping for a present for Denise. She was so happy to have this opportunity to get to know her again.

''Uh-huh. And Bobby loves you,'' Denise said. Jo felt her face catch fire and Denise laughed at her. ''Do you think you guys were invisible tonight, slow dancing together? You know what you looked like?''

She shook her head.

''Like two people revoltingly in love!'' She sighed. ''Honestly, it made me almost nostalgic for my absentee husband, who I might actually forgive now.''

Jo smiled and sat down in a chair between the piled baby shower gifts and the bed. There was a table next to the chair and she started nervously fingering the contents on top of it. She sniffed a perfume bottle. ''That's called

Happy,'' Denise told her in her usual deadpan. ''I'm trying to use the power of positive thinking around Junior here.''

She smiled. The next bottle on the table was a large medicine bottle. She rattled the pills inside.

''Those are prenatal vitamins,'' Denise supplied helpfully, abetting her snooping. ''They're supposed to be good for you, especially during the first three months because you lose a lot of nutrients when you have morning sickness. What they don't tell you, though, is that the horse-size vitamin pills are so strong they're enough to make you heave, too. It's like a double whammy.''

''You haven't been sick lately, have you?'' Jo asked, concerned.

''No, thank goodness that's ancient history. Now I can swallow my horse pill like Seabiscuit. No problems.'' She grunted. ''No problem except that I'm ready for this baby to arrive, fatherless or not.''

Jo laughed and absentmindedly opened the vitamin bottle. They did have a pungent odor. She sniffed at the opening for a moment.

Denise laughed at her. ''See what I mean? Enough to make anyone barf, right?''

She tried to laugh, but there was something about the smell, the heavy bottle in her hands, that danced disconcertingly at the edge of her memory. What was it?

Pills, vitamins.

Terry.

Jo jumped to her feet. The bottle nearly slipped out of her hand. ''Did you say these are fairly common vitamins for women to take when they're pregnant?''

''Yeah,'' Denise said, obviously a little confused as to why her bottle of vitamins had struck such a chord with Jo. ''Most pregnant women do take them. You can buy them over the counter.''

Jo tapped the bottle nervously. "And the smell...?"

"I can only speak from personal experience, and big pungent pills are it."

It was hard to believe...and yet it all made so much sense. When she'd been fiddling with Terry's stuff the night before they'd staged her death, she'd found the bottle of huge multivitamins and had even opened them. Terry was a healthy person, but the megavitamins seemed a little strange to Jo at the time. Why hadn't she read the label on the bottle?

Then she remembered. She *had* looked at the bottle. But the label had been scratched off. At the time, she'd chalked it up to being a travel bottle Terry used often. Now she wondered if Terry hadn't scratched the label off on purpose.

And then, all that time later, when Terry had called her, she'd heard a baby in the background crying. Come to think of it, she hadn't heard much besides the sound of the baby and the traffic way off in the distance. Terry had said she was at a diner, but there hadn't been any sounds of forks and plates clinking. No coffee cups hitting saucers. No conversation or laughter. No canned music.

Just the baby...

And when she'd last seen Terry, her friend had been dressed dumpily. The clothes hadn't been simply dowdy, they'd been oversize.

As pieces of the puzzle came together, her mind raced. Terry had been pregnant. She was sure of it. And pretty far along when Jo had last seen her. But she hadn't noticed because Terry hadn't looked like herself. All the things she'd noted—her tiredness, her weight gain and her shabby-looking clothes—weren't signs of depression or stress. They were indications that Terry was going to have a baby.

No wonder she'd been desperate to avoid jail! Now Jo knew who her friend was trying to protect. It wasn't her own skin. And especially not Leo Hayes.

It was her child.

CHAPTER TWELVE

"THE BABY MAKES all the difference!" Jo said excitedly to Bobby as they drove back to his cabin.

She'd started spilling the good news—the birth announcement—as soon as they'd stepped out the front door of his parents' house. She'd practically been bursting with it. Bobby was finding it difficult not to get swept away by Jo's enthusiasm, but he was still a little puzzled as to this mysterious baby's significance.

"What difference?"

"Don't you see?" she asked. "The baby proves that Terry wasn't in cahoots with Leo Hayes. She was trying to get away from him, to protect her baby."

"Whoa, there." Bobby twisted his lip thoughtfully. "Sniffing a few vitamins doesn't exactly prove all that."

"Okay, maybe it doesn't *prove*," Jo conceded, "but it at least shows that she wasn't just trying to save her own hide when she skipped out of Brazil and disappeared, like you said. No mother would want to have a baby in prison. Or have a baby taken away from her and raised by someone else."

"I'll admit it makes her motives seem less selfish."

Jo beamed at him. She was so over-the-top happy that he didn't want to rain on her parade by pointing out that it didn't matter what Terry's motives were. They were no closer to knowing what had happened to her or where she was or even if she was alive than they were before Jo had twisted the cap off Denise's vitamin bottle.

It also didn't make Jo any safer, and her safety was of paramount importance to Bobby now. When they arrived back at the cabin, he silently checked each room carefully to make sure there were no signs of a break-in. He didn't want to take any chances that their hideout had been discovered.

Unfortunately, there were no messages from the Houston police about Leo Hayes when they got back. Or from Doug giving him any information he had been able to dig up on Nina Monteverde.

But Jo was still too keyed up to care about the delays in apprehending Hayes or finding out about Nina. He couldn't help smiling at her enthusiasm. "You'd almost think it was *you* who'd had a baby, you're so happy about Terry's bundle of joy."

She laughed as she settled onto the couch. "Terry and I were such good friends, I almost feel as if I have a new little niece or nephew out in the world now." Her forehead wrinkled suddenly. "I wonder which she had. I hope everything went okay."

He sat down next to her and patted her leg. Big mistake. Touching her, even innocently, reminded him of being on the couch with her this afternoon. Or of holding her in his arms as they danced at his parents' house. He felt he was just functioning on the edge of restraint anyway.

A cough hitched in his throat and he scooted a little farther over.

Jo, who seemed oblivious to the conflict going on inside him, merely gravitated closer to him, undermining all his good intentions. "There has to be documentation somewhere of the baby's birth, doesn't there?" Her eyes widened. "If we could figure out where the baby was born, maybe that would bring us closer to finding Terry."

He shook his head, hating himself for having to be the one to throw the damper on her high spirits. It was so good to see her this way. She was like the old Jo. Looking at her now, with her eyes shining and that incredible smile that made her whole face look like sunshine, he could almost imagine that it was eight months ago, that nothing bad had ever happened to them. But of course that wasn't the case. He didn't want Jo to start spinning optimistic scenarios in her head that might never come true.

"It could be impossible to trace her baby through birth records, Jo."

"Why?"

"For one thing, it's hard to know where to start looking. When you last heard from her, you said it sounded like she wasn't calling long-distance. But we can't be sure of that. And even if she had been calling from somewhere in Texas, who's to say she didn't take off after talking to you? She might have fled the country even."

Jo's smile faded, and for a moment Bobby would have done anything to bring it back. He couldn't lie to her, though.

"I hadn't thought of that," she admitted. "I guess I just assumed that she was somewhere nearby."

"Even if she did give birth anywhere near here, she would have used an alias. Do you have any idea of the name she might have taken when she assumed her new identity?"

Her face pinched in concentration for a while, but she shook her head. "I wouldn't know where to begin."

"Not knowing the name of the mother we're looking for is a huge drawback. Plus, we can't even say for sure what date she had the baby."

Jo nodded thoughtfully, and suddenly he felt like the wettest of wet blankets. She fisted her hands in frustration. "I wish I had noticed more about her. How could I not have known she was pregnant?" She laughed mirthlessly. "Even back when my eyesight was twenty-twenty, I apparently didn't see so well. I'm more observant now."

"You have to be, to compensate."

She let out a long ragged sigh. "Well, even if we can't trace the baby, it still makes me happy to think that she had it."

"Why?" He would think she would be worried about how her friend was getting by, especially with a child to support on her own.

The emotion in her hazel eyes tugged at his heart. "All these months when I thought about Terry, I worried about her being lonely. I knew she must be missing Nina terribly, and her friends as well. But if she's got her baby, she has family. She's not alone."

It was so like Jo to worry about her friend being alone when for half a year she not only had been alone herself but had suffered the devastating loss of her brother. Not to mention, she'd had the loss of her sight to deal with. She really was an extraordinary person.

"We could try to hunt for the baby, Jo...." he heard himself saying. Her face lit up again—making him realize what had compelled him to make the impulsive offer. "It will be like looking for a needle in a haystack, but I don't see what harm it could do."

She grasped his hand. "Oh, thank you, Bobby! I'd do it myself, only I probably wouldn't be very good at hunting through hospital records in the shape I'm in."

"So far you've been a much better detective than I've been."

"Beginner's luck," she said.

"Or maybe natural ability. Have you ever considered that you missed your true calling?"

Her auburn brows spiked up on her brow. "What? My golden-throated tones don't make it obvious I was a born chanteuse?"

He laughed. "You *are* a talented singer, Jo. You should have seen the faces tonight while you were singing. Mama was almost weeping. Even Dad looked moved."

She smiled with typical self-deprecation. "Maybe they were weeping over my accent."

"You sounded great. And believe me, if you can have my parents eating out of the palm of your hand, that's something. They're usually not the easiest people to win over."

"Are you kidding? They've always been nice to me. I like your family so much, Bobby," Jo said. "But I still think they were just being polite. My face is all banged up, so they probably think I'm on the brink of a nervous collapse or something. And they also know I'm your guest."

He chuckled softly. "I'm afraid they think our relationship is a little more intimate than guest-host." She did that little head-ducking thing she did whenever she seemed embarrassed, and he squeezed her hand to reassure her. "It's okay, Jo. I tried to tell them...."

"That we were just friends?"

He nodded, then remembered she couldn't see him and felt foolish. "Right." But there was a Gibraltar-size lump in his throat when he said it. He turned her hand over, looking at the long lines running along her palm. He felt desire stirring inside him all over again and knew he should get the hell off that couch. Now.

But he didn't move. His jeans might have been glued to the couch cushions.

She turned toward him; her eyes were luminous in the soft light. "People get crazy ideas, don't they?"

"Mmm." He was having some pretty crazy thoughts himself right now. Like how wonderful it would be to bend down and kiss her again. To pick up where they'd left off this afternoon. He remembered her breasts, round and rosy and sweet, and he closed his eyes and stifled a groan.

"I guess it's just human nature," she said.

At this particular moment it seemed like human nature to want to take Jo into his arms and make love to her, something they had never done. He'd never known what it was like to bury himself inside her, to feel her beneath him....

"Bobby?"

His name broke through his wayward thoughts and he snapped to, realizing that he was sweating. "Yes?"

She gave her hand a tug. "You're squeezing the circulation out of my hand."

He looked down and saw that he was practically clamping down on her hand in a white-knuckle grip. He immediately released her and tried to move away again. He was getting far too carried away here. *She's vulnerable,* he reminded himself feverishly. *She needs a safe place, a place where she doesn't feel pressured or threatened....*

Suddenly, he vaulted off the couch and stuffed his hands into his pockets. Damn it, he was going to be honorable if it killed him, and it just might. Especially when he looked into her face and saw that her lips were slightly parted. As he stared at her, her tongue darted out and licked one corner of her mouth. He had to close his eyes again.

Honorable, he repeated to himself.

"Well, you must be very tired," he said, abruptly drawing the evening to a close. "Think you can make it to the bedroom okay?"

She looked a little confused as she lifted her shoulders. "I guess so, sure."

"Well, if you need any help with anything, let me know."

"Okay."

Before he could change his mind, Bobby fled the room and plunged his head under the cold tap in the bathroom.

WHAT THE HELL had happened?

Jo couldn't figure it out. One minute she and Bobby were having a nice talk, an intimate and earnest discussion about Terry and families, and the next moment he was bounding away from her as fast as he could go. Like she had plague or something. One second she'd worried he was going to kiss her—worried and hoped for it, too. And the next?

He was history.

She just couldn't figure it out. She also couldn't fathom why she felt so depressed all of a sudden. After she heard Bobby leave the bathroom and go to his room, she got up and started getting ready for bed. She changed into a nightshirt and went into the bathroom and brushed her teeth and washed her face.

It had been a long day, she told herself. For both of them. They had flown to San Antonio and back, and had experienced all sorts of highs and lows. She felt like she'd lived half a lifetime just in the past eight hours. God only knows how Bobby felt.

She flashed back to the moment she and Bobby were on the couch tonight, before he'd dashed off to bed. She could have sworn she'd heard desire in his voice. Maybe she was just thinking about how *she* felt. But if she wanted him so much, could she be completely off the mark about his feelings? It couldn't be all one-sided, could it? He'd told her this afternoon that it wasn't.

And yet something kept making him scurry away from her like a jackrabbit. He was treating her with kid gloves, and she was getting mighty tired of it. It was so frustrating. He acted as if she were something delicate, breakable.

She returned to her bedroom—Bobby's bedroom—and flopped down on the bed. She was immediately assaulted by the scent of Bobby's Obsession on the pillowcase again. She felt wide-awake. Why, oh, why did Bobby have to be such a—

A gentleman.

Her breath caught. He was just being a nice guy. He was giving her breathing room, because when he'd offered to bring her to the ranch, she had refused at first. He probably thought her refusal had been about her reluctance to get involved with him again, but really it had been just the opposite. She'd feared her desire to get involved with him again because she was afraid she would end up giving away information about Terry. But she'd already spilled the beans about her friend's disappearance, so that wasn't an issue anymore.

Even the right or wrong of her having helped Terry didn't seem to be an issue anymore. Jo was pretty sure she'd managed to convince Bobby that Terry wasn't the evil diamond smuggler he had assumed she was. She wasn't in cahoots with Leo Hayes, either, and she hadn't been using Jo to cover her own butt. She was just a mother trying to keep and protect her baby.

Even some of the long-standing problems between them didn't seem so insurmountable now. Even their memories of Greg had become less painful. What had Denise said? Greg *wanted* them to be together. No one knew her brother better than Jo did, and she had to admit that Denise's words struck her as on the money. Greg had possessed a truly generous spirit. The notion that his death would break her and Bobby up would have saddened him no end. But in the immediate aftermath of his murder, she and Bobby had forgotten to think about Greg the man, and had only considered Greg the victim, whose death they both felt responsible for.

Maybe they would always feel a tug of guilt. But Bobby had told her they needed to move on and she was ready to accept that now. No matter what had happened, she couldn't stop loving Bobby. It was useless to try.

But now that she was ready to put the past behind her, where was Bobby? In the next bedroom, treating her as if she were heirloom crystal. It was nuts.

But what could she do?

Think of something else.

She focused on Terry and her baby. Terry, a mother. She would be a good one. Who was the father? Terry hadn't mentioned a man in her life. Maybe there wasn't one. It figured that if Terry wanted a baby she would go ahead and simply have it herself and raise it on her own. On her own terms. When Terry had wanted something, she had usually gone after it.

Jo remembered Terry all those years ago, asking the musicians to let her friend sing. "Just do it," she'd told Jo, long before the words had become a clichéd sneaker slogan. Terry always took the bull by the horns.

Terry, for instance, wouldn't have let Bobby get away from her.

Jo sat up abruptly, feeling as if she'd just been struck by a bolt from the blue. She certainly wasn't going to get any sleep tonight smelling Bobby's pillow.

A grin tugged at her lips. If all went well, she wouldn't get much sleep at all.

She hopped out of bed and walked toward the door, then suddenly remembered what she was wearing. A nightshirt that, if she wasn't mistaken, had a giant Tweety bird on the front of it. Not exactly a garment that would set the stage for a sizzling seduction. She needed to do better. She crossed to her suitcase and rifled through it. T-shirts, jeans, socks, shorts…

Satin.

Her hands fumbled over a filmy silk-textured top and she frowned in concentration. What was it? As she investigated further, she remembered. It was the top to a pair of emerald-green silk jammies Tammy had given her for Christmas last year. The slyboots had tossed them into her suitcase for good measure, probably never really thinking that Jo would need them.

Or maybe hoping that for once in her life she would.

Jo, who for all her brassiness in conversation and her experience working an audience, had woefully little experience in one-on-one seduction. She'd had boyfriends in college, so she wasn't Little Miss Innocent. But in all her experience, she'd never had to manufacture the fireworks herself.

Well, here went nothing. She pulled her Tweety bird shirt over her head and changed into the green pajamas. The fabric was so light against her skin it felt almost like nothing. She went over to Bobby's dresser and ran his comb through her mass of hair, more out of nerves than any real hope of taming it into order. She powdered and perfumed and prayed she wasn't making a terribly embarrassing mistake.

Then she slipped out of the room and felt her way down the hall. She had to concentrate to remember which door was his. She didn't want to play her big love scene to a broom closet.

She tapped lightly on his door.

Bobby called out immediately, "Jo, are you okay? What's wrong?"

She slipped inside. "I'm fine." She felt her way slowly to the bed and perched uneasily on the edge of the mattress.

He let out a long breath. "You scared the hell out of me. I thought maybe you had come in here because you heard a noise or something."

She shook her head; anxiety set in. Her sexy green pajamas obviously hadn't entered his radar yet. Bobby was still in cop mode. But she wasn't ready to throw in the towel yet. She resolutely insinuated her hands around his broad shoulders and clasped them at his nape. He wasn't wearing a shirt. Excitement kicked her pulse into high gear. She wondered what else he wasn't wearing.

"That's not why I came in here," she managed to say in what she hoped was a purr but feared sounded more like a squeak.

"Then why—"

His words stopped abruptly. She could almost hear his breath catching.

Bingo.

She smiled and scooted herself further onto the bed.

Bobby was as still as a statue. About as responsive as one, too. "Jo…" His deep voice growled almost in warning.

She wasn't listening to him. Instead, she concentrated on all the things that made him irresistible to her. He'd said she was a good detective tonight, and right now she considered all the things she hadn't noticed about Bobby when she could see. Like the fact that just the gravelly drawl in his voice could cause a frisson of desire to snake through her. Or that the muscles in his shoulders rippled deliciously when she stroked a fingernail over the skin there. And that there was nothing quite so sexy as the faint scent of cologne mixed with toothpaste against the backdrop of a world that smelled of clean sheets and sage and soap.

She traced the sinew of muscle along the top of his shoulders with one nail, enjoying the tension in his body. He was like a cat readying itself to pounce, yet holding himself back. She liked the threat of danger in all his coiled restraint.

Bobby swallowed. "Jo, you shouldn't have come in here...."

She tilted her head and blinked innocently. "Why? Is there something about me in your bed that you don't like?"

A strangled groan sounded in his throat. "No...it's wonderful. You're wonderful. It's just..."

He reached down and touched her waist. His hand through the silky cool fabric settled on the curve of her waist.

She leaned toward him. "Then what's wrong?"

"Everything's wrong," he growled. "I didn't bring you here to seduce you, Jo."

She arched her brows at him. "Who's seducing whom?"

His other hand went to her waist and he pulled her to him. "You're vulnerable right now, Jo."

"Mmm, I know," she said, nuzzling her nose in the crook of his neck. She gave his salty skin a few little nibbles. "In my frame of mind, I would just be hopeless at fighting off your advances."

He groaned and stalwartly ignored her. "All that you've

been through—the loss, the trauma. You're still not a hundred percent.''

The finger tracing his shoulder moved down his chest, swirling around the dusting of hair there. He sucked in his stomach and she grinned.

''Maybe not, but I know what would make me feel better.''

''Jo...''

She straightened up and pressed her lips against him. As it happened, they landed on his cheek. He was doing his damnedest to be noble, but that fact only made her all the more determined to be bad. All the months they were together, she and Bobby had been so cautious around each other. Then their relationship had stalled during a crisis.

But now she wanted to kick-start it again. She wanted to throw caution to the wind for once in her life.

For once in his life, too.

She arched up and pushed her hands down, rubbing them along the muscles of his thighs through the sheets. The bedcovers were pooled around his hips. Her chest brushed his slightly, and his hands reflexively tightened their grip around her middle. The sensation made a jolt of pure heat surge through her, and for the most fleeting of moments she wondered if she wasn't getting in over her head.

''Damn it, Jo,'' he said raggedly, ''I brought you here to help you. To protect you.''

She reached up and traced the waistband of his boxers, tugging it slightly. ''Bobby, I'm placing myself entirely in your capable hands.''

He muttered something that she didn't catch. Not that it mattered. His nobility finally unraveled. His hands began to explore, hungrily. Excitedly.

She kissed him again, and this time he turned his mouth

to her, kissing her back. The warmth of his lips was like a prize, a triumph. Heat sizzled through her, along with a thrill of anticipation. They'd never made love. What would it be like? She'd dreamed of this more times than she could remember—practically every time her head had touched the pillow at night since last Thanksgiving.

She tilted her head and he plundered her mouth thoroughly. In his body, his ragged breathing, she felt his unspoken need to devour her. And she shocked herself by realizing that's what she wanted, too. To be one with Bobby. She just didn't want it to end too soon.

She pulled back slightly and he tensed. "Is something wrong?"

She shook her head as she slowly undid the top button of her silky top. She couldn't see Bobby's eyes, but she could feel that dark gaze fastening on her, watching every movement of her fingers as they fumbled with the little round button. The anticipation in the air was palpable, as if they were witnessing the unveiling of a masterpiece at a museum.

Bobby reached forward and helped her. He undid the button quickly, then the second and the third. When he pushed the little pajama top off her shoulders and guided it down her arms, she heard the intake of his breath.

"You're so beautiful, Jo," he whispered. "You're all I've ever dreamed about and wanted."

His words surprised her because they so mimicked her own thoughts, her own experience. Her own dreams. She'd had other men before Bobby, but since meeting him, he had consumed her thoughts. She couldn't conceive of wanting or loving another man now.

She reached a hand forward to touch his cheek and he turned it, kissing the palm. His warm lips against her skin were completely unexpected, and sexier than anything she could have imagined. Electricity sizzled through her. She was a goner.

"I've wanted you so much," she said.

"I wish I'd known," he answered.

"That's why I had to come in here tonight," she said.

He whispered her name again and gathered her in his arms. He pushed the sheets away so that she could lie next to him on the bed. He was achingly gentle as he kissed her again. And he kissed her thoroughly. Not just her mouth, but her cheeks, her forehead, her eyelids. Her chin.

His lips blazed a path down the sensitive skin of her throat and nestled for a moment in the crook where her neck joined her shoulder. All his patient kisses caused a ferocious desire to build inside her. Guided by her, he dipped down and finally kissed one taut nipple. She moaned in pleasure, and reveled in the feel of his wonderful soft-rough skin against her hands. His back was like fine buttery leather, irresistible to the touch.

He licked and teased one breast until it was a rigid peak, then turned his attention to the other one. His ministrations were a delectable, exquisite torture. Fire built inside her, making her impatient, almost demented with yearning, yet she didn't want to deprive herself of one single second of Bobby's lovemaking.

And he apparently wasn't into deprivation, either. Not now. It was as if they had shut the door on the past, and there was just now. Them. Together.

He took his time. The desire coursing through her was palpable and wild, and she gritted her teeth to keep herself from begging him to take her. She couldn't stop herself from curling her legs around his waist and arching toward him. She'd never needed anyone this way. She felt as if she were going to fly into a million pieces.

Sensing her need, he pulled away from her breasts and

torched a path down her torso, stopping to tease her belly button for a moment. She unwound her legs long enough to allow him to pull off her pajama bottoms and panties, which he did slowly, dragging them down her legs with aching care while she would have simply kicked them off without a second thought. His way was better.

He then worked his way back up her legs, stroking and kissing her until she thought she would go insane. It was as if he were determined to sample every square inch of her. The closer he came to the core of her desire, the more he seemed to slow.

And then, unbelievably, he stopped. She rose up on her elbows, confused. She was practically panting as he moved to lie next to her. "Bobby?"

He ran his hands through her hair. His voice was so gravelly it sounded as if he'd swallowed sand. "Jo, are you sure?"

Was he joking? She nodded numbly. She'd never felt so sure of anything. Never known such need. She could barely speak.

"There's one problem," he said, causing her heart to leap to her throat. Problem? She couldn't think of a problem except for the fact that she was about to expire.

"What?" Her voice was barely audible.

"No condom," he said.

She nearly fainted with relief. Condoms. *That's* what he was worried about.

He traced her jaw. "What if you become pregnant?"

The question made her feel limp in his arms as emotions swamped her. "Would it matter to you?"

"Of course it would matter," he said hoarsely. He turned and cupped her face in his hands. "It would be the best thing in the world that could possibly happen to me. But if you're not ready..."

She'd never felt so much warmth, so much desire for another human being. "This isn't just about sex, Bobby. I came in here tonight because I love you. I'll always love you. Nothing would make me happier than to have a family with you."

He said her name again and then captured her lips in a kiss.

For all her wanting to show restraint, to take it slowly, it became impossible. She felt such a rush of love for him, it was difficult to hold back. She felt frantic to be with him, to feel his nakedness against her. She rolled so that she hovered over him and pulled his boxer shorts off. Then she reached down and covered his already rigid manhood. A sound caught in his throat that only stoked the flames in her, and she slowly began to work the turgid flesh.

He pulled her down to him and they kissed again, then rolled together until he was straddling her, poised against her sensitive flesh. She wanted him so much, wanted him to fill her completely. She lifted her hips, inviting him, and he entered her with a single thrust that was the fulfillment of every fantasy she'd ever had. Bobby inside her felt completely right.

They moved together as one, in long needful thrusts that grew more frantic, more dizzying. He bent down and whispered in her ear to let her know how much he loved her, how much he cherished her, how much she turned him on. His voice was like throwing gasoline on a bonfire. Heat was a whirlwind inside her. She'd never felt so feverish, so light-headed, as if the world had tilted and she might just go hurtling off it. She was spiraling out of control.

And he was spiraling with her. When finally all the emotions and desires inside her climaxed in wave after wave of heat, she felt Bobby shudder in release as well. Exultant, she wrapped herself around him, savoring the intimate feel of their bodies against each other, the heated skin against the cool night air of the room.

She realized if she could have frozen a moment to treasure for all time, this would have been it. Sated and exhausted in Bobby's arms, sweat mingling with sweat. She'd lived thirty-two years on earth, but until just this moment she'd never known what it was to be thoroughly and completely loved. She cherished every second, savored the gentle movement of his chest as he breathed deeply.

She'd never lost hope for the future, but for a while, at least, her dreams of happiness had been obscured by all the tragedy she'd lived through. For too long now she'd lived in sadness, forgetting that life was meant to be seized and relished for every second it had to offer. For a few months, at least, she'd lost her way. Now it seemed as if Bobby had shone a light on her, allowing her to claw out of the darkness of the past year.

In his arms, she drifted off to sleep, at peace. As long as she had Bobby to hold on to, complete happiness, it seemed, would always be within her grasp.

CHAPTER THIRTEEN

BOBBY SQUINTED against the harsh daylight streaming through the windows. His heart was pumping like crazy and he couldn't figure out why. Then he looked over and saw Jo, and he knew.

She was what had him all keyed up.

Under normal circumstances he would have been exhausted. In a different time and place he might have woken up next to Jo, stretched lazily, and looked forward to a long leisurely morning of making love. But these circumstances couldn't be interpreted as anything close to normal. And leisure wasn't something he felt he had a lot of while Leo Hayes was still at large.

During the night, he'd slept fitfully at best. It wasn't only having Jo next to him that had made rest difficult, either. It was worry.

Worry about Jo.

She trusted him. Her coming to him last night was something out of his wildest dreams. She was beautiful and so giving and so…vulnerable. It was driving him wild.

For the first time in his life, he felt truly terrified. Because he knew if something happened to Jo now, he would be a lost man. She was life itself to him. God, she'd even said she wanted to have his children. The very thought of her gorgeous body pregnant with his child made him want to snuggle under the covers with her and see if they could create a baby that very moment.

Instead, he climbed out of bed and padded out of the room. He'd known it was the wrong time to get involved with Jo, but he'd done it anyway. He was so in love with her, desired her so much, that he hadn't been able to use reason when the opportunity had presented itself in the beautiful form of Jo in those sexy pajamas.

But now, in the clearer light of morning, he realized that it wasn't just for her benefit that he should have maintained his distance. It was for purely selfish reasons, too. Because he wasn't sure he could handle it if anything happened to her.

All last night he'd kept bolting awake from dreams of Jo. Not erotic dreams, either, but dreams of Jo in trouble. His imagination hadn't even had to work overtime to come up with the nightmares, either; they were all culled from real life. He'd envisioned her standing in her living room after her house had been broken into the first time, with twigs in her hair and her shirt torn. That had been bad enough. But then her house had been broken into a second time, and then he'd watched helplessly as she'd climbed into a cab that had taken her out to the middle of nowhere. He'd watched her leap out of a moving vehicle, over and over and over, and there was not a damn thing he could do about it.

He was in love with a woman with a madman after her, and he wasn't sure of his ability to keep her safe. The thought of failing Jo now made sweat pop out on his brow. If he failed her now, it would be a fatal failure.

Just like what had happened with Greg.

Damn. He shook his head and went into the kitchen to make coffee. From the way things had started, he suspected it was going to be a very long day.

When the coffee had brewed and he was slicing a loaf of bread to make toast, Jo emerged from the bedroom.

When he looked up from the cutting board she was leaning against the kitchen door. Her hair was completely disheveled and her cheeks were blotched with red. But she was wearing her pajamas from last night, and the sight of her, rumpled and beautiful, her lips rosy from being kissed thoroughly many times, slammed into his senses like a two-by-four.

God, he loved her.

He crossed the kitchen and took her into his arms. Kissing her good-morning took a while, and for a moment he considered dumping the coffee and toast in favor of carrying her back to his bedroom. But he couldn't do that. There were other things on his mind now. Like how he was going to keep them safe for the next fifty or so years.

"How are you feeling?" he asked her.

"Hungry!"

He directed her toward the kitchen table. That, at least, was one thing he could take care of with some assurance. "Have a seat and I'll have breakfast up in no time."

She chuckled. "Do you think you're going to spend the rest of your life waiting on me hand and foot? I'm not helpless, you know."

He felt suddenly awkward, worried that he'd offended her. "I know you're not. I'm sorry if I made it sound as if I was babying you."

She touched his arm. "I'm just trying to lighten your load. Wouldn't you like me to do something? I'm not a complete loss in the kitchen, you know. Cut up fruit, maybe?"

There was a cantaloupe sitting on the counter and he eyed it and the knife block loaded with clean sharp knives dubiously. "Could you handle a melon?"

"Oh, I think I could manage." She shrugged. "And if I can't, what's a finger more or less?"

His breath hitched, and he was about to swipe the cantaloupe and the knife out of her reach when he realized that she was laughing at him.

"Believe me, Bobby. I'll be careful. Just show me where the knives are."

He pointed her toward the block and got out another cutting board, but she took it from there. Still, it was hard for him to think about what he was doing, he was so panicked at the idea of Jo hurting herself. His gaze kept darting to the side, where she hovered over her cutting board. But she handled the chore deftly, while he had now slowed to a snail's pace.

For Bobby, it seemed a harbinger of things to come. How was he going to be able to function now? He would be consumed with worry. He would never be able to leave her, never be able to get anything done.

He'd never realized that lust combined with worry could be such a paralyzing mix.

"Maybe I should help you," Jo suggested, obviously sensing that he wasn't functioning at top speed.

He shook his head. "Sit down and drink coffee," he commanded her. "You're my guest."

She chuckled. "That's what I am?"

Heat burned his skin as he remembered making love to her last night. "Okay, my honored guest. What do you want to do today?"

"Honestly?"

"Of course."

She grinned. "Well, my first choice would be to jump back in bed with you."

His heart did an acrobatic flip. "That could definitely be arranged."

"Also, I'm ready to start hunting through birth records,

if that's possible. Maybe we could go back to Houston? I figure we could start by going through the big cities."

"It's going to be a long project, Jo. We don't know what date we should start looking for."

She frowned. "Maybe if we ever hear from Nina, she'll know more."

"Right. But until then, we can't even be sure what month Terry gave birth. And Nina might not know, either."

"Well, we know it was after September and before Christmas."

"True." If Jo had heard the baby crying over the phone last Christmas, then it had to have been born not long after Terry had disappeared. "That does narrow it down."

Jo was all optimism. "I have a good feeling about this, Bobby. I'm really beginning to believe I'm going to see Terry again."

"I hope so," he said. "I really do."

His cell phone rang and he dove for the counter where it was sitting to pick up. Doug was on the line.

"Hey, Bobby," was the extent of his greeting. With characteristic directness, he launched into the reason for his call. "I've got some news on your Brazilian woman."

Bobby listened eagerly. "Great. What did you find out?"

"Unfortunately, it's not good. Not good at all. From the interviews our man in Rio has done with people who know her, it seems she hasn't been around for over a week, at least. She was seen hanging around an American, a bounty hunter, name of Rick Singleton. Ever heard of him?"

"No."

Doug sighed. "Well, this Rick Singleton and Nina Monteverde took off in her company jet for the States—Texas-bound—last week."

"So she's here?"

"That's the bad news. The plane seems to have disappeared. No trace of it since it fell off the airport's radar north of Rio. They think it might have crashed in the jungle."

Bobby felt his heart sink into his boots. Crashing in the jungle wasn't good. Even if the passengers had miraculously survived the crash, it would be virtually impossible to find help there if they were hurt. And it would be a long walk to get back to civilization.

"I'm sorry," Doug said. "This woman a friend of yours?"

Bobby glanced nervously toward Jo, who was standing stock-still, listening intently. "The sister of a friend of a friend."

"Well, could be she's okay. Weirder things have happened."

On the other hand, the plane wreck matched up with Nina not answering her phone. But what were she and the American doing? And was the plane crash just a coincidence?

He thought about Leo Hayes and wondered. April Smith told them he had been out of the country last week. Could he have sabotaged the airplane?

"You said she might have some information on a murder case. You still on that?"

"Yes I am," Bobby said. "The murderer, Leo Hayes, is still at large."

Doug grunted. "And you're working on catching him from a ranch in Angelina County?"

"Believe me, I've got so much office equipment here, my little house on the Circle G looks like a satellite of Company A headquarters. Which reminds me, if you get any additional information on Nina Monteverde, let me know."

"Will do," Doug said, ringing off.

Bobby put down his cell phone and turned to Jo, dreading what he had to say to her. Especially when he saw that her brow was furrowed with worry. She sensed something was wrong already.

"What is it?" she asked. "Did your captain have any word about Nina?"

"Nothing for sure," he said. Then he placed his hands on her shoulders. "Unfortunately, Jo, what he's got so far isn't good. A plane disappeared last week carrying Nina and an American bounty hunter."

She stepped back, pressing her hands to her mouth. "Oh, no," she whispered. "Then this man thinks Nina is dead?"

He shook his head. "The plane hasn't been found, so there's no telling. They think it crashed in the jungle."

The dread look on her face told him that she understood the implications. "If they crashed last week and the plane hasn't even been found..."

A tear spilled down her cheek and he gathered her into his arms. Poor Jo. This was one more loss for her to handle. She sniffled and it was like a little dagger plunging into his heart. He wanted to protect her, but it seemed he was always the bearer of bad news.

"I shouldn't cry," Jo said, shaking her head. "You said we don't know for sure that she's gone. Maybe they survived the crash and are headed for help."

"That's a possibility."

She closed her eyes, squeezing them shut as if she could squeeze out all the pain of Nina's disappearance, then looked up at him. Her eyes widened.

"What's the matter?"

"I saw you again!" she exclaimed. "As clear as a bell."

"That's terrific."

She looked less thrilled than the other times when she'd regained a little sight. And when she looked away from the light, he could tell by the way her face slackened in disappointment that her vision was gone again. "At least it's happening with some regularity now," he told her. "Right?"

She face contorted into an impatient expression. "I just wish I could see *now.* So I could be more help trying to sort out all this mess and find Terry."

He pulled her to him for another hug. "If I could find one person to stake my life on, it would be you, Jo. Terry's lucky she had you for a friend."

"Has," she reminded him before she tilted her lips up for a kiss.

LEO HOVERED OVER the little transmitter in his hotel room, so astounded he could barely move a muscle.

They had his name? Already?

Damn it! He hated cops. Hated them. Stupid clods.

How had they found him out? He thought he'd covered his tracks. He'd worn gloves. He hadn't left any evidence that he knew of... Except the lost marble. But that was ridiculous. He could have lost that anywhere. And what would it prove?

His thoughts were reeling. And he couldn't shake the curious way the Ranger had described the dear departed Nina. *She's the sister of a friend of a friend.* But the Ranger hadn't told his thickheaded captain that the friend of the friend, Terry, was already dead, too. In fact, he'd made it sound as if she wasn't dead. But that was crazy. He'd read the article in the newspaper. He'd been in Rio during the funeral. He'd seen Terry Monteverde's grave.

Leo's head was spinning, throbbing. One person in Rio would have the answers to his questions, but he wasn't going to stoop to asking her now. He was beginning to think she'd double-crossed him from the start. In fact he was starting to wonder if there was anyone in this whole damn world he could rely on besides Leo Hayes. Sometimes it seemed like he was the last trustworthy man alive.

And now look. The police were on to him. He would be hounded now for murdering a stupid cabbie and that whole night had all been an exercise in futility. His first bungle since he'd sloppily cooked some books in his twenties.

Well, he didn't intend to go back to jail again, that was for sure. He shivered at the thought. Memories of his stay in the relatively low-security facility still gave him nightmares. Leo had resorted to things he never would have imagined himself doing, just to survive. On the other hand, he'd learned skills that had served him well on the outside. That was one thing he could say for the American penal system. There was no better place to learn how to be a criminal.

But he wasn't going back for a refresher course. No thank you. The cops could search for Leo Hayes all they wanted. He was Ben Blythe now and he had enough money in a Swiss bank to last him years if he needed it. He could leave the country for a good long time. Go someplace like Mexico or Thailand, where his money would last awhile.

Fine. But he was damned if he was going to let some Ranger get away with killing off Leo Hayes and letting Jolene Daniels make off with his diamonds, which would be enough to live on for years once he got his mitts on them.

Hiding out on a ranch! He looked down at the pad he'd

been jotting notes on before his thoughts had overtaken him. Circle G. Angelina County. Robert Garcia.

Surely that was all he needed to find out where the two of them were.

"COULD I STAY at your place when we go back?"

Bobby looked at Jo standing in the doorway of the old shed and felt his insides turn into mush. She was wearing a tank top and shorts that showed off her long legs. She was freshly showered—he knew because he'd been in the same shower—and she absently twirled a strand of damp curly hair around one finger.

After breakfast they'd whiled away the whole morning making love, yet he already wanted her again. It was crazy. This morning he'd thought he wouldn't be able to relax until he knew categorically that she was safe, and yet every time he caught sight of her, unquenchable desire kicked in. And Jo wasn't shy about how much she enjoyed sex, either. Just the memory of being in the shower with her, their bodies lathered and slick from soap and sweat, tempted him to punt his last-minute yard work and carry Jo back into the house, caveman-style.

Her question about where she would stay in Houston threw him, though.

He'd been hovering over the lawnmower in the center of the shed, but now he straightened. He had agreed that they could head back into Houston as soon as tonight, but he'd just assumed she would be staying with him.

"Of course," he said, crossing to her.

Her hazel eyes glittered up at him. "You wouldn't mind? I can't go back home and I wouldn't feel right staying with Tammy."

He drew her to him, loving the way her breasts pressed softly against him. "I want you to stay with me."

"It'll only be until the police catch Hayes, of course," she said quickly, nervously. Then her brow puckered into a frown, as if she were remembering something. "Oh, and maybe a few extra days so I can get my house fixed up again. Maybe some new furniture..."

"Jo," he said, cutting her off. "Don't worry about how long you have to stay. I'd be happy with forever."

"Oh, but—" She stopped, gulping, and looked up at him as if she were actually trying to see him. "Are you kidding?"

"No." He lifted her hands to kiss them and smiled. "In fact, I think I'm proposing."

She smiled. "You *think?*"

He tilted his head, trying to gauge whether that little grin of hers meant good news or bad. "I'm sure. But I don't want to rush you."

She lifted her arms and encircled his chest. "Let's see, it's been almost six days since my house was broken into. I would say that's pretty pokey of you, Bobby."

He smiled, loving the smell of her hair, the feel of her arms, the happiness inside him. But there was a nervous edge to it all, too. If he promised her forever, would he be able to keep that promise?

"You never answered my question."

She lifted her brows. "Which was...?"

"Will you marry me?"

She smiled and leaned against him. "You don't have to ask me just because I need a place to stay, you know."

He laughed. "I'm not. I'm asking because I love you."

He bent down and touched her lips briefly, persuasively. Suddenly, all thoughts of anything else were forgotten.

When they came up for air, Jo hugged him tight.

"Say yes, Jo," he said, nuzzling her. "I'd still agree to wear the gorilla suit if that's what it would take."

She laughed. "All right, you convinced me. But no gorilla suits are required."

"The answer is yes?"

"Yes!" She smiled at him. "You knew it would be."

If only. He let out a breath that until that minute he hadn't realized he'd been holding. In fact, he knew now he'd been holding it since the minute he met Jo.

He grinned. "My parents are going to be so happy."

"Not as happy as I'm going to be, Bobby. What should we do to celebrate?"

He cast a sidewise glance at the lawnmower. "I don't know about you, but I'm going to cut the grass."

She laughed. "Very romantic!"

But she obviously understood that it was a chore he wanted to get done before they returned to Houston. Otherwise, his father would be coming over here, and he didn't want to make more work for his parents.

"Tell you what," she suggested. "While you do your he-man chores, I'll take a walk to the pond and think about white lace and wedding bells. Then we can take off, right?"

He agreed. "You all packed?"

She nodded.

"Okay. But stay on the path and don't go beyond shouting distance. This won't take long, I promise. Then we'll go back to Houston and paint the town red."

She kissed him again. "Have I told you in the past twenty seconds that I love you?"

He couldn't hear it enough. After he watched her walk toward the pond, he turned back to the lawnmower, eager to get the work finished so he and Jo could go back to Houston. His mind, however, was thoroughly distracted by the fact that he and Jo were going to be married. What kind of wedding should they have? Maybe they should wait until Jo was out of the woods, safety-wise, until they started planning.

But that sounded ominous, and he didn't want to believe that anything bad could happen. He would keep Jo with him at his house. She would be safe there. Leo Hayes had no way of knowing that she was with him.

Now if he could just keep her from going to Tumbleweeds…

He pondered how he was going to manage to make Jo temporarily retire as he bent over the mower to fill it with fuel from the gas can.

He should have waited to take a shower until he'd finished mowing. Chores were the last thing on his mind, however, when Jo suggested a mutual scrub down. Face it. When she was naked in bed with him, she could ask him to jump into a volcano and he'd do it. With bells on.

The shed door creaked and he smiled as he screwed the fuel cap back on. ''Back already?'' If she was going to try to seduce him away from work, he was an easy target.

Out of the corner of his eye he caught sight of brown trousers. Jo had been in shorts. His heart skipped and he tensed, straightening.

That's when the tire iron came down on the back of his head.

CHAPTER FOURTEEN

SOMETHING WAS WRONG.

Jo stood at the edge of the pond where she'd come with Bobby once before and counted all her blessings. There were so many. Bobby. The future. The possibility that they could find Terry, who had a baby. The chance that they could have a child themselves. That was the most amazing possibility of all. She felt that if she and Bobby could have a family together, her life would be complete. And completely happy.

There was so much joy to look forward to. A whole new life was out there waiting for her to snatch it up.

But she just couldn't shake her worries. Was she a complete neurotic? Or maybe she was so accustomed to angst that it was now a habit she couldn't let go of. Bobby wanted to marry her. She had a new lover, a wedding to plan, all the good things in life to look forward to.

In the back of her mind, however, there was Nina. It seemed a stunning coincidence that Terry's sister would be involved in a tragic plane crash the very moment Jo had started looking for her. Could Leo Hayes be behind the plane crash? It wouldn't surprise her. The man seemed capable of anything.

That's what she couldn't shake. Leo Hayes was still a pall hanging over her head. No matter how happy she was, her future wasn't worth two cents while that man was at large. Maybe that's why Bobby, for all his responsiveness, hadn't seemed as happy as she was today. Why their lovemaking had held an extra twinge of urgency. Why he wasn't looking forward as much as she was to going back to Houston. Bobby was a realist, and he wouldn't have forgotten that there was still a killer out to get her.

She had been so involved in thinking about Terry, and then Nina, that she'd almost forgotten that she was in danger herself. Or maybe forgetting was a kind of self-preservation. She simply couldn't stand any more fear in her life.

She bent down and picked a rock up off the ground to toss in the water. She was about to pitch it when she caught sight of a mallard duck and stopped. It was beautiful. Its green head had almost a metallic shine to it.

Her breath caught and she blinked, staring at the bird again, yet half expecting to lose her focus. But if she turned her head in just such a way, she could still see the bird. Perfectly.

Sheer elation exploded through her and she let out a whoop of joy. It was an omen, she was sure of it. A good omen. Forever more, this would be a red-letter day on her calendar. She couldn't wait to tell Bobby. She gave a little skip forward and her toe stubbed against a tree root.

Then she was falling.

Her arms wheeled in wide circles as she tried to catch herself, but she hit the ground with a thud. Once she realized that she'd hurt her pride more than her body, she pushed herself up from the dry ground and laughed. All right, so she hadn't made a complete recovery. At least there was no one out here to witness her latest display of klutziness.

She felt around for her walking stick—obviously, she still needed it—and stood again. More carefully this time, she headed back to the house.

As she neared the cabin, she frowned. She couldn't remember hearing the lawnmower running. What had happened with that? Maybe Bobby had changed his mind about doing the yard work. Maybe he'd decided they needed to get back to Houston sooner than planned. She walked more quickly toward the house to find out what was up.

There was the smell of smoke in the air. As if someone were burning trash. She shook her head in surprise. July was not a good time to be doing that chore. Many counties in Texas had burning bans this time of year.

She knew the path in front of Bobby's cabin better and made faster time as she neared the house. She did have to stop every so often and check out the place from the corner of her eye, though. For instance, as she stood in the shade of a pine in front of the house and turned about forty-five degrees, she could make out the little wood cabin, which was just as she remembered it from last year. Except now there was green all around.

She caught a flash of color in the distance. Something dark blue. She turned her head and tried to see. Down the road, several hundred yards away, was a car. She hadn't noticed it before. Of course! That was probably why Bobby had abandoned the lawn mowing.

They had company.

She entered the house quietly through the front door, not wishing to disturb Bobby and his guest if they were talking, but she didn't hear anything. They could be out back, though. If she remembered correctly, Bobby had a little red picnic table in his backyard.

Hot and thirsty after her walk, she crossed to the kitchen. In the doorway, she saw a man's shadowy form and turned to try to see him better.

She obviously surprised the other person there because

she caught a spinning movement out of the corner of her eye. She tilted her head and felt a jolt of uncertainty as she focused on the man. It wasn't Bobby. This guy was dressed all wrong, wearing a suit in the heat of the day, and he wasn't nearly as tall as Bobby. Or broad. Instead, he was almost slight. About her height, with light-brown hair…

As the description of Leo Hayes sank into her consciousness, her body stilled. The room was so quiet. Deadly quiet. And then, like a scratching at first, she heard the light, muffled click of marbles.

Her spine went cold.

Any tiny shred of hope she'd had that this was not Leo Hayes, that she was just having a horrible hallucination, disappeared at that moment. The clacking sound made a shuddering fear sweep through her. She wanted to move, but couldn't. She was like a mouse in front of a rattlesnake. Her heart beat like a wild animal's, and her skin felt hot and clammy all at once.

Where was Bobby?

What should she do?

"I was wondering when you'd get back," the man said. The clicking continued. "I would have gone after you, but it's hot out today. Fiery, you might even say."

That voice. That flat, sickening voice. It brought bile to her throat.

She turned to run. And she screamed. She screamed her head off for Bobby. "Bobby! Bobby!"

In a heartbeat, Hayes had her. He grabbed her bad arm and wrenched her around, causing such white-hot pain to shoot through her that her voice cut off abruptly. She clenched her teeth and felt his hot breath as he hissed in her ear.

"Your protector's out of commission, lady. It's just you and me now."

Her stomach lurched. "Where's Bobby? What did you do to him?"

Hayes let out a creepy chuckle and sniffed loudly. "Hmm, what's that smoky smell? Ranger flambé?"

Nausea roiled in her. He was psychotic. She remembered the cabby. She thought of Nina. Then she remembered Bobby holding her and laughing and making love to her and she wanted to weep. Could this animal make a joke of killing her happiness?

She was suddenly filled with such rage that she turned and kicked at him, hard. She'd been aiming for a leg, but her foot barely grazed him.

He laughed again. "You people are a riot," Leo said, pushing her away. "You're so inept!"

"How did you find us?" she asked, backing into the kitchen.

She had to buy time. She groped with her hands along the counter. She could see the shadow that was Leo following her, but he didn't grab her again. Instead, he was toying with her, allowing her a modicum of freedom because he thought she was blind, helpless. He thought he could take his time, bat her around like a wildcat with wounded prey. Jo wanted to scream, but it felt futile.

Save your strength, she thought. Where was a phone?

She could see, a little, but it was difficult because she was so frantic. Her whole body felt like it was quivering. It was hard to force herself to turn and focus. And maybe it was better if Leo thought she could see nothing. As long as he thought he didn't need to grab her.

She kept thinking of Bobby. Was the old shed burning? Is that what Hayes had meant? Had he killed Bobby first and set the little building on fire? Jo remembered smelling gasoline in the shed. Bobby was probably using it for the lawnmower.

She wanted to cry, but some instinct of self-preservation made her try to focus on what was happening. On what Hayes was telling her.

"Those idiot Rangers think they're elite policemen." He cackled. "They couldn't catch a cold. I walked into the place in broad daylight and bugged the captain's telephone."

She couldn't believe it. "How?"

"I borrowed a phone repair truck." He laughed again. "They *might* find the lineman eventually."

Another murder. The man was on a rampage. A quiet, demented rampage. What was she going to do?

"It's your fault, you know," he said calmly.

She was shaking so hard she was afraid her voice would falter. "Why?"

"Because you made me do it. If you'd just told me where they were when I first asked you, everything would have been much easier. But when you started running to the police, making problems, I had to get creative."

"I didn't know what you wanted."

He laughed. "Right. Tell me another one."

"I still don't know," she said quickly. "Terry didn't give me anything."

These were apparently not the words Leo Hayes wanted to hear. His hand slapped angrily against the counter, making her jump. "She had to have given them to you! Do you think I'm an idiot? Where else could they be?"

"At the bottom of the Gulf of Mexico," she said. "Have you ever thought of that?"

He grabbed her left hand and squeezed. Hard. She bit her lip in pain and tasted blood. "Don't screw me around now, lady. I'm giving you exactly ten seconds to tell me where those jewels are. Before Terry disappeared they were in the Monteverde vault. I know because I was the one who made sure they were put there! After she fled the country, they were gone.''

He was pinching her so hard her eyes teared. She feverishly searched her mind for any response that might keep her alive, but she couldn't give him information she didn't have. And she would die before she told him Terry was alive.

She would die, she repeated to herself.

''Maybe someone stole them.'' She ground the words out, barely recognizing her own voice now.

''Yes. Terry!''

He wrenched her wrist further and she reached back reflexively with her other hand. She intended to punch him. Instead, her hand hit something. Something solid and wooden.

Oh, God, she thought. The knife block. Hours before she had been making breakfast, cracking little jokes about injuring herself with a knife. Now the block represented her last hope.

''A-all right,'' she stammered. ''I'll tell you if you'll just stop hurting me.''

''I'll stop hurting you when you tell me.''

She ducked her head. Out of the corner of her eye she saw her bag and her purse propped in the hall against the doorway to the bedroom. Ready to go back to Houston, to that happy life she'd been so optimistic about. And now…

She couldn't think about it or she would never get through this alive. She would be too upset and do something stupid.

''They're in my bag,'' she told Hayes. ''In the inside zipper compartment.''

She thought he would let her go then, but he didn't. "*What* are?"

Fear suffused her. She still didn't know what this crazy man was after. But she remembered the kaleidoscope. "The diamonds," she blurted out. If it was the wrong answer, she'd be a dead woman.

He gasped and let go of her arm. Suddenly, she was thrown against the counter as he ran across the room to rifle through her bag. She wouldn't have long now.

She turned and grabbed the handle of the largest knife. It was a ten-inch butcher knife, as sharp as a razor. The blade glinted in the light through the window over the sink. She put it on the counter in front of her, covering it with her body. Hayes thought she couldn't see. He wouldn't be expecting that she would grab a weapon so quickly.

Behind her, zippers were ripped open and foul curses rent the air as Hayes discovered that she'd lied to him. He growled and his footsteps stomped toward her. She tried to swallow but her throat was too dry, her heartbeat too wild. She felt light-headed and weightless as fight-or-flight adrenaline kicked in. She readied herself to turn, to slash at him.

As she was turning, however, he was already swinging at her with his fist. He hit her across the temple, jarring her so that the knife only hit his shoulder.

A high shriek like a wounded rabbit's pierced the kitchen. "You bitch!"

He grabbed for the wrist of the hand that clasped the knife. She held fast, but Hayes was surprisingly strong. His hands pinched on her wrist until she could feel her own hand going numb. She kicked at him and he shrilled back at her. Red spattered the linoleum at their feet, giving Jo a jolt of satisfaction. She'd gotten him. At least she'd managed to hurt him a little.

He gave her arm a final wrench, however, and the knife clattered to the floor. Hayes dived for it and Jo tried to run, but he caught her arm and pulled him back against him. Sharp stainless steel pricked her neck, taking her breath.

"That's right. Don't move a muscle," Hayes said. As she stood frozen, she could feel the hot moist air from his deep gulping breaths against the back of her head. Her body was pressed tight against his and the pressure of it caused a shudder of revulsion. But though she was half turned toward the door, toward freedom, she couldn't move. She was pinned by that razor-sharp blade of steel.

"Now." His voice was tight with fury. "You can tell me where they are, or you can die."

She closed her eyes. He might think he was giving her a choice, but she knew better. He would kill her either way.

JO SCREAMED HIS NAME.

Bobby came to in a hell of acrid smoke and flames. He pulled himself to his hands and knees, then nearly passed out as dizziness assaulted him. He had to shake his head to try to make sense of where he was. Someone had hit him. Jo was screaming.

Dear God. It had to be Leo Hayes. How the hell had he found them?

Not that it mattered now. Bobby pulled his T-shirt up over his nose and mouth and tried to withstand the urge to take deep breaths of the poisonous air. The shed was an inferno.

He cursed. He had to get out of here. He could no longer hear Jo screaming.

He ran to the door, but it was shut...and no doubt padlocked from the outside. He threw all of his weight against the heavy wooden barrier but it was no use. There was only one hope left, and that was the narrow transom opening over the door. It was the only window in the old shed, and as far as he knew it had never been opened.

Swiftly he retrieved the ladder leaning against one wall and set it against the door. As he climbed toward the transom, the smoke got thicker, hotter. His clothes felt heavy with sweat, and he shouldered the heavy iron-and-glass transom to unstick it. Finally, it gave way. There was just enough space for his body to squeeze through the opening, and he wasted no time.

For a brief moment he hung from the other side, taking deep gulps of fresh air before he dropped to his feet. The landing stung but he stumbled toward the house. Then he stopped.

His SIG-Sauer was in a case in the living room, but he couldn't be sure what would be happening inside. He might not have time to retrieve it, or worse. Hayes may have found it already. Bobby sprinted to his car, snatched his department-issue Colt .45 from the glove compartment and headed around the house. Just as he reached the back door, he heard a shrill, animal-like shriek. It wasn't Jo. Which meant that, maybe, she was still fighting.

He cocked his revolver and pushed quietly through the door and crept along the hall toward the kitchen.

A man's tense voice said, "Now. You can tell me where they are, or you can die."

The words sent a bolt of fear through Bobby. He sidled around the corner of the kitchen and the sight there sickened him. Leo Hayes was holding a butcher knife to Jo's throat. Bobby could hear her quick shallow breaths. He could smell her fear.

Rage coursing through him, he stepped forward, gun clasped in front of him. "Let her go, Hayes."

Hayes twisted in surprise and Jo jerked. Bobby saw a line of red on her neck and nearly lost it.

"*I* know where your damn jewels are. Let her go!"

"Where?" Hayes said. He eyed the gun with arrogant indifference. He was insane. "And don't bullshit me, or this knife's going further in."

"They're with Terry Monteverde."

"Bobby, no!" Jo cried.

Hayes's eyes bulged.

"That's right. She's still alive, Hayes."

A sob broke in Jo's throat, and for a split second, as Bobby's words and Jo's reaction registered, Hayes's hold on her slackened. It was the break Bobby had been waiting for. Aiming for the side farthest from Jo, he pulled the trigger.

Both Jo and Hayes recoiled. Jo jumped back, however, nearly clawing her way onto the counter behind her, while Hayes doubled over. The butcher knife clattered onto the linoleum.

Bobby ran to Jo. "Are you okay?" He pulled her into his arms.

She was pale, in shock. Her skin was white as a sheet except for the angry cut across her neck. Tiny droplets of blood gathered along its edge. Bobby unraveled a wad of paper towel from under the counter and pressed it to her. Then he kissed her cold, trembling lips.

"Bobby," she gasped. Suddenly it seemed as if the world around her were registering again. "Oh, my God, Bobby, you're here. You saved my life."

By a hair, he thought, feeling ill at how close he'd come to losing Jo just when they'd found each other again.

Her brow contorted in puzzlement. "How did you manage it? He said you were dead!"

"I nearly was. He set fire to the shed with me in it."

They looked down to where Hayes was lying, his body an awkward heap on the linoleum. Blood pooled out from his brown suit, and a gurgling rattle came from his throat.

Jo's expression turned to one of horror again and tears streaked down her face. "Call 911. Quick."

Bobby couldn't find his cell phone. He'd probably left it outside when he'd been preparing to mow.

Suddenly, it didn't matter. Sirens sounded in the distance. Within moments, there was a commotion outside and Bobby's mother and a fireman were standing in the kitchen, gaping at the scene.

The fireman started mouth-to-mouth on Hayes, while Marisol hurried to Bobby and Jo.

"We saw smoke and called the fire department," she said. "I made Denise stay home and came over."

Bobby nodded, but Jo remained silent.

His mother pushed him aside and looked at the wound on her neck. For the first time in his life, Bobby heard his mother swear in English. She glanced angrily at Hayes. "That man? Who is he?"

The fireman looked up at her, shaking his head. "Was, ma'am. This man's dead."

THEY RETURNED to Houston late in the afternoon. For the most part they drove in silence. Jo felt an enormous sense of relief. Leo Hayes was dead. Clearly, he had been the one who'd set Terry up on the original smuggling charges, and he also could have been the reason Terry was frightened for her life. Jo and any number of people could now testify against Leo on Terry's behalf and work to clear her of the charges against her so she could go back home.

Terry would be exonerated. But when they found her, she would have to be told that her only sister was gone.

Jo knew from experience how hard it was to lose your only sibling.

When they were on the ramp heading into Houston, Jo finally spoke. "I guess you should take me back to my house."

"Your house?" Bobby repeatedly incredulously. "You can't go back there."

She turned and tried to look at him. Dark hair. Incredible body. Strong, slightly bristly jaw. A shiver of desire went through her, reminding her for the first time since Leo Hayes's death that they had made love last night and this morning. That they were going to be married!

"There's no reason for me not to live there until the wedding."

"Your place is a mess," Bobby reminded her.

"I have to clean it up sometime."

When they reached her house, Bobby walked her to her door. "Mind if I come in?" he said.

"No, of course not."

They went into the house, and through the corner of her eye Jo finally got a look at the damage. Everything was everywhere, just as it had been described to her. It was a depressing sight, and reminded her of all she'd been through in this past week. All the fear. The highs and lows. Her legs trembled beneath her.

Just when she thought she might lose it, Bobby's hands were on her shoulders, bracing her. "It's all over now, Jo."

It was as if he knew her thoughts. She leaned back against him. "Is it?"

He turned her around to face him and drew her into an embrace, one she fell into gladly. She pressed herself against him and inhaled a deep breath. He squeezed her tightly, and she could smell the smoke still in his skin.

The things this man had done for her. She couldn't even begin to thank him. "Bobby, you saved my life," she said.

He lifted her chin. She couldn't see him directly, but she knew the emotion that was in his eyes as he looked down at her. She knew because she felt the same thing deep in her heart. "I saved myself."

She shook her head.

"Yes, I did," he insisted. "I've been so lost without you these last months, Jo. If anything happened to you now, I don't know how I would have been able to stand it. It wasn't heroism, it was selfishness. I love you, Jo. I want you with me every second from now on."

They were the sweetest words she could have hoped to hear. "That's what I want, too."

She tilted her head up to his and he captured her lips in a long, emotional kiss. His tongue plundered her mouth, and the heat that rushed through her seemed to erase all the ugliness, the fear of that day. In his arms, she felt safe. Loved. Cherished.

"So what do you want to do? Should I help you clean?"

She shook her head. "I think I'll get professionals to help me sort this one out. Right now I'd just like to pack a bag and go home. To your place."

She heard him let out a breath and he drew her to him again. "From now on, home is wherever we're together."

She laughed. "Good. Because this home is definitely more than I want to tackle right now."

She picked her way toward the bedroom. "I'll throw some more of my stuff in a bag."

"Should I help?"

"That's okay. Why don't you grab a beer or something out of the fridge."

"Your answering machine is blinking."

"Could you listen to it?" she asked. It was bound to be

from Tammy or Willie, and she wasn't sure she was up to returning such a call right now. There would be too much to explain—too much that she didn't want to think about today. She edged more quickly toward her bedroom. "I won't be long."

She went through her bedroom, snatching up articles of clothing and shoes from the floor. There was an old tote bag hanging on the closet door, and she threw the items in it haphazardly. No wonder Hayes had wrecked her house. He'd been searching for diamonds. They could have been anywhere.

But where were they really? she wondered. That was still a puzzle. Terry wouldn't have taken anything that didn't belong to her, would she?

"Jo."

Bobby stood in the doorway, strangely still. The odd tone in his voice sent a chill through her.

"What's wrong?" She half expected Bobby to say there was a menacing message from Leo Hayes on the machine.

But what he said was almost as startling. "It was from Nina, Jo. She's alive. And she's right here in Houston."

THE FIRST THING Bobby noticed about Rick Singleton and Nina Monteverde was that they didn't look like two people who had just stumbled out of the jungle.

In fact, from the magnetism in their eyes when Rick and Nina stared at each other, they looked like two people who had just stumbled out of a bedroom. Rick Singleton was about Bobby's height, but he had sharp green eyes and a hungry look about him. Not a man to tangle with, Bobby decided. Which made him all the more surprised that gentle-looking Nina, who resembled a prim school librarian more than her tempestuous, beautiful sister, obviously *had* tangled with the bounty hunter.

They were still tangled, as a matter of fact. Even as they talked to Jo and Bobby in the lobby of their hotel, they could barely keep their hands off each other.

They'd stayed overnight at the hotel after failing to locate Jo at her house the night before. As the police drone in Rio had reported, their plane had gone down and may have crashed in the jungle. But they hadn't been killed. Rick had landed the craft, barely, and the two had managed to survive the jungle and reach help. They'd headed straight for Houston to warn Jo that she could be in danger. By the time they'd reached a telephone, Jo had already fled town for Bobby's ranch.

"I guess we can chalk another murder up to Leo Hayes," Bobby said. He was gladder than ever that the man was dead; he only wished Hayes had lived long enough to make a few more confessions. It would have tied things up a little more neatly. On the other hand, once they searched his office and house again, and interviewed a few more of his acquaintances, there was no telling what they could turn up.

"I'm so glad you're all right," Jo told Nina. "We heard about the crash and assumed the worst." She frowned, her hazel eyes clouded with worry. "But I'm sorry I can't help you find Terry."

Nina, it turned out, also was in the dark as to Terry's whereabouts. She had hoped that since Jo had helped Terry fake her death, she would know where her sister was.

"I'm just glad Leo Hayes never found out she was alive—or where she was hiding."

Jo hesitated before asking, "Did you know Terry had a baby?"

Nina nodded, and for the first time since they'd begun discussing Terry, her face broke into a beaming smile. "A little girl named Hope Katherine. That's how Rick and I met. Terry left Hope with her father, Mitch Barnes, and then disappeared. So Mitch sent Rick to look for Terry in Rio."

"Mitch will be in Houston soon," Rick said. "He wants to talk to you, Jolene."

The news that Terry had left her baby with her American father worried Jo. "I took comfort from the fact that Terry had her baby with her," she said, sighing sadly. "But now..."

"She probably left the little girl with Mitch Barnes because she felt she was in danger from Leo Hayes," Rick guessed. "Now that Hayes is dead, Terry can come out of hiding."

"I know she'll want to see her little girl," Nina said.

Jo frowned. "But how will anyone be able to find Terry to tell her?"

Rick released a long, ragged breath. "I know some people, the Garretts, who run an agency called Finders Keepers. Maybe through Hope's birth records..."

Emphasis on the maybe, Bobby thought. He hugged Jo to him tightly. "Don't worry. She'll be found."

She looked up at him, and her hazel eyes seemed luminous and genuinely optimistic again. "I know she will, Bobby. In fact, I'm beginning to think anything can happen."

So was he. In a week, he'd gotten Jo back. Jo was recovering her sight. It was like a miracle. Surely God would allow one more miracle and enable them to track down Terry.

"Besides," Jo said, smiling at Nina and Rick, "I *know* now Terry will have to turn up."

"Why?" Nina asked.

Jo brushed a light kiss against Bobby's cheek, and for a moment the worry fell away from her expression and he basked in the love that he saw there. A surge of pure emotion swept through him. God, he loved this woman. He sent up silent thanks to heaven that he had been able to keep his promise to Greg to keep her safe. And also a promise to continue doing so for the rest of his life.

"Because Bobby and I are getting married," Jo said, smiling as she looked up at Bobby with an expression that held love and understanding and so much trust in their future. "And Terry's the person I've always wanted to be maid of honor at my wedding."